P9-ELX-137

DISCARDED

a matter of days

ALSO BY AMBER KIZER

Meridian

Wildcat Fireflies

Speed of Light

*Gert Garibaldi's Rants and Raves:
One Butt Cheek at a Time*

Seven Kinds of Ordinary Catastrophes

a
matter
of
days

a novel by AMBER KIZER

DELACORTE PRESS

PEMBROKE PUBLIC LIBRARY

This is a work of fiction. Names, characters, places, and incidents either are the product of the author's imagination or are used fictitiously. Any resemblance to actual persons, living or dead, events, or locales is entirely coincidental.

Text copyright © 2013 by Amber Kizer
Jacket art: photograph of road copyright © 2013 by Elise Bergsma;
virus cell art copyright © 2013 by Markovka/Shutterstock

All rights reserved. Published in the United States by Delacorte Press, an imprint of Random House Children's Books, a division of Random House, Inc., New York.

Delacorte Press is a registered trademark and the colophon is a trademark of Random House, Inc.

Visit us on the Web! randomhouse.com/teens

Educators and librarians, for a variety of teaching tools, visit us at RHTeachersLibrarians.com

Library of Congress Cataloging-in-Publication Data
Kizer, Amber.
A matter of days / Amber Kizer. — 1st ed.
p. cm.
Summary: In the not-too-distant future when a global pandemic kills most of humanity, a teenaged girl and her younger brother struggle to survive.
ISBN 978-0-385-73973-3 (hc) — ISBN 978-0-375-89825-9 (ebook) —
ISBN 978-0-385-90804-7 (glb) [1. Survival—Fiction. 2. Brothers and sisters—Fiction. 3. Epidemics—Fiction. 4. Virus diseases—Fiction. 5. Science fiction.]
I. Title.
PZ7.K6745Mat 2013
[Fic]—dc23
2012012200

The text of this book is set in 12-point Adobe Garamond.
Book design by Angela Carlino

Printed in the United States of America

10 9 8 7 6 5 4 3 2 1

First Edition

Random House Children's Books supports the First Amendment and celebrates the right to read.

To Alex
I love you

YA Fic Kizer, A. 7/8/13

a matter of days

DAY 56

I waited a few swallows, a couple of deep breaths, before standing and tugging the quilt, with its blue-and-white wedding ring pattern, up and over Mom's face. *Quiet. Peace. Finally.* Exhaustion frayed my edges, fringed my cogent mind until the world hazed a gray blue. Mom's death was a type of ending, sure, but the beginning of so much more. *Are we ready?*

I tucked the corners of the quilt down under the mattress, into the crevice between the headboard and pillows. Smoothed out the wrinkles, covered up the filth, the days of dying cleaned up with the bright rings of magical promises my parents made to each other twenty years ago.

The bulge in the middle of the bed didn't resemble a human being anymore, let alone the woman who'd loved us our whole lives. *Why didn't she listen when it mattered?* The juncos, chickadees, and nuthatches chattered like stock traders outside. Or maybe, as the world fell more silent with each death, the birds simply seemed louder, more insistent.

The day was what Washingtonians called partly sunny rather than partly cloudy, and only about fifty degrees, but I'd kept the windows open. The chilled breeze blew in the stench of rotting meat and garbage. This world was separated only by a matter of degrees of gross. I almost didn't notice. I remembered moments when the air I breathed was scented with cedar trees, the dank acidic tang of low tide miles away, or elderberry blossoms on the wind. A lifetime ago. *Can it really be only eight weeks?*

Move, Nadia, don't stop moving. So much to do. Rabbit's footsteps sounded like a herd of elephants pacing upstairs. I imagined he checked the family room one last time for treasures he absolutely had to take with him. He probably lingered over the Xbox 360, gaming maniac that he'd once been. The shooting game, Uncle Bean gave us with a stern lecture to hide it from Mom, but practice aiming, firing, and holding a weapon until we were comfortable with it.

Rabbit clattered down the stairs, dropping something heavy, swearing words he shouldn't know at eleven.

A sigh deflated my legs until all I wanted to do was melt into the floor and let the virus get me, too. *Or pills. Or booze. Or blades. Anything to not be left behind.* I leaned my back against the side of the bed and scratched my scalp. My fingernails had blood, and other grossness, in the cracks and creases. *Will they ever be completely clean again? Will I?*

Rabbit's footsteps paused outside the master suite's door.

He'd worry at the quiet. Mom's moans and screams became a part of our routine; intense, contorting pain was one of many symptoms of BluStar.

A thin, wavering voice called through the door, "Dad come get Mom?"

If Dad came to get Mom, why in the hell didn't he take us, too? Why do we have to live? "Yep, champ, she's gone," I called back to my little brother, trying not to sound as defeated as I felt.

Get up, Nadia. Be the cockroach, not the orchid. I heard Dad's voice chastise me until I pushed myself off the floor. Leaning down, I kissed Mom's forehead through the quilt. It was almost easy to say goodbye. Those last few days had been so horrific, so painful to watch, that the relief felt too big to fit inside my skin. But I was empty, couldn't even summon up tears. I'd used them all along with fervent prayers and agonizing wishes. *Who has energy left to grieve? I have to be strong. Keep it together.*

"Are we—um, are you— When?" Rabbit shouted as he threw a tennis ball against the hallway wall with the steady thrum of a heartbeat. He did it when he was most worried, most anxious. *"Not in the house," Mom would yell. "No dog to bring it back," he'd say. "A dog could chase the ball."*

I shook my head and did a few jumping jacks to slough off the haze and debilitating paralysis that made me want to sit in one spot until I died too. I had to snap out of it. *Rabbit's counting on me.* "Soon. Thirty minutes?"

"'Kay." The tennis ball bumped and echoed farther down the hall, back toward the kitchen. The empty, scavenged remains of our kitchen.

I stripped off clothes I'd worn for longer than twenty-four hours, longer than days, or years, or lifetimes. I shuffled into my parents' closet. I riffled through until I found my mom's favorite pair of jeans and the cashmere sweater set, the royal-blue one, never worn. Mom was saving it for when Dad got home from his tour in Afghanistan.

For a split second, I wished I could bury Mom in the National Cemetery next to Dad. I'd done the next best thing: put Dad's dog tags over Mom's heart and covered her in the wedding ring quilt. Granny had made it for my parents' wedding gift. It had covered their bed all my life until Mom shoved it deep into the closet when the uniforms came with casualty news. Now the quilt's memories tied my parents together, as best I could, on this day, in death.

I padded naked into the bathroom and dipped the last clean washcloth in a bucket of rainwater Rabbit collected yesterday. It was cold, but it was clean. My hip bones poked at my skin and I had divots between each rib. *I have to eat more.* Manic laughter threatened at the thought of eating more energy bars and canned soup.

I scrubbed with a loofah until my skin pinked, reddened angrily, chafed with the contact. I reveled in the sensation, and part of me wondered if that was all I'd feel ever again—pain. Physical, emotional—it was all pain at this point. I brushed my fuzzy teeth until they were slick and shiny. I tried not to cringe at the sight of the kinked frizz of my hair or the glaring sprinkle of freckles across the bridge of my nose.

I slid into Mom's clothes. *Two of me would fit in here. I might as well be the hanger.* She'd been a couple sizes larger than me to start; I'd lost a size or two over the past few months. I threaded a belt through the loops to keep the jeans up.

I buried my face in her sweater, trying to find the lingering of perfume I grew up associating with Mom, but it still car-

4

ried that new-clothes smell. *Where's her spray?* I padded over to Mom's perfume on the vanity, sprayed a little DK Cashmere over my heart, and set the bottle back on the counter. *It's lonely.*

On impulse, I grabbed a toiletry bag and dumped Mom's makeup and perfume in. I sprinted into the bathroom and dug around in the back of the drawers until I found Dad's cologne and shaving kit, out of sight, but not gone. Maybe they'd come in handy. *Something to hold on to.*

I left the window open with the curtains rustling. I almost saw Mom and Dad standing together in the drape and movement of the fabric. A large brown moth with a perfect blue stripe sunned in a stray ray on the sill. Mom would know what kind it was. *I can't ask her. I can't ask her anything, ever again.*

I avoided looking at the bed even one last time before slipping out of the room, my arms full of my parents' daily routines.

I didn't spare my own room more than a glance as I slipped on my newest pair of sneakers. I hadn't slept in there for days, weeks. Homework was still piled on my desk, and there was a nasty mound of dirty clothes in the corner. I wanted to lie down on my bed and never get back up. *Too tempting.*

I found Rabbit sitting at the kitchen table staring out into the backyard. A Steller's jay imitated a red-tailed hawk and cocked its head as if asking if we'd put out the usual peanut butter. The bird feeders were full for the first time in weeks. *We don't have time to feed wildlife. We need the food for us.*

"I filled 'em," Rabbit said, before I'd even asked the question, and didn't take his eyes off the jay. *Dad loved the birds.*

I sighed. "That's nice." I knew I sounded bitchy and distracted, so I tried again, "I mean, I know they'll appreciate it while they can. You're a good kid, Rabbit." I flipped open cabinets, checking, double-checking. We'd jammed everything we could into the Jeep. Everything that was left, that we hadn't used up or had stolen from us.

"I'm packed," Rabbit answered with a shrug. "Ready."
Antsy, more like.

I didn't blame him; the house felt oddly both full and empty, no longer home but a prison. I placed the letter for Uncle Bean on the counter just in case, exactly like he'd instructed.

Dad had promised me a summer vacation road trip after my sixteenth birthday. See the sights, visit the must-sees, and I would do the driving. Most of it. He was supposed to be sitting right next to me telling me to watch the speed limit, turn down the music, ignore the phone's vibrations of text messages. This wasn't what either of us had in mind when we'd planned our trip years ago.

"Let's go." My heart sped up, a sprint of anxiety. *Am I doing the right thing? Should we stay in our neighborhood? We've managed this far. Aren't we supposed to stay put in case of emergency?* That was the old days, when there was rescue coming.

As if he knew what I was thinking, Rabbit said, "We have to." He looked up at me with his big brown eyes, so much like Dad's. Depths of experience, more like an old man's than a young boy's, gave his gaze an otherworldly determination. "We have to find Uncle Bean. Dad said to survive the effect, not the cause."

I nodded. I'd never really understood all of Dad's nuggets of military speak he'd cram into his talks and vacation leave. Until this—now they all made an eerie kind of sense. *Be the cockroach. Survive the effect.*

We'd talked about going, about staying. Voted. 2–0. If we'd

split the vote, we'd have flipped a coin. But then fires in the distance seemed to grow darker, bigger, and finally obscured the Seattle skyline completely. We were sitting ducks in this suburb if the fires didn't go out naturally, and why would they? There was plenty of fuel to burn, enough rain to tamp them down but not to put them out. If this were November, and not April, maybe we'd be stuck to deal until spring, but we could do this. *Have to do this. Get to Uncle Bean and start over.*

"Are you sure you don't want to say goodbye to Mom?" I paused.

"I did. You licensed to drive yet?" He sent me a mischievous grin like the bratty little brother he used to be.

"How hard can it be?" I smiled. At least the streets were empty. We'd take it slow until I got the gist, but it was a long way from the outskirts of Seattle to West Virginia. And we were alone.

DAY 56

We utilized every spare inch in the Jeep—left the backseat bare for sleeping, but Rabbit had to ride with his legs on the dashboard when he sat in the front with me. I couldn't see out the back window, but it wasn't like I needed to look behind me. *Onward.*

Rabbit carefully packed the sentimental bits like photo albums on the bottom and important usables like bottled water and toilet paper on the top. He deserved kudos for the organization; his ideas packed more into the Jeep than I'd imagined possible. He'd packed, and unpacked it, while I tended to Mom. We'd known it was only a matter of time before we hit the road. Mom knew it was only a matter of time before she and Dad reunited. If we'd forgotten anything, we'd scavenge on the road, or live without it.

I stuck my parents' toiletries in a cranny under the driver's seat and tapped my pocket to make sure I had Dad's MP3 player. I didn't look at the house again. Couldn't. *I hope we have everything. Maybe someday we'll come back and the house will be here, untouched.* I shook my head; fantasy had a life of its own in this new world.

I shifted the Jeep into reverse and slowly backed down the driveway, with Rabbit calling out directions. *I'm gonna need to see out the back, aren't I?* My practice with the riding lawn mower, with pedals and steering—which Mom oversaw before—came in handy. Tiny compared with this monster heft, but better than nothing. Family cars lined the driveways and the sides of these suburban streets, as if everyone had taken the day off. Cozy and happy inside their homes. *Appearances are so wrong.*

Rabbit hopped in, his knees up to his chin as we rolled out of our neighborhood. Twisting to stare behind him, he didn't seem to breathe as our house disappeared into the distance. "Can we stop at Jimmy's?"

"Just Jimmy's?" I asked, clenching the steering wheel. *Why couldn't driver's ed have been last semester instead of next?*

I didn't know what it was like for Rabbit to look out at the deserted streets and quiet backyards, but for me it was eerie. Bananas crazy. Like a movie set, not real life. Like one of those amusement-park tours Dad loved—"This is where they filmed 'The End of the World Part Four,'" he'd say with a chuckle.

"Well, he is my best friend, and if he's there alone . . . What if just kids survived this?"

Rabbit clearly hadn't figured out that there was something in the shot Uncle Bean gave us. *We're lucky. Special.* But our survival had to do with our family and not our age. *Maybe I should have shown him Bean's letter?*

The world unfolded differently from the driver's seat. I didn't realize how little I had paid attention to streets and landmarks when I was riding shotgun.

Rabbit continued as if my silence wasn't answer enough. "If he's alone he can come with us, right?"

I pressed the accelerator harder. *We don't leave marines behind, Nadia. Yes, Daddy.* "Of course. Sure, we'll stop." *Just what I need, two boys to worry about.*

How was this supposed to work? Should we knock on the doors of everyone we'd ever known? Every friend? Classmate? Should we nurse them if they were sick? Bury them if dead? *We'll never make it to West Virginia by summer.*

Rabbit exclaimed, "You missed a stop sign!"

I slammed on the brakes. "Crap." We were in the middle of the intersection. There was wildlife, but no traffic. No humans at all.

"Are there cops?" Rabbit giggled, jokingly rubbing his forehead and knees.

"Sorry," I muttered. The whole thing was so ludicrous, I laughed, too. "Cops? Anymore?" I eased off the brake and started forward again. At the first blank traffic light, I braked and waited for a light of any color to turn on, or flash.

"It's not on." Rabbit glanced at me.

"So that means—?" I couldn't remember Mom's traffic safety quizzes. *See, Mom? Don't need to know that stuff.*

"I don't think it matters, Nadia. There isn't any traffic."

"So, I ignore the dead lights?"

"I would. What else are you going to do? Write yourself a ticket?" Rabbit shrugged.

I nodded, easing forward again.

As we drove out of our suburban neighborhood, we saw businesses we used to frequent had been trashed in panic or greed. The Best Buy we passed had boxes and glass shards in the parking lot and the doors were an obliterated tangle of metal and shattered Plexiglas. *Did anyone live long enough to enjoy the stolen electronics that no longer showed any programming, received signals, or had power?* Reduced to plastic and wires, they were useless.

"Did people steal TVs?"

"I think so." The looting they'd shown on television, while there were still reporters, was catastrophic. People thought they'd be the lone survivors, the kings of the new kingdom. *How'd that work out for you?*

"They didn't take the right stuff." Rabbit shook his head.

Each store we passed looked the same. There were probably millionaires, with tons of useless cash from robberies, dead in the houses around us or in the apartments of Seattle.

I saw only a few rotting corpses, bloated and bent, unrecognizable as the people they used to be, near doors and against walls. It seemed as if people got only so far and couldn't go any farther.

Rabbit averted his eyes and whispered, "Sucks to be them." As if trying to feign nonchalance, he fiddled with the radio dial and found only static of varying annoyance levels. He mumbled and sighed and squirmed in the seat, then asked, "Dia, um, do you think there are zombies?"

Focused on driving around a tangle of cars in an intersection, I didn't look at my brother's face. *Is he kidding?* "Where?"

"Anywhere? Here."

I slowed to a stop and set the parking brake. I turned in

my seat to face him. He glanced at me from beneath his lashes. This world was scary enough without borrowing nightmares. I wanted to make sure he heard my answer. "Only in movies, Rab. No one is going to attack us and eat our flesh." *I hope.* The run of apocalypse movies and books in the last few years didn't inspire confidence. I knew so little now, maybe those had been early documentaries. I'd kill us before that happened, but I didn't think that would comfort Rabbit.

He nodded, but still appeared unconvinced.

I knew I was about to overshare and maybe scare him worse, but I didn't know what lay ahead of us. I thought of Mom's endless lecture when she could still talk in coherent sentences. "There may be bad people in the world. They may try to steal our food, or the car, or hurt us, but that's because they're desperate, bad people."

"Why didn't the bad people die and the good people live?" Rabbit asked in a voice that sounded much younger than his eleven years.

I wish I knew. I shook my head, as much to clear my thoughts as to buy time to formulate an answer. "I don't know. I can't answer that. But I can with complete and utter conviction tell you that there are no zombies. No zombies."

"Promise?"

"Promise. No zombies."

Earnest and reassured for the moment, he nodded.

I started driving toward Jimmy's neighborhood and we passed a whole family laid out in their front yard. Or what used to be a family. Maybe. Hard to tell with all the human puzzle pieces.

"No zombies?" Rabbit ducked his head.

"Nope, just dead bodies. They're not going to get up and say boo." Before Mom's dead body, Dad's closed casket was the closest I'd come to the dead. After BluStar started, the 24/7 television news bulletins of the sick and dying had been everywhere, while the virus took hold and there were still relatively healthy, or only recently infected, people to report on it. For a while things worked. I assumed computers and backup systems didn't need humans to keep going. At least for the very short term.

"Turn here. His house is up there. The brown one." Rabbit pointed.

Jimmy was a blond kid who forever had food caught in his braces and sported a cast on either arm. My dad had called him a pistol. *Why am I already placing him in the past tense?*

I pulled into the driveway and noticed right away that the house was frozen in time, drapes pulled. "Do I honk?" It felt rude to hit the horn with the world hushed and heavy.

"I'll go knock." Rabbit unbuckled his seat belt with a deep breath.

"No, you won't. You will stay in the car. I'll go." My little brother couldn't be braver than me. Not today.

He didn't argue. "There's a key under the mat."

"Nuh-uh. I am not going in there. I will knock." Other people's houses were creepy in the best of times, which these weren't. A light sweat broke out along my scalp.

"What if he can't get to the door, then what?" Rabbit raised his eyebrows like I was a moron. *Sure, Jimmy is alive, but trapped out of reach, waiting for rescue. I'm stuck in a Nickelodeon movie. Cue the happy ending music.*

I rolled my eyes and wanted to stamp my feet. "Fine. I will

open the door. I will call out. I will listen, but I am not going into a house I've never been in." Because the queasy feeling in the pit of my stomach told me Jimmy and his family were not inside. Or they were inside, but dead. Rabbit's stricken expression had me amending. "If I think he might be in there and alive, I'll go in, deal?"

Rabbit nodded, seemingly satisfied.

I dragged my feet up to the front door. I kept waiting for the eerie music and strobe lighting of bad slasher flicks. The world didn't feel right anymore. Like it spun faster on its axis, or gravity had increased tenfold.

I knocked and waited. *Nothing.* I leaned in and tried to see through the window beside the door. Nothing out of the ordinary.

I glanced back at the Jeep and Rabbit motioned. I knew he wanted me to open the door. I swallowed, bent down, and found the key under the mat. I said a quick prayer that zombies really didn't exist and turned the knob.

DAY 56

When I was little, I used to leave my Strawberry Shortcake dolls in the car in the sun with the windows rolled up. I didn't do it on purpose, but I took those dolls everywhere. Mom threw up once because the sweet chemical perfume of fake fruit in the hot car was overpowering. I'll take fake fruit, Mattel-style, over decomposing human any day.

The blast of putrid air doubled me over and I puked into the wilted potted pansies. No one was alive in there. No way.

I shut the front door and jogged back to the vehicle. Sweat dripped down my forehead as my stomach continued to spasm. Rabbit handed me an open bottle of water to swish out my mouth.

We didn't speak. There weren't words.

I put the Jeep into reverse and Rabbit plugged his MP3 player into the car's sound system. He picked Long Goodnight's latest—last—and turned it up until the entire vehicle shook with the beats. Somehow the silence outside deafened us all the same.

I cruised up the on-ramp for I-405 south to 90. Hitchhikers lay in ditches and a few cars hugged the shoulders, but otherwise it was us and a few rats, crows, and the occasional possum up early crossing the road.

Two weeks into the pandemic, everyone was ordered to stay home. Off the roads. Most people complied, more afraid of what was "out there" than what was in their own homes. By that time, there wasn't a safe place to run to and very few people tried.

I watched the gas tank ebb to half-full. "Crap." *Hadn't thought of gas.*

"What's wrong?" Rabbit hit the pause button when I swore.

"Gas. We're gonna run out. And then what?" *Nadia, how'd you forget this detail?*

Rabbit patted my shoulder. "Chapter seven of that survivor book—we sip on it."

I shook my head. "What?"

Rabbit reached under his feet and brought out one of the volumes of survival guides Bean shipped us before we'd known what was happening. "We sip on it from another car's gas tank with the tubing stuff that was in the car."

Obviously, we couldn't drink gasoline, so I braked and stopped in the middle of the interstate. "Show me."

Rabbit handed me the book and pointed.

"Oh, *siphon* it."

"Yeah, with the tubing."

"It will either work, we'll get high, or it'll kill us." I spoke out loud without thinking.

"Beats walking across the country, doesn't it?"

"Good point. Next car we see let's stop and investigate." Fears that the only cars on the road would be ones without gas, or contain the dead, went unspoken. Worst case, we'd get off the interstate and go into a residential neighborhood and look there. *I really need to get over my aversion to poking around in other people's junk if we're going to survive. They don't need it anymore.*

"Hey, there's a state patrol car in the median." Rabbit pointed. "Somebody's in there."

I bleated the horn. If a cop was alive he'd respond. "No movement."

"That sucks. To die out here waiting for speeders?"

I pulled over, shut off the engine, and handed the manual back to Rab. "Can you get what we need? You know where it all is."

"Sure." He hopped out and opened the side door like this was routine.

I slowly walked over to the trooper's car and knocked on the window even though I no longer knew what was holding his hat up. The headrest, maybe? *I can do this. I can do this.* I pulled on the handle, but the car door didn't budge. "It's locked," I said.

"Here." Rabbit handed me a hammer. "Break the window."

"Stand back." I whacked on the glass until it broke into small pieces and the hat, with skull and bits, fell onto the ground at my feet.

"Gross!" Rabbit stumbled backward.

I unlocked the door and plugged my nose with one hand while I leaned down and popped the gas lever and the trunk. I slammed the door shut, jumped back, and leaped around, shivering and shaking. "There has got to be a better way!"

A flock of crows settled on the wires above us, interested in our activity, or maybe dinner. I gagged.

Rabbit found a blanket in the trunk, along with a gas can, and covered up the cop's head. "You stick this end in, suck on it until there's gas, and then put it in here. Got it?" He showed me the stick figures in the manual. "Want me to do it?"

"No." If one of us was going to die from gasoline poisoning, it would not be him. I took a couple of deep breaths and then sucked on the tubing's free end. I coughed and spit but finally got gas running out of the tank and into our commandeered gas can.

"Cool!" Rabbit smiled at me like I'd asked him to bathe in mint chocolate-chip ice cream. *Ice cream. God, I miss ice cream.*

I sucked enough gas to refill our tank and we continued on after I cleaned my mouth out with the last of the minty mouthwash. Rabbit pulled out a map and laid it across his lap, marking our route. *Maybe someday kids will study it like we did the Oregon Trail.*

"We need to stop for the night, Rab. I don't want to drive the mountains in the dark." The sun's arms lengthened and the world gilded. Without power generating an aura of ambient light, dusk was our early warning system for a deeply disorienting black night to come. *There is no black like clouded nights with no electric lights.*

"And snow." Rabbit didn't look up.

"Snow?" Tension stiffened my spine and clenched my hands.

"It's been chilly this week, and it *is* only April. Or is it May?"

I wasn't even sure what day it was. Sunlight started to drift away from us. "Sleep in the car or find a hotel?"

"Car."

The next rest area we spotted, we pulled in. Five cars dotted the parking lot along with a couple of eighteen-wheelers. Shadowy remains were evident in only a few. I wasn't getting close enough tonight to find out if the others were totally empty, or if they contained a gloppy pile of someone's loved one in the upholstery. Believing the vehicles empty meant sleeping better. *Maybe.*

"Let's check out the vending machines!" Rabbit undid his seat belt and bolted across the parking lot. From here, nothing seemed vandalized. After locking the doors of the Jeep, I followed with the hammer. *No quarters.*

Rabbit shone a flashlight through the glass, into the lobby area. "Hey, there's a pop machine, and the snack ones look full!"

I smiled. *Christmas presents in April. Or May.* Times changed; I hadn't kept up with the calendar. The door's chain was padlocked, but the window out front wasn't even shatterproof. "Be careful of the glass, Rab," I reminded him as we stepped inside.

"Sure."

Rabbit went to work on the vending machines and I raided the bathrooms for paper products and anything else useful. We made several trips to the car, then sat on the grass by battery-operated lantern and ate a dinner of chips, trail mix, Sno Balls, and root beer. "You want real food, too?" I asked, too tired to dig out the burner and canned soups.

"Nah." A yawn cleaved Rabbit's cheeks and his words. "I'm just sleepy."

Sleepy underestimated my exhaustion. The last week with Mom I'd slept five minutes at a time. I was beginning to see double. But could I relax enough out here to sleep? *God, I hope so.*

We brushed our teeth in the women's room. The men's was occupied, and the last thing I wanted Rabbit seeing before sleep was a possible zombie to dream about. "Wash your face, too."

I flinched with every sound as raccoons and other nightlife began to materialize out of the woods. *There are no zombies. There are no criminals out there tonight.* It would help if I knew someone else had survived. Unfortunately, I couldn't check email or voice mail to find out. *You're getting punchy, Nadia. You need sleep.*

"Yes, Mom." His teasing wrecked the little bit of peace we'd both found. "Sorry."

"It's fine. Take the backseat."

"But I can fit in the front better than you?"

"I can't stretch out either place. One of us should be comfortable." I shrugged and fluffed his pillow, unrolling one of the sleeping bags to make a bed of sorts. I left my shoes on, pulled on a sweatshirt, and reclined the seat as far back as I could. Not bad. Not good, either.

"Night, Rabbit. Sleep in and then we'll get going, okay?" I wanted to get over the Cascade Mountains tomorrow.

"Night. Don't let the bedbugs . . ."

"Bite." I switched off the lamp and a profound claustrophobic choke of night engulfed us. I hit the car door locks quickly. *Combat breathing: inhale four counts, exhale four counts. Yes, Daddy.*

"It's dark." Rabbit's voice quavered.

I swallowed and forced my voice to remain calm. "Close your eyes. It's not as dark then." I took my own advice and a giggle escaped. In a weird way I was right.

"Can we have a light on?"

"We have to save batteries, Rabbit. But here"—I grabbed a small flashlight from the door well and handed it to him—"take this. Keep it off, but anytime you want to check, you can, okay?"

"'Kay." Instead of a teddy bear, or a Transformer toy, my brother fell asleep clutching a flashlight, his fingers reaching out to touch mine.

Even though fear fought to keep my eyes open, in moments I was asleep and dreaming. Those first days came rushing back.

. . . The driver's-side door swung open, and for a split second, I thought I saw Dad. At first glance, as an identical twin, Bean was Dad's mirror image.

"Hi, kiddos. Let's go inside." Uncle Bean ushered us inside, carrying a canvas messenger bag. Usually freshly laundered and pressed even out of uniform. But now his slacks were wrinkled and stained. His eyes a stormy gray. His lips flat. *Like Dad's right before a deployment.*

"Nadia, I need to talk to you. Like an adult. Listen, I need to give you all shots." Bean set his bag down and leaned into the sofa like he hadn't slept in days.

"You came all the way here to give us shots? For what?" I asked.

He shrugged. "Yes and no. There's a new bug." He extracted a metal shoe box with a thick buckle. *An old munitions can. Dad has five in the garage holding nails and tools.* On top was a sealed envelope of thick, creamy stationery. "I need you to promise me that you won't open this until after I call to wish you a happy birthday."

"Huh? I don't understand." I took the box and held it in my lap.

"Pay attention, okay? Sometime in the next few weeks, I'll call to wish you a happy birthday. When I do, I want you to start keeping track of a week, okay? Count down seven days, then read this letter. Open the box. But not before I call."

"Seven days after you call, read the letter? Is this like a scavenger hunt? My birthday isn't until July."

"Go hide the letter and the box someplace your mother and your brother won't find them. And when you do open them, do it by yourself. Promise me. This is very important. It has to be a secret. Classified."

. . . Bean wouldn't do anything to hurt us. He was a medical doctor and worked for the military like Dad. Only his job wasn't so much with patients as in the lab. I knew his work was dangerous. Mom always threw Bean's military "experiments" in Dad's face when she blew up. . . .

"That's a big needle." Rabbit's lip quivered, his bravery momentarily stunted. He hated needles.

"I know, buddy. It'll take a second and then it'll be over." Bean filled the syringe and wiped down Rabbit's bicep with an alcohol swab.

"What about Mom?" Rabbit asked. Mom was a nurse working double shifts at two of Seattle's biggest hospital emergency rooms.

Bean didn't pause or make eye contact with me. He seemed rushed. "I'll leave a dose for her, too. See if you can get her to inject herself?" He quickly jabbed Rab.

"Ouch. That burns!" Rabbit rubbed his arm.

"Sorry, kiddo." A second syringe was ready to go and Bean patted the chair for me.

"What is it?" Rabbit continued massaging his muscle.

Bean handed a glass vial to me. "See if you can convince your mom? Please?" Then he turned to Rabbit. "Come on, champ! Here's a new video game for you—promise me you'll practice as much as possible, okay?" Bean swung Rabbit up into his arms forgetting the obvious indignation of a tween boy.

"Cool, a shooting game. Mom'll freak!" Rabbit grinned.

"Let's not tell your mom about it, okay? You listen to your sister. Do what she says? She's really smart and she'll take care of you. I promise."

"Okay." Rabbit stuck his tongue out at me even as he agreed. . . .

Mom slunk into the house like a ghost. Pale. Drawn like a pencil outline on white paper.

"Uncle Bean was here." I didn't have to say more because I knew what was coming.

"What? When?" Her eyes snapped open and tension pulled her frame up as she stalked toward the kitchen.

I followed, speaking quietly, hoping Rabbit didn't hear. "This afternoon. He gave us shots."

"Shots?" She slammed the refrigerator door closed. "Why didn't you call me?" . . .

My third-period classroom swirled into view. . . .

"What factors might contribute to a pandemic? Any ideas?"

"Overcrowding. People on top of each other."

"Do we have that issue right now? Where?"

"The earthquakes in South America and China displaced millions of people."

"Good, good, what else?"

"The droughts in Africa and India forcing people to move into cities?"

"What's the problem with cities?"

. . . A delivery truck pulls up outside our house. . . .

"You kids live here?"

I nodded.

"Where do you want all this?"

"Are you sure it's for us?"

"You Nadia Jones? It's for you. Don't worry, kid, none of this is cash-on-delivery. Somebody named Bean paid for it."

The UPS guys pitched in hauling boxes. "You guys preparing for Armageddon?" one joked.

Rab shook his head. "Nah, just a big family camping trip."

Bean calling . . .

"You're scaring me," I said.

"I know. I'm sorry. But it'll come clear."

"When?"

"I don't know yet. How are you guys feeling?"

"My arm is sore and I'm really hot."

"Headache? Cough?"

"No?"

"How about Rab?"

"Rab, how do you feel?"

"Like I live in a Costco. Otherwise, fine."

"Remember—out of sight and tell no one." Why in the world did Uncle Bean think anyone was going to care about packs of dried fruit and cases of bottled water?

"That was weird." Rabbit eyed me.

"Uh-huh. . . ."

The next morning . . .

"Nadia? You okay? The bus is almost here?"

"Sick. Covers. Hand me." I scrunched my eyes against the invading light from the hallway.

Rabbit carefully pulled up the sheet and got me an extra blanket. "You want me to call Mom?"

"No, just sleep," I mumbled. . . .

I scrolled through television channels as the clock flipped digits. I needed to do my homework. I clicked to the next channel, a twenty-four-hour-news one I never watched.

I sat up and leaned forward. Those were bodies. Human bodies, in piles like trash being burned. White hazmat-suited ants swarmed around. I turned up the volume.

"England's countryside has taken on a macabre hue of black smoke. The minister of health had this to say: 'It pains me to stand before you today.'" He paused and hacked into a white handkerchief, sweat poured down his reddened face. "'We are experiencing a crisis on our shores we haven't seen since the Black Death spread across our island in the Middle Ages.'"

". . . When Bean was here, what did he say to you?" Mom perched next to me, her expression troubled.

. . . Gone for thirty-six hours straight, Mom came bustling in with more energy than I'd seen since Dad's funeral. She had a feverish, almost manic glint in her eyes. She rattled around in the kitchen cabinets, shoving papers, take-out menus, coupons. Packets of fast-food ketchup and soy sauce rattled to the floor. "Where's Bean's phone number?"

"Why?" I leaned against the doorframe and clasped my elbows.

"Just help me find it." She bit off the words without looking up.

I scooted over to the counter and wrote the number down on the back of a napkin. "Here."

"Is this his cell or his home?"

"He doesn't have a landline, Mom, only a cell." I spoke quietly, as if trying not to spook a lion. My mother didn't believe in cell phones, but I think that belief stemmed from the expense, not because she really had anything against them.

"Okay. Thanks." She huffed out a sigh and wrapped her sweater more tightly over her scrubs. She picked up the phone and said, "Go find your brother and keep him company."

Clicking on the phone to eavesdrop on Mom and Bean . . .

"There isn't much time before we get to flashover. It's already hitting Asia and Africa. England has a mortality rate exceeding ninety percent."

"That's not possible—"

"We've never been here. It's a new world."

"How long? Weeks?"

"Days."

"Okay, thank you. I've never thanked you for all you've done. I'm sorry. For everything."

"I'll accept your apology when I see you the next time. Tell Nadia I said happy birthday. . . ."

Mom argued, "But it's not close to her birthday—"

I laid the phone down; I couldn't risk clicking the button. I'd swing back through as quick as I could later and shut it off.

Start the countdown clock. Seven days and read the letter, open the box. . . .

. . . I found Rabbit glued to the television. Watching footage of riots in Hong Kong.

"Jimmy says we should go to church on Sunday."

"Huh? Why?" I looked for the remote but couldn't find it. Rab didn't need to be watching this.

"Because we're going to die if we don't ask forgiveness."

"You're not going to die."

26

"We all die."

"Eventually. Not now. Besides, what do you have to be sorry for?" I saw the remote clenched in his white knuckles.

"Not going to church. Susan says her parents say this is the end of days. And there's going to be a revolution."

"Jesus, who are your classmates? The cult of horrible news?"

"They're talking about the government doing experiments and—"

"Rabbit?" I knelt down and gently touched his hands. They still gripped the remote. I purposely put my face between his and the screen now showing people in Brasília suffering from an outbreak of bubonic plague. "Look at me?"

He met my gaze, his brow furrowed with panic and worry.

I untangled his fingers from the remote, never breaking eye contact. "We don't need to go to church. People are sick, but that doesn't mean it's the end of days or an alien invasion or that there's going to be a civil war. Okay? Bad stuff happens all the time and we get through it, right? We're the cockroaches. We'll get through this, too. . . ."

. . . Rabbit moved the curtain away from the front window and pressed his face against the glass, trying to see the ambulance better. "It's the crazy cat lady. She's turning into a Smurf. Blue spots all over her."

Three emergency responders piled out of their truck all decked out in spacesuits. They moved in slow motion. I couldn't see well around the ambulance, so I shifted.

"Nadia?" Rab called from the front door.

They loaded cat lady onto a backboard and masked her face to help her breathe.

One of the guys saw me standing there and lifted his helmet to yell at me, "You'll need to let all the cats out!"

"Why me?" I shouted back.

"Someone needs to or they'll die too," he bellowed in reply while moving away. Maybe I misheard. Maybe he didn't really say "die too"—wouldn't she get better? Come home? . . .

Mom showered for almost an hour. "It's bad, Nadia." She hung her head as tears fell down her cheeks. "They sent us home tonight. Canceled all shifts for the rest of the week."

"Who's taking care of patients?"

"There weren't enough of us left anyway. Most people were calling in sick to take care of their own families or were ill themselves."

"What is it?"

"I don't know. No one's seen anything like it. Someone said bird flu, but we had twenty cases of XRD TB in two hours today."

"XR what?"

"Drug-resistant tuberculosis. Almost everything coming through our doors doesn't respond to medication, or is secondary to this virus. Nothing works. They're calling it BluStar because of the blue star-shaped bruises it leaves along the skin. . . ."

Curfews . . . Riots . . . Helicopters dumping flyers of news . . . No water . . . No power . . . The fall of complete silence except for Mom's screams at the end . . .

DAY 57

We stripped that rest stop of gas and anything remotely useful. We felt like vultures. Rats. Criminals.

At least, I did; Rabbit, not so much. "It's not stealing. Not anymore."

Clearly, my brother was more pragmatic. "I know, it's just that—"

Rabbit imitated Dad's deep voice. "Be the cockroach, Nadia."

I punched his arm.

"He was all about surviving." Rabbit said this toward the window, as if the scenery might reveal new truths.

"At any cost?" I leaned back a little. The second day of driving gave me more confidence behind the wheel.

"For us, yes. Think of it like shopping with an unlimited credit card. We can make it fun." Rabbit slouched down and slanted a glance my way, as if waiting for my reaction. "We have to."

"Hmm . . . shopping with an unlimited budget? That's a good point. . . . When did you get so smart?" I asked, knowing he'd gotten the genius genes from Dad.

"You just haven't paid attention." Rabbit grinned. He waggled his eyebrows. "Let's go to the mall. I need new . . . Airwalks."

I pretended to think before shouting, "New makeup!"

"Shades!" He pantomimed putting on a pair with boy-band panache.

"Unlimited Seven by Seven brand jeans." As if we could even afford one pair in the real world.

"American Eagle all for me!"

"Gap!" I giggled.

"Nordstrom!" Rabbit cracked up like a little kid. A game of Name That Store made the miles seem shorter.

"Barnes and Noble!"

He shook his head, feigning disappointment. "You're a dork—going for books. GameLand is so much cooler."

"I can read books without electricity." I sobered as reality crashed back in.

"Oh, you just ruined the whole thing." He snorted and dropped his feet off the dash and onto the pile of survival books and maps.

"We'll get used to it, won't we? The no-power thing?" I asked.

"We have a choice? Then, I'll choose a generator and solar panels and running water and refrigeration and—"

"Bean said Pappi's got it all figured out," I announced with more assurance than I felt. I'd learned fast that being an adult sometimes meant projecting an illusion rather than truth. "Bean will know what to do, too."

"Anyone can, he can," Rabbit agreed as he pointed out the exit to the next highway. *Through the mountains at the lowest altitude possible.* "We just have to get there, right? Then, it'll all be fine." His voice was steely and determined.

"Right." I hoped. The temperature dipped as we gained altitude up into the foothills of the Cascades, where the wind blew with icy fingers and the rain seemed chunky when it hit the windshield. We didn't turn on music, and I kept the headlights on even though I wasn't sure they helped me see better. There were lots of places a car could drop off the side and never be seen. *Not like there is anyone to rescue us. Stop being a pessimist, Nadia.*

We kept going until a fresh blanket of white snow covered everything. I swore.

"I guess no one's plowing the roads, huh?" Rabbit sat forward in his seat and gazed out at the highway in front of us. The lane markers were gone, but the snow couldn't have been more than a few inches since the path of the road was visible, if all white.

"What do we do now?" My driving skills were pushed to the limit with rain, and I shuddered at the possibility of sliding off a mountain with my brother in tow. *Survive BluStar. Die in a car accident. Ironic.* I stopped the Jeep on a particularly straight and even stretch. An uncommonly warm spring meant there wasn't a ton of packed snow. What we didn't know was what the weather had been like up here for the past months. Could be inches or feet.

"Put the tire chains on?"

"Chains? We have chains? How do you know this stuff?" I questioned.

"They're under the bench seat. You took care of Mom for those last days, Nadia. I packed up Bean's stuff and read a ton in all those books. It's what I could do." Rabbit sounded older than our parents.

I nodded. I'd simply assumed he'd stayed away from Mom's bedroom because he was scared, not because he'd been working on getting ready for this trek. "Are there instructions for these chain things?"

"Of course." He handed me my winter jacket and zipped his own up before plunging into the elements to dig the chains and pamphlet out. His mutters sounded something like "I should have put them near the top, not on the bottom."

I almost believed he could make this trip without me. It was more comforting than disturbing to think he'd be okay. *Just in case.* We closed the doors to keep out the wind as he handed me the instructions. "These are in Japanese."

"Flip them over." Rabbit almost rolled his eyes.

I did, but it wasn't much better. "That's Spanish. Fine print is English. Are these stick figures or hieroglyphs?"

Finally, the only thing left to do was try. We followed the instructions, and by the time we finished, I was bathed in sweat. I peeled off my coat and Mom's cardigan and kept my window down a few inches until it was too cold.

I swallowed, turning on the ignition. "We have to do this." Silence stretched as we made our way down the middle of the road.

"It's only like six inches of snow. We can do this. 'The key is to drive slowly and at a steady pace. Don't hit the brakes,'" Rabbit read from a travel book's section on mountain driving.

He craned his head against the window and stared up the mountainside. "What about avalanches?"

I lifted my foot to stamp on the brake but caught myself. *Avalanches? Seriously?* "We'll have to cross that when we come to them, but no loud music. I don't really want to get buried until it thaws out."

"Good news is that we have plenty of food, water, and supplies to, you know, live."

Terrified of getting us both killed, I tried to lift the serious tension of being. "But you'd start to stink and I couldn't handle that!"

Rabbit picked it up and ran for a few miles, bantering about farting and belching and all things boy. I was happy to hear him talk about normal stuff, but our ten-miles-an-hour speed had me fretting about gas supplies and hypothermia.

The snow packed down under the car and we finally reached the ski lodge at the summit. We had a long way to go before we were clear of the mountains.

"Nadia, it's already five. We're not going to make it down in time. Before dark."

I turned into the parking lot. "You wanna spend the night up here?"

"Well, I can't imagine a lot of people were skiing right before they died, so it might be empty."

Good point. I drove deeper into the deserted parking lot. At least, I thought it was deserted, but the piles of snow could have hidden cars and trucks and an army of abominable snowmen. Animal tracks littered the snow like we'd missed a party.

"What if we get snowed in?" I asked, thinking aloud. I parked and turned off the Jeep.

Rabbit was already unlatching his door and slipping out into the falling twilight. "We stay a while. Or dig out. I don't know. They have to have snow shovels around here. Take a deep breath, Nadia. Would that be so bad?"

I followed him, inhaling through both my nose and mouth. And for a split second I had no idea what he was talking about. Then the clean crisp air hit my lungs. No smell. That wasn't entirely true. Pine and ozone filled my lungs. No death. No rotting flesh. Just air. "Oh my God, I forgot." This is what the world used to smell like.

❀　❀　❀

Rabbit threw himself down into a snowdrift and made a snow angel. "Let's see what's inside. Can I take a bath?" My brother used to fight bath time.

"We'll both take baths." I, on the other hand, wanted to shower eight times a day for the next month. We'd melt snow, worst-case scenario, to fill the tubs.

Rabbit nodded. "We need cutters for the locked chains on the doors. We shouldn't keep breaking the windows of places."

"We'll look for some at the mall, but for now just get us in a door. We'll patch the window with wood, or cardboard, or something."

"Aye, aye." Rabbit grabbed the hammer and ran toward the front entrance.

I grabbed our backpacks with fresh clothes, and a couple of lamps.

By the time I'd walked over, Rabbit held the door open. "Welcome to the Snow Chalet, do you have a reservation?"

"As a matter of fact, I do. It's under Dork." I smiled, closing the door behind me.

"Isn't this place amazing?" Rabbit kicked off his boots but left on his coat—the air was warmer than outside, but only because there wasn't wind blowing. A large fireplace dominated one end of a reception area. The space was littered with sofas and chairs. Huge dark wooden beams lined the walls and supported the ceiling like sentries.

Each carrying a lantern, we wandered around picking stuff up and opening doors. There was a musty unused smell, but no death. My nose told me I wouldn't walk around a corner and be jolted back into the present. *Heaven.*

"Hey, there are tons of candles in here, and firewood." We'd stumbled into a honeymoon suite decorated with understated hearts and old-school romantic lighting. A two-way fireplace split the sleeping area and bathroom; yet another area was cozily made into a living room with a couch and recliners. Dried wilted red-black roses covered the whitest, fluffiest king-size bed I'd ever seen. *Someone planned to stay here and never made it.*

"Let's sleep in here." Rabbit set his lantern down, found matches in a drawer, and started lighting candles. "We can put a fire in and warm up. Get more wood and have both fireplaces blazing!"

"I'll go see if there's anything left in the kitchen, or grab food out of the car."

"Grab pots, or something, to melt ice in?"

"For bathing in that swimming pool of a tub, right?" I sighed and wished for hot water and Jacuzzi jets and tons of bubble bath. At least we'd be clean, sleeping in clean sheets. "Aye, aye."

"Wait, there's a minifridge over here." Rabbit lowered the candle. "And a snack cabinet."

"Minibar. Dad said they're expensive and we should never ever eat anything out of it."

Rab visibly shrank.

"Quick, what's in it?" I smiled. *No one's billing us for the stay.*

He wrestled open the doors, "Chips, Snickers, nuts, Coke, and a moldy orange."

"I'll skip the orange. But I really am getting sick of snack food."

"How is that possible?" Rabbit looked crestfallen. "Me too."

"Let me see if there's real food around here, then we can have dessert." I ruffled his hair, or tried to. It was a greasy, dirty mess.

"Do I look as nasty as you do?" I wiped my palm on my jeans.

"Oh yeah, worse." Rabbit snickered.

"Thanks. You okay here while I go out?"

"Yep, I'll get the fire going, and find more wood and stuff. . . ." He trailed off, seeming vulnerable, yet brave.

I turned away.

"Wait!" Rabbit raced over to his backpack and pulled out a pair of Junior Ranger walkie-talkies.

"You brought those?"

"They're my walkie-talkies. I just—I mean, I—I couldn't." *Leave them behind, perhaps?* Rabbit and Dad hiked the forests of the Olympic Peninsula with a walkie-talkie attached to their belts. "Man time" I'd never envied until Dad was dead.

"It's a great idea." We practiced a little. I saw Rabbit standing taller, appearing less fragile since we could talk to each other at any time. "Ring if you need me."

"You too." Rabbit started balling up old newspapers and magazines to build his fire.

I used a flashlight instead of the lantern, but there was still a lot of ambient sunlight bouncing off the snow. I wondered if I'd ever get used to the silence. I unzipped my coat but didn't take it off. My toes were icicles in my socks; the sooner I found us food, or went to the car to grab cans of soup, the sooner I'd be back in the suite.

Behind one door, I found a cart that probably belonged to room service or housekeeping. I wheeled it in front of me, part armor, part efficiency. I had to keep reminding myself of that "no zombies" thing.

I headed away from the guest rooms and back toward the reception area. I remembered seeing a bar and what might be a dining room. The kitchen had to be close to that.

I crossed a polished dance floor, and even though wires lay like a coil of plastic snakes, all the DJ equipment was gone. So far electronics topped the list. *Yummy.* When would I stop being shocked at the things people carried off?

The bar was empty of booze. One last party, or an enterprising employee? Had they raided the kitchen, too? I pushed the swinging doors open with my cart. The smell hit me first. A hint of garbage, not people rotting, but food waste like slimy salad greens and fuzzy broccoli. It made sense that I might find moldy produce, but only if there was anything left to spoil.

The industrial-style stainless steel kitchen was so clean, I felt like I'd stepped into a surgical theater. My flashlight picked up and bounced spurts of light, casting shadows on the walls like an animated movie. I'd never been in a restaurant kitchen. *Why would I? Add that to the list of things I know nothing about.* Restaurant kitchens didn't matter in my old life. My only thoughts were to hope the cooks weren't spitting in my food or dropping it on the floor. *I'll take a menu and a chance right about now. What happened to "Domino's delivers"?*

I opened food lockers and found a few jars of olives, garlic paste, a couple big tins of dry curry mix. Crumbs and not much else. I kept hunting. Maybe they'd been in a hurry with the dance-party raid.

Perseverance paid off. At the back of one locker, I found marshmallows, stale and crusty, and unopened graham crackers. We already had chocolate bars in our vending machine stash. I moved baking soda and vanilla extract to see the very back of the pantry.

"Bingo!" I shouted, and did my version of a happy dance.

"You okay?" The walkie-talkie crackled with Rabbit's question.

I hadn't realized I'd yelled so loud. "Food, I found food! Real stuff!" *Okay, well, kind of real.*

Rabbit didn't need to hit the transmit button for me to hear his whoop of delight across the building. "What is it?"

I began piling items onto the cart and realized it might take two trips. "Soups. Cheese. Chili." Moldy bread was unsalvageable, but jars of peanut butter and jam joined crackers and unopened packages of cured meats like pepperoni and salami. I left half the cheese—the moldy parts I cut off—behind.

"Should I come?" he asked.

"You have the fire going?"

"Yeah, and a bunch of candles."

"Stay put. I'm coming to you." I grabbed a pot and bowls, cutlery, napkins from the bins by the door on my way back. The darkness outside the windows didn't feel oppressive; instead I found comfort in knowing that no one could sneak up on us.

"It's like Christmas!" Rabbit held the suite door open and helped me roll the very heavy cart across the threshold.

The heat filling our hideaway was so unexpected, it felt tangible like a cuddly blanket. I'd been chilly for so long I wanted to purr and stretch, but I restrained from unwinding my scarves and unzipping my coat just yet.

"There's so much food here." Rabbit carefully unloaded my finds onto the little table.

"I think someone squirreled it all away and then didn't come back." *Or couldn't come back.* Who would think to look behind the flavorings and leavenings for real food? *Me.* Mimicking Rab's favorite saying, I declared, "Sucks to be them."

Rabbit smiled. "Chicken noodle soup and toasted cheddar cheese sandwiches." Dad's only culinary accomplishments and Rabbit's favorite meal.

"No bread. But we can make 'em on the flat crackers?"

Rab's shoulders dipped with disappointment, but he said, "Sure."

"We have s'mores for dessert." I wanted to bring the smile back to Rabbit's face.

A ghost of a grin accompanied his nod. "I tried the taps and there's no water."

"Frozen pipes, maybe?" I suggested. Sounded plausible to me, and it was my best guess. Hot running water was asking too much. I worked on dinner while Rabbit filled a couple of huge stainless steel bowls with icicles and snow from the balcony and dumped them into the bathtub to melt.

My grilled cheese crackers were black on one side and the soup boiled itself a layer of noodle on the inside of the pot. Cooking over a fire inspired thoughts of raw vegetables and sushi—no-cooking-required-type foods. If I didn't scrape the sides of the pot the carbon charring wasn't too noticeable.

"So the good news is . . ." I let my statement hang until Rabbit glanced up.

"There's good news?"

"No dish washing." At least, not now.

"What do you mean?"

In the early days, Mom made us continue to wash and act normally. Which made no sense at the time, and certainly not now. "We've got lots of extra dishes and no one is going to yell if we let the used ones stack up." I knew as the quasi adult I should make us stay civilized and wash up after each meal like at home. But I didn't care about doing dishes. Until it meant eating on a clean plate or having to reuse a dirty one, I was on cleaning vacation. "Just for a little while."

Rabbit nodded. "If we had a dog he could lick 'em clean."

"Kinda clean, maybe."

"Jimmy's dog licks the plates cleaner than the dishwasher." He swallowed a couple more spoonfuls of soup, but I knew he was thinking about his dead friend and the closest thing to a pet Rabbit ever had.

Rabbit set down his bowl. "Was he, um, in there?"

I hadn't seen or heard Max bark. I shook my head. "They probably let him out and he went to Disneyland instead of hanging around at home."

The look Rabbit shot me suggested he was past the fairy-tale-type lies.

I inhaled and considered. "Tell you what, if we find a dog along the way and it wants to be part of the family, we'll keep it, okay?"

Rabbit set down his soup and threw his arms around me. "Really? Truly?"

"Sure." I hugged him back, not remembering the last time we'd touched. Contact was all but forbidden weeks ago and it was oddly funny how out of practice I felt.

Rab hung on longer than he ever had. Longer than *before*. "Cool." He took a full crunchy bite of cracker and melted cheese. Extra sips of juice helped add moisture to our mouths. "Are we ever going to have bread again?"

Add that to the list. "Sure we are. There's been bread for thousands of years, we'll figure it out."

"Thousands?"

"Everyone had bread, all over the world. Every culture. We can figure it out eventually."

Rabbit sighed wistfully. "But not Seattle sourdough."

"It gets its taste from fermentation, Rab. I think all our bread will probably be sourdough. Think about the gold miners—they didn't have electric ovens and they invented sourdough."

Rabbit quietly put more of the long-lasting fake logs on the fire and tossed in a couple of pinecones that promised to "turn the fire into a romantic light show." We watched the greens and blues bounce around.

"That is definitely romantic," Rab pronounced without a hint of a smile.

Giggles turned to chuckles to full-out belly laughs, almost

41

instantaneously. My eleven-year-old brother declaring anything romantic was laughable. But in our current situation, I guffawed until I was this side of peeing my pants with hysteria.

"What? What?" Rabbit joined me in the fun, but I could tell he thought I might be losing my mind.

We collapsed trying to get our breath back. Warm, full, and relaxed, the world pixilated and I fell into a deep sleep, devoid of the usual nightmarish flashbacks. At least for a while.

DAY 58

I rolled myself tighter, burrowing into the covers, pressing the pillow against my ears. *No, brain, stop. Go back to sleep.* Too late to stay lost in slumber, my brain clicked on and started spinning with the weight of this new life.

Tucked into a tight fetal position with Rabbit smashed against me so completely I felt his vertebrae poking into my knees. I almost pushed him away to stretch my legs when I heard sniffling. The mewling, quiet sounds of an animal in pain ready to give up the fight. I forced my eyelids open. There was enough light to see my breath cloud around my face. I didn't want to leave the cocoon made by the little body heat we generated under the blankets.

I should have piled on the down comforters from other rooms. I should have pitched a tent or built a fort. I remembered thinking of all the things I should do as my eyes closed and my stomach quieted.

Cold. Fire equals heat. Reality came crashing back. I lifted my head to see that the only glow came from a tiny single ember. The rest of the coals were dark and probably cold to the touch.

The mound of blankets sighed and snorted. *Rabbit. He's crying. In his sleep.* I didn't wake him. It wouldn't matter. There was nothing I could do to stop the tears, or the pain, and he needed sleep. Even if it was broken by sobs.

Better than the screaming nightmares—his or mine. *If we watch each other's dreams, like a horror movie, will they be the same?* I forced myself to move through the sharp-edged air. I tucked my blanket over Rabbit's nest and wrapped a wool shawl from the armchair over my head and shoulders. My coat was buried somewhere in Rab's pile.

Get the fire going. Stoke it. Have food ready for Rabbit. I didn't want to go far from Rabbit in case he called for me. Which meant mining the suite for flammable materials. I picked up a stack of magazines from *before*. Smiling, loving Valentine's Day couples and artfully plated desserts and headlines like *Make This Year Special* and *The Perfect Gift He Didn't Know He Craved* and *Life Is Short, Make the Most of Your Love!*

My heart leapt into my throat. *Love?* I'd never been in love. Might never be in love. Might never meet another teenager. Might be the last girl on earth. *What if we are the only people left? What if this is it? Waking up in the middle of the night cold? Crying? Needing fire and food and what happens when it all runs out or spoils or —?*

My heart rate sped up. My lungs shallowed out in panic. I caught air in my chest for fleeting moments, but a deep breath eluded me. A fresh sweat broke out along my hairline. I closed my eyes and forced my hands to relax their grip. *Survive the effect. Be the cockroach. Adapt.*

I ripped pages from the glossies and loosely crumpled them; tight balls captured less air and took longer to catch fire. I carefully placed an end near the glowing ember and watched the edge smolder and smoke. I waited, balling more paper, adding, blowing. The lick of flame crinkled the paper and ignited. Soon, I felt flashes of heat across my nose and face. I added the last of the color-making pinecones and bits of kindling until a small but steady fire snapped and popped in the fireplace.

How does Rab sleep through all that noise? He'd stopped crying; his breathing evened out. I needed to go find more big chunks of wood for the fire, maybe a pot to make soup, or tea. The bottles of water in the minifridges would run out quick. I felt like Scrooge, already wanting to count and recount every single supply. Stupid, really, because if we were careful, and replenished our supplies whenever possible, it would be months, if not years, before we ran out of everything. *Hopefully. Maybe. Then what?*

I tucked my feet back into my boots, laced them up, grabbed a pad of paper, and started writing a note for Rabbit when he woke.

Rab, I'm in the hotel gathering wood and food. Call the walkie-talkie.

I placed the note by the bed along with a walkie-talkie. Then stopped. *What if he doesn't see it?* It was one of those smallish jot-down-a-phone-number hotel tablets. He might not see it.

My heart skipped a beat. Being left alone was his greatest fear, he'd told me sometime around day forty. I copied the note five times and placed them all around the bed. Even left one by the fire in case he decided to stoke it when he woke.

The temperature in the hotel must have dropped another ten degrees. I wrapped my scarf around my neck and itched my greasy, dirty scalp. I missed daily showers. It was amazing how much more optimistic I felt when squeaky-clean and fresh. *How'd the pioneers do it? Days of struggle and stinking messes?*

I unloaded the cart I'd rolled in and inhaled courage. Odds were that no one was checked in when they died. It didn't matter what I told Rab, I kept waiting for things to jump out at me. Maybe it was Rabbit's mention of zombies yesterday, or the reality of leaving our house and everything familiar to venture out into the great unknown, that threw me off my game. But I kept holding my breath and tiptoeing as if hoping to not wake the dead.

I went back toward the lobby. There must be an office, with information and a layout of the resort. Plus, I thought I remembered seeing stacks of perfectly cut wood by the massive fireplace in the front room.

A click click click caught my attention. I froze. Like pebbles being thrown against glass. Then like marbles tossed across linoleum stairs. Hail? Rain? I made my way toward the windows, but the flashlight caught my reflection on the glass.

"Crap!" I shrieked, jumping back. "It's you. Just you."

I pressed the LED beam against the glass and tried to shine

it out into the world. The beam skittered across ice pellets and chunky raindrops. A thick slush of marbles and Magic Shell ice covered the parking lot. *Um, not going anywhere today.*

I sighed. *Wood. We need wood now.* We were safe in here, dry, and there was food. The ice would turn to rain eventually and we would move on. Was having a ski chalet all to ourselves so bad? Not really.

I stacked the cart with huge tree trunk rounds, leaving behind the heaviest ones, and made my way toward our suite. I stopped at the one next to ours and went in. Raided it for any comforters and then relieved the minifridge of its innards, including bottles of water. *We'll build a tent of sorts to sleep in.*

I clicked open the suite door and rolled the cart in, trying to keep it from tipping over. The bed was empty.

"Rab?" I called.

"Dia?"

Who else? "Yeah."

Rabbit poked his head out of the bathroom. He gripped the fireplace brush like a weapon. "I was scared."

"I left you notes." I pointed at the pieces of paper he'd gathered up.

"But what if they got you while you were out there?"

"No zombies, Rab." I sighed.

"Then why were you so quiet?"

"You were sleeping," I snarked. "I was trying to be a good big sister and let you sleep. If you'd rather, I can sing at the top of my lungs and wake you up with my stylings of Vlad King of the Vampires' 'End Times.' That can be arranged."

Rabbit nodded as if I wasn't being bratty. "Is that a real song?" He laid down his weapon.

"Nah," I lied. It was the last major chart topper before, well, *before*.

"Is it snowing?"

"No, it's lumpy rain." Lumpy rain was a mix of ice and rain and purely a Northwest creation. He knew exactly what I meant.

"Are we leaving today?"

I shook my head. "Not in this we're not."

"Is that bad?"

It wasn't like we were on a time line of someone else's making. This was our trip. *Our rules.* "Doesn't have to be."

"That's good, I like it here." He smiled. Rabbit used to smile all the time. He'd annoy me with his always-present grin. Now, I never saw it.

We made it into a game, racing around as the black grew gray outside and the icy rain turned to snow and then stopped. Rab took a cart and I took mine and we shouted over the walkie-talkies as we collected anything and everything that might be useful. Candles, laundry soap. In the staff break room, there were lockers full of clean uniforms, T-shirts, socks. As if people were just off for the weekend and coming back in on Monday.

What day is it? I didn't know. I couldn't remember. For a moment I panicked, I let the fear of the unknown blind me. Days of the week. They didn't matter. Monday was exactly like Tuesday and Wednesday and Thursday. No one knew where we were. No one knew we were alive. No one cared, except Uncle Bean. And Pappi, if he'd survived in his West Virginia bolt-hole.

I found the emergency procedures manual. "Bingo."

"What?" Rab stood in the doorway.

"This binder. Tells us where everything is and what to do in case of emergencies."

"So?" He jumped from foot to foot like I was taking too long.

"So." I flipped through it, checking the index. "'In case of power outages, use the keys in locker fifty-two to unlock the shed and turn on the generator.'"

"Generator?"

"Power, Rabbit." I tried to keep my excitement tamped down. Odds were someone had already used the generator, or it was frozen, or because it was us it simply wouldn't work. I scanned the information about what the generator was hooked into. "Water."

"Water?" Rabbit scurried over and tried to read too.

"Water!" I yelled, allowing myself a tiny little happy dance.

Rab's eyes widened and a grin split his lips. "Really?"

"Only one way to find out." We headed toward the staff room.

"Which locker?" He raced down the line pulling open the unlocked ones and glancing inside with his flashlight.

"Fifty-two." Turned out the resort had its own propane generators to run both lights and its own well. It looked like the water heaters and in-floor heating systems also kicked on when the generators were running. Now all we had to do was pray that there was enough propane left. *Any* propane left.

I didn't have to have lights, and there wasn't any television, radio, or computer info to gather so that would cut down on the draw. But it had been months since we'd had an actual shower—spit baths with rainwater heated to not-cold-but-not-even-lukewarm sucked.

There was a time when the city had turned off the water to halt the spread of the disease. Right before they'd come to the house. I shook off the memory.

We bundled up. The keys were clutched in my hand. We read the directions and I knew what I had to do.

Rabbit stamped his feet. "What are you waiting for?"

Still I hesitated. *What if it doesn't work?*

DAY 60

It was only forty-eight hours, two days, but we took four showers, washed our clothes, and flushed the toilet every time we peed. We cooked spaghetti noodles, slathered them with jarred alfredo sauce, and added chunks of canned chicken. There were canned green beans and rings of sweet pineapple. We even found a boxed scone mix that we were able to bake, slather with strawberry jam and wildflower honey, and eat in bed, along with mugs of hot cocoa.

The snow turned to a light rain and I saw bare patches on our Jeep and in the parking lot. The world wasn't white anymore. *Time to move on.*

Wrapped in one of the resort's logo-covered bathrobes, socks, and long johns, I folded our clean clothes in neat piles for the morning.

Rab readied another board game. "I'll be banker."

"Okay."

"I'd like a hotel on Boardwalk to start."

"Okay." I was distracted. I knew it. Couldn't help it.

Rabbit tossed down the dice in a huff. "You aren't paying attention."

"I'm trying, Rab. I'm really trying."

"What are you thinking about?"

"We have a decision to make." I hadn't planned on giving Rabbit any say. I thought I'd decide no problem and just tell him. But it was his life, too, his journey, and I was fast realizing I wasn't autocratic and dictatorial. Not anymore.

He sat straighter, looked me in the eye, and said, "Brief me, Marine."

I snorted. "At ease."

He slouched back down comically, but the serious expression in his eyes didn't change. He simply waited, with Dad's patience.

"Bean said we have two options in our route to get there. For long-term survival, we need to find unoccupied land, like a park or a forest. That way, if we have to we can hunt, and we'll have access to foraging, drinking water. We'll be able to stay away from the majority of people who might have survived."

"Keep going."

"That's our best bet. But militias and other wacky folks who might know about this strategy could be there too. And territorial." I didn't add mention of the guns and execution of interlopers that Bean said might be worst-case scenario.

"They'll shoot us or make us slaves," Rabbit said as calmly as if he'd asked me to pass the toothpaste.

Startled, I nodded before catching myself. "How do you know that?"

"Because that's what always happens in video games. Assuming we're not dealing with aliens or zombies."

"I think we can assume that."

"So it might be safer if we can't make it to the mine, but we're not going to run into Jesus unless he drives a tank and accessorizes with a flamethrower." Rab grinned at his own vivid word picture. The kid cracked himself up. Often.

"Right."

"Option B?"

"We stick to populated areas where we can find gas and scrounge supplies, but odds are we may run into people who want what we have or need help."

"They'll slow us down or even keep us from getting there. You're worried we'd have to say no to strangers who want help. And there are going to be more bodies if we do that."

Moments like this gave me a new appreciation for how perceptive my brother was. "Probably. Yes."

He nodded, then thoughtfully declared, "I'd rather get over the creepy dead guys than the ones who want to make us slaves."

"Good point." *The dead don't kill or rob.* "I think we need to get a little farther away from Washington and closer to West Virginia."

"So we stay near small towns, and maybe medium-size ones, but steer away from big cities."

I saw his logic. "Do the same with the parks—stay in little ones that no one would hole up in long term, but leave alone the ginormous ones people might be possessive over."

"Works for me." He finished dealing out the fake money, although now it was as real as any currency.

Late that night we crawled into our blanketed fort, which kept cozy warmth around us even in the wee hours.

When dawn broke on the third day there was a part of me that wanted to stay forever but also a part that was itching to get going. This was just a stop on the journey and not the destination. It wouldn't work long term for us to stay in the Cascades, not like this.

"It's time to move on." Rab spoke to me even as his attention was fixed on the landscape outside the windows.

"You think?"

"The rain washed all the snow away." Nothing white, only lots of greens and browns.

It took us a couple of hours to load the car with the treasures we'd collected. Most wouldn't fit. The truth was we hadn't used much of what we brought with us, so there wasn't room to restock.

At the last minute, we loaded the rest of the supplies we'd gathered onto one of the carts and parked it by the information desk along with the notebook on how to turn on the generator. Just in case there were people behind us. Maybe they'd say a prayer for us in gratitude.

I cleared my throat. "There's another full gas can in the shed. Do we leave it in case someone else comes?"

Rab shook his head. "What would Dad say?"

"He'd tell us to take it because we're the only ones we know for sure need it."

Unfortunately, I thought that would be the rule of life in this new world. What we knew for sure was us, and only us.

We filled the gas tank of the Jeep and belted in. "Ready?" I asked.

"Yep."

We drove down the other side of the mountains, making good time with clear skies and empty roads. I didn't worry about the speed limit as I got the hang of driving. The farther we got into Eastern Washington, the warmer the temperature. Bright sun, fluffy clouds, and heat had us changing into T-shirts and driving with the windows down.

"We need gas. There's a big blank spot coming on the map." Rabbit showed me.

Lots of potential for nothing and no one.

In Quincy, we pulled into a neighborhood that looked hollow, as if a strong wind might blow through and knock all the facades down. It took five cars for us to find enough gas to fill up, but there was a long stretch of open road ahead before 28 crossed into 90 and Spokane.

Rab lowered the map with a frown. "Dia?"

"Yeah?" I didn't take my eyes from the road as I steered with one hand and took a drink from my water bottle.

"Did you notice that we're on the road that passes by Fairchild Air Force Base?"

"Oh." I slowed down until the Jeep idled. Military bases were designated evacuation sites early on in the rampage. But the dead weren't what caused my hesitation.

Rabbit didn't really have to continue. "If I were a crazy person looking for guns and tanks . . ."

He trailed off, but I picked it up and ran. "You'd go to military bases looking for caches of firepower?"

"Yeah, probably."

"Me too." I nodded. "What're our options?" He was navigator, and if I was being honest, I wasn't all that good at reading and understanding maps. Give me step-by-step GPS software directions and I called it good.

"Right, let's cut south at Harrington and catch 90 that way."

I agreed and we drove on. Running alongside the road, packs of dogs resembled an old National Geographic special.

"Are those wolves?" Rab asked as I slowed down to get a better look.

A bloodhound, a couple of silver Weimaraners, and white and black cocker spaniels ran with mutts of every kind. All were muddy, matted, skinny, and no longer resembled anyone's beloved pets. "No, I don't think so."

They circled a cow and calf who bawled for rescue. I hit the accelerator knowing what was coming. "Turn up this song, I love it."

"You like this song?" Rab quizzed me, as if not even he liked this particular tune.

I hit the volume as Rab turned in his seat to watch the dogs. "Rab, turn around." *I sound like Mom.* But he ignored me. "Turn around." I raised my voice until I shouted on this side of hysteria. I didn't want him to see the scene playing out in the rearview mirror.

"Dia, I'm not a baby. They're hungry. They're going to kill the cow and eat it."

I blinked. "I know. We don't have to watch, though." *We've seen so much worse in the past two months, why does this bother me?*

"How are you going to hunt for us if you can't handle watching animals hunt?"

"I can do it." Dad taught me. "I don't know. It's different." I wasn't sure how, but it was.

The cow and dogs left long behind, Rabbit couldn't let it go. "I'm not a baby," he declared.

"I know. I know." Maybe, but I didn't know how to see him as an equal. The last two years my world had narrowed to taking care of him. Competent non-babies didn't require that level of care.

The miles slid by. Abandoned cars and the occasional human skeleton.

Rabbit's stomach growled. "My ass hurts, Dia."

"Mine too." With over two hundred miles behind us, I finally felt hungry. My stamina wasn't what it once was. Rabbit had also been sick, but he'd bounced back much faster. The lingering effects of the virus, or the shot, didn't seem to weigh him down like anchors. Maybe I was feeling that last sleepless week taking care of Mom, or the continual nightmares, but I wanted a nap. Sleep without the sound track of Mom's screams or the Smell-O-Vision of this rank new world.

Rab held up the map. "There's a wildlife refuge—mostly birds—up ahead. I think it's one of the small sites, not useful for the crazies. Can we camp there tonight? Then go into that town tomorrow?"

"Why not? Can you get us there?" I wasn't looking forward to seeing what was left, or not left, of the next medium-size town on the map. Not as large as Seattle, but far larger than anything we'd passed through so far, it even had a couple of college campuses.

Did kids die in their dorms or did they get home to say goodbye?

Not for the first time I wished I could search online or turn on cable news for numbers—how many people survived this thing? Would we run into crowds? Did all military personnel have the shot, or just a few select people like Bean said? Did everyone evacuate to the cities along the coasts like they were supposed to?

What if there were people with planes and information about the rest of the world? What if we could just hop a jet and be in West Virginia by tomorrow? Not bloody likely, and if anything, Dad would have screamed in frustration that I was willing to trust my life and that of my brother to someone else, someone I didn't know. *"Seize your destiny, Nadia. It's yours and yours alone."*

"Nadia, turn here." Rabbit grabbed at the wheel.

"Don't!" I slammed on the brakes. "Don't touch the wheel while I'm driving."

"Sorry, but you weren't listening." Rabbit shrugged.

Survive BluStar and die in a car crash. Brilliant.

I turned and followed Rabbit's directions to Turnbull National Wildlife Refuge.

"What if we meet some anarchists?" Rab's voice trembled.

"Some what?" I followed the signs toward the outlook area. "Did you say anarchists?"

"What if?"

"That's why Bean made sure we had guns and could use them."

"Video games aren't the same." Rabbit shook his head.

They'll have to be. Dad's lessons were abbreviated at best.

DAY 61

Really loud frogs and some animal that sounded like the Loch Ness monster had a baby with Lady Gaga were the only overnight sounds. No people, dead or living.

"Nadia?" Rab asked.

"Yeah?" The gas gauge was under half-full and heading south faster than I felt comfortable with. We needed gas.

"I have a bad feeling."

"I told you not to eat that candy bar for breakfast." I shook my head.

"Not that kind of bad feeling."

I pulled my foot off the accelerator. "About what?"

"I don't think we should go into this town."

"It's called Cheney. You said it was the next nearest place

on the map and there was a college, so there might be kids still alive, supplies."

"I don't know. Let's go into Spokane instead."

"But I thought we agreed to stay out of big cities?"

"We did."

"This isn't that big. It's more like a town, right?"

"Still."

"Are you psychic?" My frustration bubbled over.

"No."

"Then we check it out. We need gas."

Rabbit nodded, but the clouds on his brow didn't lift and he turned off the music.

We drove across Front Street and railroad tracks. Burned husks of cars and strange signs were spray-painted on the sides of buildings. As we drew alongside a road that edged the town, there were roadblocks. Military-style vehicles. *Maybe Rab's right?*

"Dia?" He sat up straighter and locked the Jeep's doors. "Let's use the AC." He hit the buttons to raise our windows. I wanted to tell him he was overreacting, but I was ready to hit the buttons too.

Cars, trucks, wood, and wires cobbled together a fence of trash. I continued along the street.

"Look for any signs of life. People," I instructed.

There were bleached bones poking out of shoes and jeans littering both sides of the mound.

"There were people." Rabbit pointed.

"What the hell happened here?" I gazed around, trying to imagine what drove people to such lengths. It looked like a war zone. Houses were trashed or burned-out shells; skeletons sat in cars as if they'd died protecting stuff.

Barricades of tires and furniture, bags of rotting garbage, razor wire, mattresses covered in stains, windows and doors, chicken wire were piled. Bricks of concrete that seemed to come from sidewalks or homes' foundations were mixed in, as if when someone died, the contents of their home were puked into the fence in front of it.

Sidewalks were obliterated under piles of people's useless junk, like electronics, and heirloom desks.

"This was on the news," Rabbit said. "Towns doing this. Trying to shield themselves safe against the virus."

In theory it made sense. Band together to keep the outside out and healthy people in. But by the time anyone realized they needed something like it, there was already at least one sick person. The idea only worked when the invader was visible— viruses were smarter than humans in many ways. Invisible to the eye and skilled at adapting, they hitched rides on carriers before ever making them sick.

A stench weaseled its way through the ventilation system, its fingers tickling our noses and closing our throats. After a few days of not smelling this, it was almost overpowering to be reacquainted with it.

"I'm going to throw up." Rabbit gagged.

"If you do, I do, so you can't. You can't!" I hollered, fighting my own upwardly mobile stomach. The high heat of May in Eastern Washington wasn't helpful. Or maybe it was helpful in that it sped up the process.

"Eventually the smell will get better," I repeated.

"You keep saying that."

"I mean it." Uncle Bean had assured me that nature would take care of the mess as quickly as it could.

Rabbit grabbed the air freshener hanging from the rearview mirror and sniffed it crazily. "I'm not smelling buttercream. I can't smell anything but dead shit."

"Don't swear," I chastised him.

"Seriously? You're gonna nag me for swearing?"

A sign sprayed with red paint leaned against the fence. TURN BACK. THERE IS NO ONE AND NOTHING HERE FOR YOU.

"What's that mean?"

"I think they got the zombie memo."

Rabbit cracked a smile. "Look at that one." He pointed to another sign.

CROSSING THIS LINE WILL GET YOU SHOT. DON'T MAKE US SHOOT YOU.

"Are there people here?"

"If there are, they aren't selling Girl Scout Cookies or lemonade to folks going by, are they?"

I slowed the car and rolled down my window.

"What are you doing?" Panic gripped Rab's tone and he caught my arm.

"I'm going to yell."

"And get shot?"

"I'm staying on this side of the stuff."

"That doesn't really matter."

"Says who?"

"Dark Forces 6: Humanity's Last Hope."

"I'm taking advice from a video game?"

"You got a better idea?"

"Yeah, I'm going to see if there's anything alive."

"Bad idea."

"Thanks, Monsieur Mario Brothers, for that prediction. Can you do something useful, please, and find us water in the back?"

62

Rabbit shook his head. "I'm not getting out of this car."

"Climb over." I sighed. Unhooked my seat belt.

"What are you doing?"

"Getting out so they can see I'm not sick."

"Tastier with ketchup that way." Rabbit grabbed my shirt. "I will leave you here if they drag you away. I am *not* brave."

"I'm not going to be eaten by zombies."

"Just consider it a warning."

"Fine. Let go of me." I opened the car door and stepped into the heat. The sun baked everything under her rays. I saw heat rippling and felt my scalp prickle. I smelled putrefying flesh and warm sewage. "Hello?" I called at the top of my voice. "Anyone alive?"

I felt like an idiot. But I didn't like this place. There was something wrong. Something off.

"Come on, Dia."

"In a minute, I said."

"I don't like it." Rabbit held out a bottle of water over the car door. "We can make it to the next place to get gas—let's just go on. Someone didn't want people going in there—I think we should respect that and get the hell out of here."

A pop sounded, like a car backfiring. The crash of breaking glass forced my feet back.

"Nadia, they're shooting at us!"

I jumped back into the Jeep and floored it.

For miles neither of us spoke. Breaking the silence, Rab said in a small voice, "I guess we're not the only survivors."

For the first time I wondered if that was really a good thing. *Maybe there are worse things than zombies to worry about?*

We passed through Four Lakes, and it was clearly close enough that anything of value had been ransacked and collected by the Cheney crazies. There were no cars visible. The gas gauge dipped slowly lower. Driving through neighborhoods that looked trashed would only waste gas. *What if we run out? What then?*

"We keep going." I nodded, speaking aloud.

"I don't know that I want to go into Spokane." Rabbit studied the map in his lap.

"I don't either, but I'm not sure what choice we have. We have to find gas or we're going to be walking." I sped up, hoping that we'd come across an answer if I went fast enough.

"Take the next exit!" Rabbit yelled in excitement.

"Spokane International Airport? We can't take a plane." I rolled my eyes.

"No, but lots of people went to airports, right? And left their cars? Isn't there a parking lot or something we can raid?"

"That's brilliant." I grabbed his shoulder and shook him.

"Thank you!" Rab smiled.

Besides, there's not a lot of supplies and stuff to guard there— low crazy-low corpse factor, right?

I was beginning to understand that assumptions were a bad idea in this world.

I bypassed the parking garage and instead took the exit toward outdoor parking. Fewer places to get trapped. And we could go to the parking garage if we needed to. Monster trucks—the kind with chipped paint, gun racks, and hay in the back—were the vehicle du jour. The good thing was they were easy to siphon gas from, and we were able to fill the Jeep and the extra gas cans.

"Nadia, that's the same Jeep." Rab pointed.

I shrugged, not paying any attention.

"They have a rack on top and a bike rack on the back."

I glanced up. "So?"

"So we can put more gas cans on top, maybe other stuff, too? Right?"

"That's really smart," I said. "Any idea how to get them off there and onto ours? Or I guess we could just load our stuff into that Jeep?"

"Oh, please. Give me fifteen minutes and we'll be ready to roll." Rabbit crossed over four lanes of parked cars and sure enough, even though he had to break the windows, he got the racks off and onto ours in under a half hour. I just did what I was told.

Back on the road we couldn't decide if we should go into Spokane or avoid it. Now that we knew there might be people, and they couldn't all be shooters, there was a huge temptation to find others. A black cloud ahead of us looked like millions of birds swarming.

"What is that?" Rab sat farther forward.

"I don't know." Whatever it was, it didn't look friendly and happy.

"Birds?"

"No, not birds." They weren't big enough, and I couldn't see a single wing outline.

"Are those bugs?"

Oh no.

"Those *are* bugs." Rabbit grinned. I could tell he was torn between being a gross boy and being horrified. There were predictions in the early days about the increase in numbers of bugs that ate carrion or used it for breeding. We'd seen it in our neighborhood.

Maggots no longer gave me the total creeps. For weeks, they were common any time we left the house. "Flies," I said, turning on the headlights and the windshield wipers to help see into the wall of iridescent black.

"Are they coming this way?"

"Uh-huh."

"We're going to drive through them?"

"I don't think we can go around them." The fly cloud seemed to stretch from one side of the landscape to the other.

"This is going to be disgusting, isn't it?" Rabbit almost clapped his hands. *Boys.*

With the ping of large raindrops, and the splat of flyover bird bombs, thousands of flies smashed against the Jeep windows. It was impossible to stop from flinching and ducking in reaction to all the hits.

Rabbit's giggles and groans had me loosening my grip on the steering wheel.

"New this year at Disneyland, the Bug Splat, the ride that will have you laughing your guts out." Rab's sense of humor was fully intact and so like Dad's that it sometimes surprised me.

I smiled as Rab dialed to a song on the MP3 player.

"Sound track," he said as the first beats of Queen's "Another One Bites the Dust" came pouring over the sound system. We rocked out three times before the edge of the flies brightened.

"I guess we know what all the maggots became. You know they think this is the best thing to ever happen to them." He grew silent.

"Perspective?" I immediately thought of one of Mom's last lectures.

Rabbit nodded. "Depends on how you look at it. Let's turn here and go south."

"Take 195 south?"

"I don't want to go into Spokane. What if it's like Cheney?"

"It might not be bad."

"But don't you think those flies mean something?"

"They mean it's a good time to be a fly. But sure, we can take 195." I slowed and took the twisty ramp to get onto the smaller highway. There were even fewer vehicles on the sides of the road. We rolled down the windows again and paid attention to the scenery.

"What was that?"

It took me a moment to recognize the brown rolling hills and sand traps. "A dead golf course."

"Why's it so brown?"

"No one to water and feed it, I guess."

"That's sad."

Of all the things Rab had seen and been through, this is what he found sad?

"You're a weird kid."

He grinned. "Tell me something new."

For lunch Rab ate cold SpaghettiOs out of the can, while I munched on a granola bar. I missed salad. Fresh fruit. *Thank goodness I'm not vegan.*

"Welcome to Idaho."

"Wow, we've done a state."

"Yep." I tried not to imagine how many more we'd need to cross.

"We can spend the night at the St. Joe River tributary." Rab showed me on the map. "I could use a bath."

We had a couple hours of sunlight left, enough to make camp, stretch our legs, and wash off in the river. With clean hair and clean clothes, I could almost forget why we were here. Exhaustion clawed at me, and even brushing my teeth twice didn't get rid of the strange metallic taste in my mouth. The Jeep was too hot to sleep in, so we rolled out sleeping bags on a tarp. I slept with my sneakers on and the car keys tied around my wrist.

"What's that noise?"

"What noise?" I asked, without opening my eyes.

"That, over there."

I heard it, but it sounded distinctly like something Rab might joke about. "Rabbit, stop that."

"I'm not doing anything."

"You're making whining noises." I didn't even have the energy to roll my eyes.

"I am not."

"Go to sleep." I was exhausted. I couldn't handle any more antics from Rabbit. I couldn't do it. "Don't make me lock you in the car."

"Seriously? You'd do that?" He almost sounded hurt.

Like hell. Of course not. "Sure." *Why am I the person elected to get Rab and myself to West Virginia?* I wanted to go back in time. Demand a redo. Give Mom the shot sooner no matter the consequences.

"Fine." Rabbit burrowed down into his sleeping bag and I drifted off.

I woke sometime later—it might have been hours or seconds—to growling and hissing. "Rab?" I whispered.

His voice was as quiet as a sigh. "It's a big cat. Standing over there." He tried to point.

"Don't move." Why hadn't I slept with the handgun? *Because I thought I might shoot myself?* I reached for a large stick, trying to figure out if I could throw it hard enough to do any damage before the animal ate us.

Growling grew louder, more insistent. *From a second animal? Ah, crap, they're a pack.* "What's that?" There were two voices, not just the hissing. Like a fight. They sounded like adversaries before they battled to the death. The thought nauseated me. "Don't move, Rab."

I tried to remember to breathe—oxygen makes the brain work better. *Shallow breathing kills common sense.* There was a tinny smell in the air. A sort of bloody tincture that seemed familiar. Blood? Pus? I worked the zipper down until I could throw off the sleeping bag and get to my feet quickly.

I didn't know what to do. *Think, Nadia. Think.*

Play dead? Cover your head? Protect your stomach? Protect your brother. I had to sacrifice myself, a pound of my flesh. Hopefully, Rab could get the gun or throw rocks, or something, from the car. There was no choice. Lying here silent wasn't improving our chances.

The growling intensified; the hissing quieted. Then a chilling scream rent the night.

Something nudged my foot, snapped tension into my body like a taut bowline, and I tossed the bag. A surprised yelp told me that the animal was covered for a minute.

I grabbed Rab and tried to lift him, running toward the car. He'd gotten bigger and I'd gotten weaker—not a good combo. "Get in the car!" I hauled him, then turned to face the animals.

He giggled. I knew stress affected different people differently, but laughing? Really? Did he have to?

Rab didn't even try to close the driver's door before his giggles turned into full-blown guffaws, so hard he sounded near tears.

I picked up a rock, squinted into the night. "Get the gun! Quick!" Did he not know how dangerous this was? I was putting myself in front of him, the least he could do was refrain from finding my impending death humorous.

"You—you—" Rab clicked on his flashlight.

I saw a shaggy black tail sticking out from the unzipped sleeping bag. *Aren't cougars a tan color?*

I shoved Rab over and climbed in, slamming the door behind me. *Where's the gun?* I wanted metal and glass and locks between me and the damn creature out there.

"Uh, Nadia?" Rabbit barely got the words out between strangling bellows.

"Thanks for saving your life? You owe me one?" I bit off the words.

"Um." Rab pointed. "Look."

I turned in a huff, expecting to see slobbering fangs and slanted yellow eyes and maybe even signs of frothy-mouthed rabies.

Poking out the edge of the sleeping bag were a shiny black nose, white muzzle, tan markings, and a giant pink lolling tongue. From the other end of the bag a bushy tail wagged insistently, as if we'd stopped playing a game midway through. *A dog?*

"It's a dog." Rab scrambled out of the Jeep and around it, toward the animal.

"Careful. We don't know what it wants. It growled a minute ago." I tried to grab Rab, but he outmaneuvered me and all I clutched was a handful of empty jacket.

"He wasn't growling at us." Rab skidded to his knees a couple of feet from the dog and slowly raised a fist like he'd been taught. Mom had a thing about dogs after all the bites that she'd seen coming through the ER: *Always curl your fingers under when meeting a new dog; they damage less if offered a fist.*

I clicked on a lantern. Still tangled in the sleeping bag, the dog stumbled forward. It licked Rabbit's hand, quickly moved up his forearm, then mopped his face with a tongue the size of a hand towel.

My brother's giggles were delighted like opening presents on Christmas morning. He started to scratch under the dog's chin, and with a satisfied groan the dog relaxed against Rab and lay down. I inched closer.

"See, it's a pet." Rabbit undid the blanket, freeing all four of the dog's legs. "He's hungry." His coat was matted and covered in burs, with sticks and mud crusted in places. He smelled like he'd rolled in putrefied flesh and rinsed with dead fish.

"My sleeping bag is going to smell like disgusting dog now." I sniffed at it as I rolled it up. *Maybe I'll switch mine with Rab's tomorrow.*

"We owe him." Rabbit waved off my complaint.

Oh really? "How do you figure that?"

As if explaining to a wall, Rabbit talked slowly and deliberately, "He chased off the puma."

"He did, huh?"

"That was the growling. That scream—a puma. Dog made it go away. He's a hero."

"Okay, get him a can of something with protein." I relented. It wasn't like Rabbit was really asking permission from me—he'd do it anyway.

"Chili?" Rabbit scrambled to find a can.

Good God, a boy and a dog in a car with chili in the mix? "Sure. If that's easiest to grab." I knew our caravan had now become three—Rabbit had a good memory, and no way was he going to forget I said he could keep a dog. . . . Of course, I'd had no idea the dog would be the size of a large pony. I took over petting the dog, who watched Rab's every movement with utter devotion. *Even before he knows there's food on offer.*

The dog whined and crawled forward a little. Rabbit dumped the contents of the can on a paper plate and slid it over. Dog scarfed the chili without breathing.

Rabbit glanced at the pieces of paper plate left and said, "We should give him more."

"Not yet, we don't want him to get sick," I answered. "You can give him more, but let's make sure that stays down. I don't think he's eaten for a while."

Rab nodded, and Dog tried to stand. With a yelp, he lay back down.

"What's wrong with him? Was it the food?" Rabbit seemed ready to cry. "He's really hot, Nadia."

"I don't know. There was nothing wrong with the chili." I squinted at the dog. "I can't see anything in this light and under his fur." Again I caught that whiff of blood and infection. *That sweetish vinegary stink that shouts bacteria is present, accounted for, and winning. Where is he hurt?*

"He's okay being petted, right?" I started trying to triage, like Mom used to drone on about.

Rab nodded, the dog's head resting in his lap. "Just not walking."

"Is it his feet?"

"Here's a flashlight." Rab shone the bright LED first on the dog's back feet, which seemed fine. But when he pointed the beam at the dog's front feet, they were both swollen to almost melon size. And I could see angry oozing wounds. *Uh-oh.*

Rabbit gasped.

"Okay, let's see if he'll drink water first. He's got to be dehydrated." *Fever? Do dogs get BluStar? The apes and monkeys in zoos all died of it. Do other animals?*

Rab grabbed a bowl and poured some of our precious bottled water into it. "Come on, doggy, drink it."

The dog lifted his head and lapped at the water. He laid his head back down without finishing it.

"I think he's given up." Rabbit sounded near tears.

God, damn it, you do not give a kid a dog and then kill it. Not fair. "No, he hasn't." *Maybe he has.* "He knows you'll take care of him and he can rest now. I'm sure it's been really hard for him and now that he has a friend he can relax."

"We."

"What?"

"We will take care of him. Not just me. You promised." Rabbit stared at me.

"I know I did." I sighed. *No sleep tonight.* "We need to clean his paws if he'll let us, but Rab, if he doesn't let us he might get sicker." *And die.*

"He'll let us. I know he will."

I nodded, not convinced. But I wasn't going to watch him die without trying. Rabbit couldn't take much more. I folded the sleeping bag into a mat for the dog. I needed Rab to help. "We need a big bowl, a pot to boil water in, the salt, and find a clean T-shirt we can make bandages with. And tweezers in case there's something in there we have to dig out. Put your headlamp on, we need our hands."

I started building a fire. "And Rab?" I waited until I saw his eyes. "We need a pair of Dad's socks from your stash to keep his feet clean, okay? None of ours are big enough to fit."

I saw the headlamp nod. I knew Rab had packed a few pieces of Dad's clothing as mementos. *Who am I to judge? I packed perfume and cologne and a dead MP3 player.*

I got the fire going strong with a fire starter we'd taken from the resort. I wasn't going to go all flint-and-sticks medieval unless I absolutely had to.

Dog continued to breathe shallowly and watched all our movements with curious eyebrows and halfhearted tail wags.

Rab laid a piece of tarp on the ground, collected everything I asked for, and offered Dog another drink.

I went to the Jeep to find one of Uncle Bean's survival books. I thought I knew what to do, but I needed all the backup I could get. The early rays of dawn speared the sky.

When I returned from reading about cleaning and binding infected wounds, Rab spoke quietly while petting the dog. I missed a step, tweaking my ankle. I hadn't realized quite how lonely Rab was. We weren't close before. Too many years, too much technology, and too much responsibility got in the way of a close relationship. That was changing. *Needs to change.*

"Shhh, we're going to make it better, Teotwawki. Nadia is really smart, she'll know what to do."

The answering whine wasn't exactly confident.

"What'd you call him?" I asked, kneeling down next to my brother.

"Teotwawki." He shrugged.

"Where'd that come from?" *English, please?*

"Teotwawki," Rabbit repeated.

That's helpful. "Which means?"

" 'The end of the world as we know it.' Teotwawki. I'll probably shorten it eventually."

"Oh." I needed to remember that Rabbit spent a hell of a lot of time online and watching CNN with Mom in those early days. He probably knew more about the whole thing than I did. "That's unique. Let's start with the easy-to-reach. Clean the parts that don't hurt so he can get used to our touch, okay?"

Rab took cool wet rags and tried to spit-bathe the worst of the mud and knots off Teotwawki's coat. "These tangles are terrible."

"See if you can just cut them off." I wasn't sharing my hairbrush with a dog.

"Really?"

"It's hair, Rab. It's not going to hurt him, and it probably annoys him to move with all those rat nests."

This was a dog used to fluffy beds and special treats and toys. Not used to sleeping in holes and hunting for his food. He was a purebred, and his rhinestone collar wasn't exactly this year's must-have fashion for strays.

When the water had boiled long enough I took it off the heat and measured some out into a bowl. I hoped it would draw the infection out, soften the wounds, and give me a chance to see what exactly was going on. *At least, that's what the chapter on infected wounds says.* They were referring to humans and gangrene. Not exactly sure what that was, but if it was gangrene, then Dog was toast anyway because I wasn't amputating his leg. Even I had my limits.

"Rab, it's time to try this."

"What do we do first?"

"I need you to hold his head so he doesn't bite either of us, okay?"

"He won't."

"Rab—"

"Fine. Hold head, got it."

I looked Dog in the eye and explained, hoping he'd know instinctively we weren't enemies. "Teotwawki, I am going to put one paw in this hot salty water and hold it there. It's going to hurt, but it'll help."

As I picked up his paw, he whined and tried to wag his tail, but other than increased tension in his frame, he didn't move.

I tried to be as gentle as I could. He pulled against me for a breath and then relaxed.

"It's okay, Twawki. It's okay, boy." Rab muttered non-sensicals and sweet nothings into the dog's ears while stroking between his eyes and down his head.

"Rabbit, I need you to reheat the pot of water and get me a roll of paper towels. Okay?"

"Sure." Rab scrambled up. "The ones from the rest stop?"

"Doesn't matter." I needed something disposable to wipe the ooze and guck off. Bits of gravel clinked into the bowl and had long since changed the water from clear to pink frothy gunk like peppermint ice cream dropped on the ground and melted.

Rab handed me wads of paper as I took Teotwawki's paw out of the water. With my headlamp pointed at the wounds,

I saw the shredded pads on his foot like open masses of hamburger. Spoiled hamburger. The smell gagged me.

"Holy cow." Rab backed away as if he too was appalled. "How'd he walk at all?"

"Dump this out, wash it with the boiling water. Don't use too much, okay? When we finish with this paw we have to do the other one."

"Should I see if he wants water?"

"I don't think he's going to drink anything until we're done, Rab." These were feet I'd seen on those horrid medical reality-TV shows Mom watched with titles like *I Shouldn't Have Lived* or *Superhuman Immune System Fought Off Slime Mold of the Toenail.*

"There were glass shards in here." Rab came running back with the clean bowl.

"What?"

"At the bottom of the bowl there were pieces of glass. I buried them so no one else would step on them. You want me to go get them?"

"No, but we better make sure they're all out. Hold his head again."

I smushed and pushed and wiped and cajoled. Used the tweezers to get two more long icicles of clear glass out of his foot. When I stopped, I wasn't even done, but thought Twawki had taken enough torture on that paw.

"How do you think it happened?" Rab asked.

"I don't know, maybe he walked on something." *Maybe he had to break a window to get out of his house.* "I think there are probably more pieces in the other paw and maybe even in his skin or other places."

I rinsed the paw, hesitating when Teotwawki whined and lifted his head as if to lick his foot. "Don't let him lick it, Rab, it could make him sicker."

"'Kay."

If I disinfected the wound with hand sanitizer it would hurt. I didn't like it in a hangnail, I couldn't imagine the pain of filling a wound with it. And I had no idea if it would help. *Plan B?* "Do we have any Neosporin?"

"Yeah, I grabbed a couple of tubes."

Can we find more? Do we use it on the dog, or wait and use it on us if we need it?

"I'll get one." Rab didn't let me decide, but I had an uncomfortable moment where I was sure he read my mind.

I filled the crevices with goo. Using more than I probably needed to get at the rest of the infection. Rab handed me strips of T-shirt that I wound and tucked to hold the ointment against the wound and give Teotwawki some protection. "Now, Dad's tube sock." I held out my hand.

Rab handed it over with only slight hesitation. I dragged it up over Teotwawki's leg and then rolled the top down. "He might try to take it off."

"Then we duct-tape it so he can't."

"Really?"

"Yeah, duct tape fixes everything." I gave him a small smile.

The morning air heated with the rising sun. I wiped sweat out of my eyes and peeled off a layer of clothing. May already felt like August. "You want breakfast first or are you ready for me to continue?"

"I don't think I could eat right now." Rab's brow furrowed,

"Let's clean him up and get on the road before that puma comes back."

"Sure." Worked for me. In silent tandem we found a rhythm cleaning out the second paw, which, thankfully, was not as bad as the first. Rab clipped all the balls of hair he could reach, carefully handling them in case there was more glass, which there was.

By the time we finished, my neck was cricked and my fingers were cramped from holding the tweezers so long, but Teotwawki was as cleaned up as he could be. Cleaner than he'd been in a long time.

"Have you changed your underwear today?" I asked.

"Dia!"

"Well?"

"No," Rab mumbled.

"Let's heat up a little water, wash, and change our clothes before we get on the road." We both smelled like pus and rotten earth.

"What happens to Twawki?"

"I imagine he'll sleep where he is."

"But—"

"Until we get him into the Jeep to go with us." I flashed Rab a smile.

Relief sagged his shoulders until we assessed the size of the backseat hole, checking it for the still impressive girth of a malnourished Saint Bernard. "He won't fit."

Nope, he won't fit at all. "We're going to have to make room. Any ideas?"

His expression thoughtful, Rab nodded. "Yeah, I think so."

"Sitting on your lap doesn't count."

"Dia!" I watched Rab struggle to get something out from under the backseat.

"Want some help?" I asked, checking our supplies. *We used too much water. We'll need to find more soon.*

"Don't be mad," Rabbit said.

My stomach sank.

DAY 62

Don't be mad? How do parents do it? That phrase told me to get mad immediately and that I'd probably stay that way. But anger took too much energy. "What?"

"I can't get my XPlay out without taking out a bunch of other stuff."

"You brought your gaming system?" I blinked. And here I'd thought Rab had packed the Jeep with only the essentials and the things we'd agreed on.

He nodded. "I thought maybe Pappi might have—"

"A monitor? Power to spare? A desire to challenge you in *Zombie Dance Masters 12*?"

"I guess. I just needed it, Nadia," he answered in a small voice.

I wasn't mad. I'd brought a few security blankets too. Rab lived for that gaming system; it was at times a better friend to him than any human kid ever had been, including Jimmy. Especially after Dad died. I think mastering the next game level felt like the only thing Rabbit controlled in his world. "I get it. But I guess you have to decide which you'd rather take with us."

"I don't need to decide. We can't leave him here. Plus, you promised."

I smiled. "I know. Just testing you. I'll help." We cleared space, tossed out a few bags of dirty clothes and food wrappers. I spread cleanish clothes and blankets out on top of the bench seat instead of stashing them and created a relatively comfy bed. It wasn't big and it was cramped, but it would work.

"Are you hungry yet?" I asked.

"I'd go for ice cream." Rabbit licked his lips.

"Yeah, me too. Want a PowerBar?"

"Nah, not the same."

I sighed. I knew it. "Tell me if you get hungry, though, okay? We can't stop eating because the food's all the same."

Rabbit nodded, but he was focused on the dog. "Um, how are we going to get him in here?"

I glanced over at Teotwawki and saw he was watching us with avid attention, but his weight was firmly on his elbows. If he tried to stand he'd likely undo all the good work. "We pick him up."

Rab's jaw dropped. "He's huge."

"He's not that big." *For a horse.* I opened both back doors of the Jeep and assessed the situation. "I'll take his front two-thirds and you take care of his butt."

"'Kay."

I knelt down and the dog licked my face with his ears back and tail thumping. "It's okay, Twawki. Please don't bite us." I wedged my arms underneath his elbows and prominent rib cage. Under all that fur he wasn't as sturdy as he looked. With the right food he probably would weigh another fifty pounds. "On the count of three."

Rab took a beating as Twawki's tail kept whapping him in the face.

"Two, three." We lifted and Twawki all but used his hind end to jump up into our arms. We sidestepped and finessed until Rab had the dog's butt on the seat. I pushed Twawki along, deeper into the nest. We closed the door and he leaned against it with a happy bark, his head on the windowsill. We high-fived and clambered into the front.

"Do we have everything?"

"Yep, think so."

I glanced over at the neat stack of electronics, games, and controllers Rab had made by the boulder. "I'm sorry, Rab."

"I'm not, I'll take Twawki any day." But he didn't make eye contact or look back as we drove away.

Gassed up twice, three pee breaks, and lunch on board, we made it another hundred miles before we came across a few houses.

"We're looking for water and gas, and we need dog food," I said.

"Where do we find dog food?"

"Look for a yard with a doghouse and toys and stuff."

It took three tries to find everything and it was only enough to get us a few clicks down the road. Late-afternoon sun baked the world around us in tans, browns, and grays.

Rabbit turned down the music. "What's that?"

"A roadblock of sorts, I think." I leaned forward and tried to read the sign propped against a couple of cars and sawhorses.

"What do we do?" Rab asked.

Twawki growled low in his throat, then thumped his tail. *Is that good or bad?*

"Well, we can turn around, or we can see if it's an old road-block, or if there is a survivor to man it, waiting for people." I held up fingers as I rattled off our options.

"Uh-huh."

"What do you think?" I asked, slowing down.

"Not everyone still alive can be mean and insane, right?"

"Probably not." *Although both traits might tip the scale more toward survival.*

"Let's check it out. We just don't get out of the Jeep," Rabbit pronounced, sitting forward in his seat. "Wait, there's movement. What is it? A deer? A bear?"

"I can't tell. I should have brought Dad's binoculars." *You and me both know those would have been more useful than Dad's MP3 player tucked against the base of my spine.* "Rabbit, grab the gun, okay?"

"Is that an old—"

"Lady?" My hands tightened on the wheel as we rolled closer. She took off her big floppy sun hat and waved it in greeting, then bent down and lifted up a piece of cardboard. "Can you read that?"

"Yeah, it says 'Will share our food for information.' Do we trust her?"

She seemed friendly. No gunshots rang out. "Grannies can be desperate criminals too, Rab." But were we going to head into this new world thinking ill of everyone we met? Or were we going to take a few chances and hope for the best?

"Let's vote," Rab demanded.

"Okay. I say we approach cautiously, but don't follow her anywhere. We can give her information and we don't need her food."

"Twawki?" Rab turned in his seat to ask the dog's vote.

Woof!

"I think that's a 'proceed as suggested.'"

Where does he come up with this stuff? I nodded and continued toward the old woman.

"Hi, I'm Miss Tre. Where you coming from? Where you going?" She used a walker to hobble over toward the driver's-side window.

"Uh, we're—"

She gave us no time to answer before continuing. "I have to stay here on guard duty." She seemed uncertain for a moment. "You're the first I've seen. You don't know how lovely it is to see such young, fresh, and new faces. The girls will be thrilled, just thrilled. Would you like some cool tea? Let me shoot off my rifle and one of the kids will come escort you up to the farmhouse. I'm Miss Tre, did I tell you that already? What are your names?"

She was harmless. Dotty. Maybe simple, but innocuous. "Do you know how to shoot a gun? Miss Susan showed me, but I've forgotten."

Rab glanced at me. "Uh—"

"Yeah, I can fire it." I gave Rabbit a look that I hoped said to slide into the driver's seat and be ready to move out if he needed to. His short nod led me to believe we were on the same

85

page. Twawki didn't keep growling, but he wasn't exactly showing signs of wanting to be Miss Tre's friend, either.

I climbed out and took the rifle from her. Laid it against my shoulder. "Does it matter where I aim?"

"No, into the air is fine."

I saw a V of Canada geese flying low overhead. I took aim and fired. I hit one and it tumbled out of the sky. I rubbed my shoulder and shook my ears to clear the ringing. I guess the practicing worked.

"Nice shot," Rabbit said.

"Here she comes now." Miss Tre pointed into the distance.

Across the fields a horse and rider covered the ground at a full gallop. From here I couldn't tell if the rider was a man or a woman, but Miss Tre seemed pleased. "That's Miss Othello. And Princess. You can give me the gun back now."

I assumed Princess was the horse and Miss Othello the rider, but in this upside-down world I guessed it could go either way. Still holding the rifle, I tried to climb back into the Jeep, but Miss Tre's walker was in the way, with her leaning on it. *How'd she move that fast?*

The warning bells in my stomach began to ring. "Rab?" I said. Twawki heard it in my voice and began his low growl.

Miss Tre wrestled the gun from me. I think shock made me release my grip on it.

The rider held up a gun as she approached. "Don't move." Gray hair tumbled out of a big cowboy hat. "Where you from?"

"Uh, Seattle." *Combat breathing, Nadia, remember—four counts in, four counts out.*

"What are you doing so far from there?"

"Heading east." It was hard to concentrate with Rabbit's wide eyes fixed on the gun that the granny pointed at me.

"Why?"

"We have family in Wyoming."

"Where?"

"Outskirts of the park." *Please don't ask me what park I'm talking about.*

She jerked her chin toward the Jeep. "What's in your car?"

"My brother, our dog, stuff from home."

"Guns? Gold? Medicine?"

"What?" *Should we have all that?*

"Do you have any guns, gold, or medicine?"

"No." I tried to cover the shaking of my limbs by vehemently denying.

"Show me." She gestured with the gun. "And if your damn dog gets out of the Jeep I'll shoot it."

Rabbit startled and made a soft noise. I moved around to the back door of the Jeep. "Robert, remember four in, four out." Only Mom ever called him Robert and I needed Rab to keep his head. "Twawki, stay," I commanded in my deepest dog-trainer voice. *Please know what I mean.* He didn't move, but vibrated as if an electric current surged through him. I had a feeling that with one word from me, whatever that might be, he'd launch himself at the grannies regardless of his mangled paws.

I reached under the back of the driver's seat hoping I remembered where I'd put them. A random can of ravioli came out first and then I touched the zipper of Mom's cosmetic bag. I yanked until it slid free. I shut the car door, more to keep the dog in than to hide anything from their eyes. If they wanted to, they would toss everything out of the Jeep and take their pick.

"Here, this is our last can of food. And maybe there's gold

in there." I held out my offerings. The granny with the walker ripped the can out of my hand, dropped it into her housedress pocket, and tossed the cosmetic bag to the rider.

She unzipped the bag and held up the bottle of Mom's perfume. "What the hell am I supposed to do with this?" She cackled. They both laughed as if they hadn't in a long while.

"It's the only thing with gold on it we have." I tried to sound like an incompetent teenager. Only a moron would think the gold-painted plastic was real. Let them think I was dumb. *Let the enemy underestimate you, Nadia.* I heard Dad's commandment in my head.

She flung the bag to the ground. "This isn't real gold. You got your parents' wedding rings?"

I wanted to throw myself down and gather it all up. "No." Instead, I stood there and focused on my breathing. Keeping oxygen flowing to my brain was spectacularly hard to do.

"Do I believe you?" She narrowed her eyes and waited for me to flinch.

"They're still on their fingers—in the ground," Rabbit answered, one ounce pissed and twelve ounces instructive. Twawki added a rumble.

"Those gas cans—give us those."

"They're empty." I shrugged, trying to seem unconcerned at losing them. One was empty, the others not so much. I took a step as if I was going to untie them.

They paused and shared a look. "You kids better hook up with a caravan. You'll never survive out here."

There are more cars out here? Of course there are. "There's a group of a dozen cars behind us coming this way," I improvised.

"Why aren't you with them?"

"They're slow, lots of trailers"—I shrugged, behaving as if as a teenager my amusement was paramount—"we got bored."

Rabbit nodded and huffed a sigh that might have been bored overkill but seemed to get the ladies to see us as incompetent.

"Tell you what, for that bit of information we'll let you go. But listen up, head south through Utah. Do not keep heading this direction into Montana. There's a militia that'll marry you, kill your brother, and eat your dog."

"She ain't kidding." Walker Granny nodded.

"Thanks." I frowned.

Rabbit monkeyed over the seat as I opened the passenger-side door. I didn't want to turn my back to them, but I wanted to get out of there before they changed their minds.

"How far behind you?"

"What?"

"The others—how far behind?" she repeated as if she began to smell my lie.

"Probably a day or two now." I met her eyes and didn't flinch. She nodded.

Once in the driver's seat I hit locks on all the doors, raised the windows, and floored it in reverse. Reckless but too scared to care, I spun the wheel and turned us around. The Jeep's tires bit into gravel and dirt along the side of the road. Rabbit was thrown against Twawki, who whined. "Sorry," I said.

"Just get us out of here!" Rabbit yelled, wedging himself behind the seat.

Miles passed at a clip. I turned down the first smaller southern road I saw an exit for. Rabbit could figure out where we were later. The sun lowered itself along the recliner of the horizon. "We gotta stop for the night." I eased off the accelerator.

Rabbit climbed back over. "You did good. You didn't act scared."

"You think?"

"Yeah, better than I would have. I couldn't breathe."

"I guess we now know that roadblocks aren't necessarily a good thing." Would it have been too much to hope that survivors were kind and sweet?

"I'm sorry you had to give up Mom's stuff," Rabbit said in a small voice as he stared out the windshield.

"It's okay, we need the room for supplies anyway." My heart hurt a little. *A lot.*

"You convinced 'em. Dad would be proud."

Quick tears stung my eyes and I blinked them away. *If I start crying I might never stop.* "There's a farmhouse up ahead."

Rabbit paled. "I don't think I can handle going inside."

"We don't have to, there's a big barn back there. There's probably a place we can camp inside it." I didn't want to face the owners of the house either. "You sure you're ready to stop?"

"Yeah, Twawki needs to pee." Rabbit nodded, but I saw his muscles tense up as if waiting for the next blow. He used to be a kid who climbed trees and snuck candy and wasn't afraid of anything. Dad's death changed things. *Changed me too.*

I drove up a long, bumpy gravel driveway. We watched for any signs of life. "No one's shooting at us." A chicken trailed by six chicks dashed across the drive in front of us. I refrained from asking why they crossed the road, but I could hear Dad's laughter. *He'd have asked.*

"It's nice not being shot at." Rabbit didn't relax an inch.

"Can you drive?" I asked.

"Sure. Why?"

"I need to get out and open the barn door."

The barn was the kind that movies showed—curved dome of a roof and painted red with a smaller door for people and a large sliding one for monstrous machinery.

"Take the gun and you shoot first." Rabbit's voice was strong. "Don't be nice."

Coming from my little brother this was almost laughable, but I nodded, holding the handgun with both hands. I approached the smaller door first. It was unlocked and the only smell that blew out was of hay and animals—not rotted ones. Just what I'd imagined a barn with horses and cows might smell like.

Somewhere nearby a chicken crowed.

I poked my head inside. A large sliding door on the opposite side of the barn was open. I didn't see any animals, nor corpses of any kind. I nodded and leaned on the handle of the front sliding door. I couldn't get it loose. I didn't see a lock, but maybe it was rusted shut or something. "It's stuck!" I yelled to Rabbit, and then shrugged, walking back to the Jeep and climbing in.

"What's the deal?"

"The larger door is stuck. But there's one on the other end."

"There's a fence."

"I thought you liked demolition work?" I asked.

He grinned. "I can tear it down?"

"Enough for us to get inside, yeah." I shut off the Jeep and we climbed out. It wasn't hard to dismantle a few feet of fence. Once inside the barn we fell into our routine. Scouting around, keeping our eyes peeled as we set up beds. We knew to eat dinner when everything else was finished. We'd learned the hard way that we couldn't keep food down when we cleaned Twawki's infected paws. That night it took several hours. Again. His nose was dry and he was hot to the touch.

"Why won't he eat or drink anything?" Rabbit asked.

"I think we need to find a clinic or something."

"We can't let him die, Nadia. It's not fair." Rabbit's chin quivered, but there was only so much reassurance I could give him.

Maniacal squawking startled us to our feet.

"What's that?" Rabbit yelled over the noise.

"It's just a chicken," I said as the bird raced out of the barn continuing to sound as though it was being strangled while singing "The Star-Spangled Banner."

I moved closer to where the chicken had popped up from.

"Be careful."

I peered behind a bale of hay. A nest of perfectly white eggs was tucked between the wall and the hay. "I found eggs."

Rabbit loped over. I started picking up the eggs. Scrambled. Omelets. Deviled. My mouth watered with the possibilities. *How long has it been? Since we used up that dozen in the fridge. Months.*

"What if there are baby chicks in there?" Rabbit leaned over the hay and shone a flashlight at them.

"Would she leave them?"

"Um, I don't know."

"They're cold to the touch. Wouldn't she be sitting on them?"

"I don't know."

"We studied this in biology last year. They sit on them for weeks. I swear." And then we dissected baby chicks instead of frogs. I left that part out. "We should eat some for dinner."

The yolks were orange and the scrambled eggs were creamy. So good I almost didn't miss bacon, English muffins, or orange juice. Twawki even ate a few bites.

As the last of the light fell, chickens came scurrying into the barn. A rooster exactly like the one on Mom's dish towels pranced in and crowed at us before heading up into the rafters. Several sets of chicks and mothers found their sleeping spots around the barn. We used up water to brush our teeth and wash our faces. Made pallets up in the hay loft, leaving Twawki to sleep below. I'd learned the faster I fell asleep, the quicker the world was light again. So once Rab's breathing evened out, I turned my brain off, refused to think about anything, and forced myself to sleep.

Blood-chilling, eaten-by-a-zombie-jump-five-feet screaming woke me from a sound sleep. Below us Twawki gave a woof and whined. I hit the flashlight realizing the screams came from my brother.

I tumbled gracelessly over to his thrashing. "Wake up. Come on, Rabbit, it's a nightmare."

He beat against me, slamming his elbow into my eye. *Ouch!* I held his shoulders with one arm while pinning his legs with mine. I was afraid he was going to hurt himself, or roll off the edge of the loft. He hadn't had a night terror this bad since he was little.

"They're dead. They're all dead!" He sobbed, still so asleep I was afraid he'd never wake up. *What did Mom do?*

I yelled in his face, "Wake up! You're having a nightmare!"

He continued mewing. "We're gonna die too."

I started singing one of Mom's favorite songs from the 1980s—I was off-key, didn't really know the words, but I made up for it in volume. I tried rocking him, but he wasn't that much smaller than me anymore.

Finally, by the second verse Rabbit stopped screaming long enough to gulp air.

"Dia?"

"You're okay, you had a nightmare."

"I peed myself." His voice was slurred like he was still half-asleep.

"It's okay, Rab. I've done it too. We'll get a new sleeping bag for you. You can have mine. You want help cleaning up?"

"I'm not a baby." He dropped the sleeping bag over the side of the loft. I kept my eyes lowered so he wouldn't be embarrassed.

"Okay." I climbed down and got Twawki to eat a little more of the cold eggs. I wasn't sleeping another wink. Dawn couldn't be far away.

Rabbit made a neat pile of his soiled clothes and slunk over to me.

"You want to stay here today? Take a nap later? Just chill?"

Rabbit shrugged, petting Twawki's head. "What was in the shot Uncle Bean gave us?"

"I don't know." Something that helped us fight off the virus. Something that kept Mom alive even after she developed symptoms and was sick.

"What was in the box he gave you?"

"You've seen the map." I swallowed, not sure my younger brother really needed to hear this truth. "The gun."

"That wasn't all."

"No, not all. He wrote me a letter. And there were pills."

"I want to read the letter. Is it in the Jeep?"

I shook my head. "I don't think that's a good idea."

"I do. You promised." Rabbit's expression closed and for a moment I saw Dad's face in his.

He's right. I had promised we'd be partners in this journey. That I wouldn't be his mom. "Okay." I reached into my jeans pocket and pulled out Dad's music player.

"Does Mom know you took that from Dad's stuff?" Rabbit slapped his hand over his mouth. He looked near tears. Like for a moment he'd forgotten Mom was dead and she might get mad at me.

"No, but it doesn't matter now."

Rabbit reached over to his boots and pulled out a trinket he handed to me. Gold wings sprouted from a parachute.

"This is Dad's."

He nodded. "I thought the wings and all, you know . . . heaven."

I remembered the day Dad got this pinned on. He went from being a marine to being special forces. He spent hours polishing his uniform's buttons and pressing the creases exactly right. He was so proud.

I handed it back to Rab. "It's okay. Whatever it takes for us to get through this, right?" I slid the player out of its holder so I could reach underneath, where I'd tucked Bean's folded letter. I'd read it so often that I had it memorized. With only the slightest hesitation I handed it to Rabbit.

Dearest Nadia,

If you're reading this, then the worst is happening. The shot I gave you, your brother, and your mother is an experimental injection that I've worked on for the past ten years. If your mother is still alive she'll want to know it's based on research started during the Cold War. I work in biological weapons programs so highly classified that the marines don't claim me as one of their own, and deny any knowledge of this laboratory. I report directly to the Commandant and no one else. My unit has focused on developing a shot for the president of the United States and other government officials in case of a viral attack. The idea was to manufacture a rapid response in the body, to seek out and change the replicating DNA in the virus cells—stopping it in its tracks and giving the injected person a superhuman ability to withstand biological weapons of the most virulent types. Basically, we've been trying to put thousands of years of evolution into an injectable.

Understand there are very few people who know this. Even your father didn't have the level of clearance to be told. I was brought in because of my research and experiments with genetic code and the immune response. We have had several breakthroughs, but at the same time there was a coalition of nations continuing to work on weaponizing viruses with no known cure, and an unrelenting kill rate. An accident at a facility in China six months ago started a chain reaction that will wipe out an estimated ninety-eight percent of the human population. I have no data to know if it will affect other species or not. You did not hear about this accident on the news. No one will be told about the kill rate. The plan will be to keep panic low and tell the populace anything needed to keep them from rioting. In the weeks to come you'll see evacuations, miracle medications, government relocations—ignore all of these. Stay at the house. I repeat: do not go with anyone, anywhere. Hide if you have to.

By day forty-five the virus should have run its course across the globe. It should have burned out. If you are all healthy enough to travel, start then. If not, wait until you can.

I promised your father I would take care of you, your mom, and your brother if anything happened to him. He promised me nothing would happen to him. We both know your mother hates me for being the one who signed us up. At some point you'll need to tell her what's going on. I leave exactly when up to you. Get her to take the shot at any cost—even if you have to stab her with the needle in her sleep.

Pappi's mine is outfitted to survive and thrive in many worst-case scenarios. His time in the wars messed with his mind and made him paranoid, which means he's completely self-sufficient and prepared to live for decades without help. You do not need to be afraid of him. He is the one who taught your dad and me how to be the cockroach.

Finally, if evolutionary biology has taught me anything, it's that there will be people on this planet with a natural immunity to this new virus cocktail. So you may meet people along the way. They will be from all walks of life, all ages, and all sorts of personalities. Tell no one where you are going. You may bring up to six people with you, but they cannot know what your ultimate destination is. This is for your own safety. Be cautious of everyone. I have the utmost confidence you and your brother will be able to survive in this new world and I will see you at Pappi's as soon as you can get there. If you do not make it by Halloween I will try to come to you and get us through till spring and make the trek together.

Love,
Uncle Bean

Rabbit read it twice, then handed it back. "We need to burn this letter."

"Why? I've hidden it."

"Yeah, but if something happened we don't want bad guys showing up at Pappi's, right?"

"They don't have a map."

"Right, but still."

"You're right." But it meant losing another piece of *before*. What if there was something in there we needed to know and we forgot?

"Do you think anyone else lived? Like everyone in Africa is okay? Or Brazil?"

DAY 63

"You saw the same television news I did." The riots, the panic, the city blocks burning to prevent the spread of the unknown disease.

"I know, but maybe somewhere?"

"Maybe." I wasn't going to kill the kid's hope. There was enough of that in everyday life.

Twawki whined. He seemed weaker and thinner than earlier in the day.

Rabbit frowned, "You think maybe there's medicine here or any of that other stuff?"

"Why don't you explore the barn and I'll take the walkie-talkie up to the house?"

"I can go with you. . . ."

"Nah, keep on eye on Twawki. I think he's worried about you. Maybe they have medicine for animals here, too?"

"If it's a working farm, they might."

I wrapped a towel around my mouth and used a clothespin to keep my nostrils shut. The house wasn't open to the elements—not that I saw—so if someone was inside, they'd rotted in there. As smells go, there wasn't anything like it.

I found the remains of the farm's family in their living room. All but a man were bundled in quilts, with several rounds of shotgun shells littering the floor at my feet. Three kids, someone with long blond braids was maybe the mom, and a guy in dung-covered work boots and patched denim could have been the father. The weapon lay on the floor near his body. None of the kids looked shot, just the adults. And the dog. Couldn't really blame them for choosing death over surviving if their kids all died. If I didn't have Rab I wasn't sure I'd be making this trip.

The coffee table was covered with bright-colored papers. The same kind they'd dropped from the sky over us in the early days. Especially after the power started going out and people were told to stay in their houses, or else.

I picked up one dated a month ago informing people to head toward the nearest university or college campus. There they'd be transported to government-run hospitals and given antiviral drugs. The last lines were enough to make me laugh. *Do not panic. Everything will be all right. Follow directions.*

I opened a window, feeling better with a breeze and air changing. I took a deep breath, fairly certain that I wouldn't find more bodies upstairs. Looked like they'd gathered together in the end. I found a few wool blankets and clean sweats for

Rabbit, and checked the medicine cabinet. I grabbed all the bottles, over-the-counter and prescription. The granny had asked for gold, medicine, or guns. If that was the new currency, we needed some. I riffled through a jewelry box, grabbed a plain-looking gold locket and what might have been a wedding band. I closed my eyes. Stealing was wrong. Just because they were dead didn't make it okay, didn't make it feel better. Maybe necessary, but not better.

I carried the bottles to the sunlight and read the labels. One of them was antibiotics. Twawki was big enough he'd qualify for human weight, but would human drugs work? Rabbit and I would talk it over, but we'd need to chance it.

I found a couple of bottles of whiskey above the kitchen sink, shotgun shells, and another gun. I made several trips, putting it all on the porch.

One corner of the dining room had leather-bound books, the kind that looked expensive and were always special requests at the library. I walked over and scanned the titles until I recognized one.

The sweet, sickly smell of death clung to my hair and I twisted it in a tight French braid. Next beauty salon we passed I was finding clippers and shearing it off.

"I grabbed a book for you." I handed the book to Rabbit as I brought the last of the stuff to the Jeep.

"What is it?" Rab flipped through it.

"*The Swiss Family Robinson.* Dad used to read it to me when I was little." There were times when I felt guilty about knowing Dad before the wars started. Rabbit's whole life Dad was coming and going into combat, into places I knew never made it on the news because Mom watched it religiously until he died. As if she might get a sense of when he might come back, or where he was, based on news reports. Thing was, Dad said so many times that he was nowhere near the places we heard about on the news—those were missions for other marines. His marines—the Chemical Biological Incident Response Force, or CBIRF—never made the news, and that was the way they liked it. I didn't really understand then. *I know better now.* "The family survive a shipwreck and build a tree house."

"Thanks, Nadia." Rabbit hugged it to his chest like I'd given him something more valuable than a story. Maybe it felt like a piece of Dad to him, too. "I think we should keep moving."

"Okay." We finished loading the Jeep and lifted Twawki inside. His paws were swollen and so hot to the touch it was like a horrible sunburn radiating out.

"He's getting worse." Rabbit toed the dirt.

"There were a few pills upstairs. Antibiotics for a human."

"Can we give him those?"

"I think we have to try and then find a veterinarian clinic at the next town. See if there aren't more pills, or books, or something on what to do."

"He's gonna die if we don't, right?" Rabbit kissed Twawki's nose.

"I think he might." My voice dipped to a whisper.

"Then let's do it. We gotta try."

I mushed a couple of the pills—the right dosage for Mr. Richard Bjorn, according to the bottle's label—into a vending-machine peanut butter cookie and got the dog to swallow them.

Hours down the road, Rabbit checked on our patient for the three hundredth time. "Twawki looks better." Rabbit twisted around in his seat. Two doses of meds and we were looking at the bottom of an empty bottle.

The dog thumped his tail as if to answer.

"He needs more than we gave him. Mom always said we had to take all the antibiotics or they'd stop working."

"Yeah, a full course of meds. She knew what she was doing." Her work as a nurse wasn't lost on me. And she couldn't have taken the shot in the beginning? Still be here with us to help? "We need to go into the next town."

"What if there are people there?"

"We have the gun out now," I assured him, and myself.

"I can shoot it too. Bean gave those video games and fake guns to both of us. I practiced a lot in my room."

"Really?"

"Yeah, I didn't hardly play anything else once it started."

Dad had guns in the house. He taught us how to handle them, how to clean them, how to check to make sure they were unloaded. Mom kept a handgun by her bed whenever Dad was deployed. But promises of shooting ranges and lessons disappeared in the smoke of grief that suffocated our family.

"Me too. I played one late at night." When I should have been doing homework or chores or sleeping. I was beginning to think I should have had real conversations with Rab a lot sooner. Maybe things would have been different at home if I'd bothered to listen to his answers and ask questions.

The gas light popped on the screen. "We're low on gas."

Rabbit glanced down at the map in his lap. "There's a train station five miles ahead. There might be a parking lot with cars."

"Is it in a town?"

"Outskirts. Like a suburb thingy."

"Let's check."

The flocks of birds were our first clue.

"What are those?"

"Crows?"

"No, the other ones circling."

"Vultures?"

"Like in cartoons?"

"Yeah, they're real." But why were they circling up ahead? They ate carrion, dead animals—including people, I was sure—but there shouldn't be anything left. Mom made certain we understood decomposition and what to be afraid of. The myths surrounding disease and dead bodies might work to our benefit since we knew better than most people.

"There's a train parked at the station."

"Should we keep going?" I stopped and we watched from a distance.

"Anything?"

"Nope, but they could be hiding."

"Where's the next gas stop?"

"If we go south instead of east? Ten miles that way, for sure."

"East?"

"Dots on the map, but nothing big."

"Okay, so we need these cars."

Rab nodded.

"I think you should drive us closer." *That way I can shoot.*

"I can shoot too." Rabbit shook his head, reading my mind.

"I know, but I'd feel better if you could get away. If I have to get out of the car again, right? If you're already in the driver's seat, then it'll save time."

"That makes sense." Rabbit crawled into the backseat with Twawki.

"What are you doing?"

"We don't want them to see we're kids, right?"

Good point. I slid over and then he climbed back into the seat. I held the gun with both hands.

Birds flew up in a mass. Dogs and raccoons dove out of our way, their faces bloody.

"There shouldn't be—"

"I know." Rabbit cut me off.

The train station was a mess of broken glass, graffiti tags, and brochures blowing around like confetti.

"What happened?"

Cars in the parking lot had slashed tires and broken windshields. "There may not be gas here."

I rolled down our windows so we could hear. Nothing but the sounds of angry birds, a door banging in the wind, and Twawki's low rumble as he scented the air and his hackles rose.

"What do we do?"

"Can you drive around the side of the building? I want to see the train itself."

"Okay." Rab nodded and eased the Jeep around the end. The luggage compartments were ripped open and piles of stuff were strewn everywhere underneath the train and between the wheels. It looked like the mess continued on the other side.

"Rabbit, if you see any movement you floor it and get us out of here, okay? We can always come back later."

He nodded.

"Drive around the front of the train. Let's see the other side."

"I don't like this, Dia."

"I know." *Me either.*

The other side of the train was worse.

With an unobstructed view we saw what the animals were eating. Rabbit gagged and so did I.

"Back to the parking lot!" I cried.

We held a few minutes in shocked silence. "I need to go back and look."

"No, you don't." Rabbit shook his head vehemently.

"Yeah, I do."

"Why? They're dead."

"I know, but . . ." I had a suspicion I needed to follow through. "Why don't you start at the far edge of the parking lot over there? Start checking the empty cars and see if whoever destroyed this place left any gas?"

"What if they didn't?"

"We'll figure it out. If you hear the gun you drive back to the train station sign and hide in the woods there, okay? If I'm not there in two moons you go on, okay?"

"Nadia, don't say that—"

"Rabbit, I have to. We have to have backup plans. Turn on your walkie-talkie." I handed him one and tucked the other in my pocket. I didn't know what we'd do if we ran out of batteries, but at least for now this kept us in communication.

He nodded.

I picked my way around the litter. The inside of the train station was plastered with letters, photographs, and signs for loved ones. "We're taking this evac train. . . . We'll meet you in Miami. . . . We love you and we'll see you soon. . . ." They were all the same, goodbye with a little a bit of hope sprinkled on top. "If you see this girl, she is attending University of Nebraska. Tell her that her parents are heading south. . . ." These were dated months ago. When the government told everyone still alive to gather for relocation.

I kept my eyes peeled for anything useful in the luggage. But all that was left was clothing. Empty food containers littered the ground around a campfire. Like an all-you-can-eat buffet. Cigarette butts, drained liquor bottles.

I cut between cars and glanced inside. My nightmares were peaches and cream compared with what I witnessed. But the bodies on the far side of the train were what spooked me.

Six, maybe seven people, lined up. The blood spray and bullet holes along the side of the train told me everything I needed to know. There were survivors here. Up until last week or so there'd been people, including kids, who were living at this train. They'd been executed.

I jerked my head up to study the horizon. The flat land of the prairie flowed out around me. I saw no smoke, no movement, no vehicles. What I did see were a bunch of massive four-wheeler and motorcycle tire tracks heading away from the train. Thankfully, in the opposite direction from us. But were they the only ones?

A chill swept my spine, tightened the grip on my gun, and forced my feet into a sprint back to Rabbit.

"Those people didn't die of BluStar, did they?"

"No."

Rabbit nodded. "Nadia, I saw something on the map."

"Yeah?"

"Five miles west of here was a maximum security prison."

"Show me." I stared at the map. "They headed that way."

"South?"

I shrugged. "Let's get gas and get out of here."

"Should we start traveling at night?"

"You think?"

"What about headlights? Won't those be easier to see?"

"We just need to be careful." *And find extra ammunition so we can practice shooting a real gun.*

"I filled the tank."

"Let's get out of here."

"I haven't filled the gas cans yet."

"I don't care. I want to get out of here."

Rabbit stared at me for a second and nodded.

Getting used to being in the silent new world, around the dead bodies, the reminders of so much gone—that was easy compared with thinking there were still people in the world who murdered and partied on the graves of their victims. That was an evil I couldn't shake off. "Let's head north for a little while before turning east again. It might be colder, but—"

"Sure. We gotta risk going into a town." Rabbit held the map.

"I know. Twawki won't make it much longer."

Rabbit nodded. The antibiotics gave the dog a reprieve, but we couldn't keep up with the pus and he wasn't even eating now. It didn't matter what we offered him.

"We need fresh water for us too."

"We explore the next town. Whatever comes."

"Deal." I drove forward praying that whoever or whatever was next on our journey was a good thing and not a bad one. "There's smoke ahead on the horizon."

"Brush fire?"

"I don't think so." It wasn't a line of smoke. Just a plume of black.

"Smells different." Rabbit lifted his head. His nose was peeling from sunburn. Skin cancer was kinda the last thing on my mind. But I heard Mom's voice chastising me for not putting sunscreen on both of us.

"Yeah, it does." Like meat and plastic and something sweetly awful.

We'd gotten used to looking for indications of fires, including smoke plumes, in an otherwise cloudless sky.

"That must be in the town itself."

"People?" Rabbit's voice quavered. We'd learned to be afraid of the unknown. Survivors we'd seen so far came in two groups: those gone crazy with the reality and those who'd been broken so far they were starving to death in their shock. I really needed to meet someone who was trying to hold it together. Someone who hadn't let the circumstances overwhelm them. *Someone like me, like Rabbit. Are we the only ones trying to start over?*

"Let's check it out." Rabbit thrust his shoulders back, and I saw his collarbones and elbows were bonier than they used to be. I needed to get him to eat more.

"You sure?"

"I'm sure."

Worst-case scenario I'd gun the engine and we'd get the hell away from whoever was burning the bonfire. As we drew closer, the smoke that hung heavy in the air took on the distinct and almost cloying stink of human flesh.

"Keep your eyes open for movement, okay?"

I sucked at being brave. If it had been me alone, I would have stayed in my bedroom until I'd eaten the last of the canned food, downed the contents of Mom's pharmaceutical cabinet with Dad's old vodka, and let the world turn on without me. *Do cockroaches know they're survivors, or do they, too, think suicide sounds like the better option?*

"I don't see anyone." Rabbit sat tense next to me, so scared he'd likely pee his pants. I didn't blame him. I'd pissed myself once or twice in the past few weeks too.

Old houses, some turned into condos. A little white church with a postcard steeple. American flags whipped atop flagpoles at the post office. A brick K–12 school, library, and VFW meeting hall lined streets with names like Oak, Birch, Adams, and Lincoln. Combined, the town looked like a set from a classic Western turned Broadway musical.

I eased forward until we turned onto a neat and tidy main street. In the middle of the town square, next to a bronze statue of a guy on a horse, was a large pile of burning corpses and parts of skeletons. Lots of clothing. Blankets. Some all together. All ages. All stages of decomposition.

I hated being able to judge how long a body had been dead at a glance. I should be checking the clothes and shoes and deciding which were last season. "Somebody's gathering the dead and burning them." I put the Jeep in park but left the engine running.

"Someone alive," Rabbit added as if zombie thoughts still haunted him.

"Hmm."

"There's the grocery store. It seems empty from here."

Smashed glass was swept into piles. Empty garbage cans were stacked against buildings.

"What do we do?"

Twawki was so out of it he didn't even lift his head, let alone growl, or wag his tail. We were on our own for this one.

I took a breath and waited for a gut feeling to tell me. I'd learned to listen to it. The voice that said *run* when there was nothing to see. The voice that said *sleep now, nothing is going to go bump in the night.* "I think it's okay. They're cleaning up the town, right?"

"Bad guys aren't neat freaks?"

"Maybe?" I asked.

"Look at the spray paint. There are circles and triangles on the doors over there. Black *X* marks."

"A code? If we start snooping they might think we're stealing or something. I vote for waiting until we see them."

"Me too."

I turned off the engine and tugged the shotgun out of the back, to rest in my arms. I clambered out and climbed up onto the hood of the Jeep.

Rabbit's door opened and he tumbled out too. He handed me one of the beat-up gray masks we used when driving through fires. It kept some of the burning ash out of my mouth and nose.

In the distance we heard an engine start and head in our direction. A large tractor pulling a flatbed trailer piled high with more bodies drew to a stop as it turned a corner and faced us across the square.

I didn't take my eyes off the figure in the driver's seat. A red bandanna covered the driver's face, and the eyes were covered with shades so dense I couldn't tell if there were even eyeballs behind them. A bright yellow rain slicker, green plastic work boots, and yellow rain pants contrasted sharply with the leather work gloves covered in grime and goop. The person's slicker was shiny and covered in what, I could only guess. My heart raced. *Horror-movie villain, anyone?*

Rabbit stepped backward involuntarily. I tightened my grip on the shotgun and slid to my feet.

We heard a mutter and then a shouted, "Shit! I must look like something out of a horror flick." The gloves were flung off, along with the hat and sunglasses. The man jumped down from the tractor with his hands raised. "Hell, kid, I'm sorry." He stayed across the square and yelled. "Can I walk over to you without getting shot?"

"Yeah," Rabbit called out without looking at me. "Unless you put your hands down and it looks like you're going to shoot us."

"Really?" I asked, not taking my eyes off the guy.

"Carried away?" Rabbit's chagrined smile was evident in his voice.

"I'm gonna take off my jacket and stuff, okay?" The guy didn't wait but started stripping while still far away. When I saw the smiley-face boxers and sweat-drenched Mickey Mouse T-shirt under all the plastic gear it was clear this man wasn't hiding anything. No weapons. His arms and his neck and even his calves were covered in tattoos. If I'd walked past him at school I would have felt fear, but now the tats didn't even make me blink. There were other things to be afraid of these days.

I relaxed. Probably visibly slumped; I couldn't help it. I didn't put the gun down, but I started breathing again. Rabbit stepped forward, not much, but enough that I knew he no longer thought the bogeyman drove a tractor.

As the layers were peeled off, a lanky, long, and lean boy

had appeared. His hair was dark and slicked back with sweat. His nose and cheekbones were red and peeling with sunburn.

"I'm Zack." He walked toward us a couple of steps. Close enough I saw he was a foot taller than me and at least a couple of years older. Hard to tell his age.

Rabbit held out his hand to shake, as if we were meeting on a golf course.

"You know how to use that?" Zack gestured to my gun. His eyes were sunken in shadows but seemed friendly.

"Of course," I said.

"Then maybe you shouldn't be pointing it at your boy-friend?" Zack asked with a smile. I realized I'd laid the barrel in my arms and Rabbit was right at the hurting end.

"Crap." I jumped away from Rabbit and slapped the gun around. "Thanks."

"Ew! *Brother*. I'm her brother!" Rabbit shouted, more concerned with the thought of dating me than getting shot accidentally.

I waited for Zack to grin, but he only nodded. Thankfully, he didn't say anything to make me feel any more idiotic than I already did. "You guys hungry? Thirsty?"

"Thirsty." Rabbit shuffled forward a little. "I'm Rabbit."

"It's been a while, but you look like a boy to me."

"Nickname. This is my sister, Nadia."

"Welcome to Zackville, Rabbit and Nadia. Population one, now three. Who's in the Jeep?" He lifted his chin toward the slobbering mass of quivering dog.

"That's Twawki. You have any antibiotics? He's hurt bad," Rabbit answered.

"Probably. You want Gatorade? Bottled water?"

"Either, thanks. We can trade you," Rabbit volunteered.

"Trade me?" Zack faltered.

"Well, we know that money doesn't work anymore and people—"

"Why don't you drink and then we'll figure out how you can help around here, okay? I've been out here a while now, didn't know anyone else was left, so you can tell me what you've seen and that'll be good enough."

"Okay, that's fair."

"Want the tour of the town?" Zack asked me.

As if this wasn't the most surreal conversation I'd ever had. We were acting like we'd shown up at a party unexpectedly while a pile of what used to be people burned in the background.

I couldn't move or even nod. Maybe it was adrenaline letdown. But I really hadn't expected anyone to be nice to us.

"Your sister talk?" Zack asked Rabbit.

"Not so much anymore." Rabbit patted my arm like I was an old lady.

"I talk," I grunted.

Zack laughed. It was rusty and unused, more a bark of shock. His expression flashed surprise. I found myself smiling in answer.

"This will wait." Zack gestured around him. "Come on. Where you from?"

"Near Seattle."

"Home of fancy coffee? Long way to come."

"Where're you from?"

"I'm from California." Zack led us toward a building that looked like a cross between a town hall and a police station.

"Why aren't we going toward the grocery store?" I asked.

Suspicion was getting to be like my own shadow—I didn't know it was there until I turned around and spotted it, but I wore it now like I'd always had it.

Zack shrugged. "You can go to the store if you want, but there's nothing left in it. I've got everything useful down in the jail." Zack jiggled a large key ring on a piece of twine around his neck. His suspicion and distrust seemed almost more paranoid than my own. "You can come in, or I can bring stuff out. You want a Coke? Beer?" The last was said with a hint of sarcasm.

"Orange juice?" Rabbit asked.

"Sure. I think I've got some bottles of that left." Zack paused at the door.

"Is there anyone else here?" I asked.

Zack turned and met my eyes as if he understood the importance of the question. "Nope. Just me." He disappeared.

"I think we should go with him," Rabbit said to me.

"Really? What if . . ."

"Nadia, we gotta trust someone. Besides, wouldn't it have been easier if he'd, you know, robbed us immediately? It's not like he needed to know our names."

In any other world I would cross the street to avoid walking near Zack. He gave off an air of menace, like a criminal who simply hadn't been caught yet. But then again, grannies had held us up. "Okay. Let's go."

Rabbit motioned me to put the safety back on the weapon and opened the door to the station. "Hey, Zack, we're coming in."

"Cool! I'm down the stairs!" Zack yelled. His voice sounded muffled and far away.

The front offices smelled like air freshener. Paper was piled in neat stacks. Whiteboards were covered in to-do lists in short-hand: *plant gardens by May first, find solar panels or generators, wood for winter—need to install fireplace or woodstove with chimney.* I walked closer and saw stacks of library books with how-to titles that pertained to everything on the list.

We climbed down the stairs, unsure what to expect.

"So there are three orange juices left. Sorry, they're warm. I don't have power for a refrigerator yet." He'd tossed on plaid board shorts and a clean T-shirt.

"No problem, thanks." I studied the rooms around us. The three jail cells were stacked high with canned goods, jars, cartons, and plastic bins of other nonperishables. He'd moved a full-size bed next to them. The bed was unmade, sheets ruffled as if he'd slept there last night. Where I expected desks or workstations, he'd brought in armchairs. Stacks of candles and more books. The only windows down here were small, barred basement slits; the rest of the light was provided by a very bright set of lanterns. Jugs of water and a couple of buckets rounded out the decor. The place smelled like Rabbit's sweaty socks and a grocery store.

"Why are you being nice to us?" I blurted out. "I mean sharing and everything."

"Jeez, Nadia!" Rabbit guffawed.

"Hey, Toad, leave your sister alone. It's a good question." Zack moved toward the far wall. "Here's my calendar—the way I see it, if I work for fifteen hours a day until the first snow, and it's a very mild winter, I have a good chance of surviving until spring. You have any idea how many things in this world would be easier with another set of hands? This is a map of the town—I've cleared the church, the grocery store, and two sets of condos. The rest is still like it was when I found it, except—" He shook his head and didn't continue.

Rabbit nodded. "Fifteen hours a day?"

"I get up with the sun and go to bed when it sets, so maybe more than that."

"Why stay here when winter comes?"

"Why not? I figure I've got to start over somewhere, right? I know people—they'll gang up and it'll be a war zone wherever they all land. At least here if I live, or die, it's because I worked hard, or not hard enough, right?"

"Why are you burning up the people?"

Zack sat down and took a long drink of juice before answering. "I'd be lying if I said respect, or God, or anything like that. I figure I'm less likely to be haunted by vengeful ghosts if I at least try to do right by the people. I can't bury them all—I'd have to take them too far away from here and I want to use the land close by for planting food. I'm cleaning out the town of bodies so the smell will improve, make this place livable long term. The flies are driving me nuts. And just because I didn't get that flu doesn't mean I can't get something else."

"You didn't get sick?"

He shook his head.

"At all?" I pressed.

"No."

"Your family?" Rabbit asked.

Zack shrugged. "Don't know. Don't know if I was lucky or unlucky. You guys passing through, or you want to hang around?"

"Is there a veterinarian clinic here?"

"You sick?" Zack might have smiled fleetingly while he

flipped through a notebook of streets and addresses. It looked as if he kept track of where supplies could be found.

"Nah, but our dog is," Rabbit answered.

Zack glanced at me and I tried to tell him with my eyes that this was serious. He said, "There's a guy who worked out of his house. I haven't cleared it yet, but I think it had animal stuff in it. "

I wasn't sure how Rabbit would survive it if Twawki died.

Zack grabbed a backpack. "Let's go see what we can find. I've got all the human medicines in the back office, so if we don't find something there, we can work from books."

"You read a lot?"

"Not before I needed to. Now pretty much every day for something. The streets of Los Angeles didn't really have much in common with here."

When we got there, Zack didn't bother to knock and didn't seem like he even considered it.

Turned out the farm animal vet had died in his bed, but not before he'd let his bird out and left bathtubs full of water and scattered seed everywhere.

A voice called down from upstairs, startling us all. The fluttering of wings and a talkative, "Hello? Name's Al. How are you?" An African gray came flapping down the stairs as if it hadn't flown for a while. Bare-chested, it looked plucked like a chicken in the store. *Is it sick?*

It landed on Zack's shoulder and bobbed its head.

"You look like a pirate." Rabbit laughed at Zack's expression. The bird settled in like it belonged there and began singing a song about being a virgin. I tried not to let the heat that flushed my cheeks show by turning my head and letting my hair fall forward.

"I don't know where he came from. I checked all the houses when I got here . . . in case . . ." Zack didn't finish his thought, but I knew.

"Maybe he was scared?" Rabbit's expression clouded as if he knew exactly why a bird, or a boy, might hide.

"I think the office is down this way." Zack pointed and led the way.

Bright sunlight poured through big squares of old glass. We opened windows.

Al picked his way up into Zack's curly black hair and danced on top of his head. Zack tried to ignore the bird completely and I couldn't stop smiling.

"Hey, Fish, why don't you go outside and see if you can find any crickets or worms, or something, to feed Al here?" Zack asked. "Just stay by the house and we can hear you. There's nobody around."

I nodded.

When Rabbit left, Zack turned to me and asked, "What's wrong with the dog?"

"He had glass in his paws. They got infected."

Zack nodded.

"We gave him a few antibiotics, but we didn't have enough!" Rabbit yelled from outside the window.

I sighed and shook my head. "Twawki is Rabbit's new friend." I hoped Zack read into my statement all the things I couldn't bring myself to say aloud.

"Don't worry, Pig, we've got meds." Zack leaned through the open window and gave Rab a thumbs-up. "We just need to figure out what to use."

"I think we need to clean and disinfect his wounds again. I haven't been able to do much except—"

Zack touched my arm before the tears threatened. "It's okay, we'll figure it out."

His words almost made me want to cry harder. The number of times I'd needed, hoped, and prayed to have someone, anyone, tell me that everything would be okay I couldn't count.

We loaded up gauze and Betadine solution, two vet school textbooks on wounds and treatments, and anything else—tools, wraps—that seemed relevant. And then we headed back to the town hall and Zack's home.

On the way out, Zack grabbed a couple of IV bags filled with fluids and antibiotics.

"I don't know how to use those," I said.

"Trust me, I can stick him if we need to," Zack said. "Hey, Bunny, can you see if Al will sit on your shoulder for a while? See if he's hungry?"

We left Twawki in the shade while we set up our makeshift surgery center in a conference room that had massive windows and bright light. A long flat mahogany table served as the operating table. Rabbit hovered around us with his hands pushed deep in his pockets and a frown scrunched between his brows.

Zack and I returned to the Jeep and glanced at each other. Twawki barely lifted his head and didn't try to put weight on his paws. I saw the pain in his pleading expression.

"Will he bite me if I carry him?" Zack hesitated.

"No." Rabbit shadowed, anxiety rolling off him in waves.

"I don't think so." I shrugged, not making any promises.

Carefully, Zack let Twawki sniff him and lick his fingers. When he leaned over to pick up Twawki and carry him, the dog didn't struggle or even make a sound.

Zack's strength was noticeable in his lean and muscular arms. Twawki had wasted away with the infection to a whimpering mass of hair mats and bones. Rabbit followed us, humming a soundless tune that sang of worry.

"I think we should keep the kid out of here," Zack said under his breath as we situated Twawki on the table.

"I can't make him stay out," I answered in a low voice, petting Twawki's head.

Zack nodded and leaned out the door. "Hey, Bear, this is gonna take a while and we're gonna want to sleep when we're finished. Upstairs in the offices, I've stashed a lot of pillows and blankets and stuff. You think you could take Al with you and bring 'em down for you and your sister?"

"Shouldn't I help with Twawki?" Rabbit stepped forward as if to argue.

"Nah, we've got it under control." Zack gave off an air of nonchalance that I envied.

Rabbit darted in and kissed Twawki on the nose before scampering off.

I turned toward our patient and all the instruments we'd picked up at the vet's. *Why didn't Mom teach me anything useful? Where am I going to use geometry in this world?* If she was still here we'd have an emergency room nurse to do this.

"This is going to hurt—a lot. We can't risk trying to figure out sedation or anything. Is he going to bite us?" Zack repeated his earlier question while picking up a textbook.

"He hasn't tried yet." A dog bite in this world could be fatal and we both knew it. Hell, everything in this new reality was freakin' death waiting.

Zack squinted down at the book. "You a good reader?"

"Yeah." I nodded.

Zack handed me the book. "Then it'll be faster if you read and tell me what to do."

I don't know how long we worked hunched over books and supplies trying to figure out from the pictures which gadgets were which. "It says if the animal is seriously dehydrated to put them on fluids and antibiotics."

"I think he counts." Zack wrapped a leg, found a vein, and slid the needle in before I had time to think about what needed to happen.

My jaw dropped. "Where'd you learn to do that?"

"Before." Zack didn't say anything else.

We fell into a rhythm of cleaning out a paw, soaking it to remove even more infection, then wrapping it so it continued to drain. Zack found a couple more slivers of glass that had worked their way to the surface. Twawki seemed to know we were trying to help him, and aside from whining occasionally he let us work. At some point I started cutting the rest of Twawki's hair off, so tangles and clumps littered the floor. *We need to find a dog brush. If he lives.*

"I'm done!" Rabbit called. "I inflated a couple of air mattresses too."

"Thanks, Rab," I answered, trying not to gag over a particularly putrid abscess Zack had sliced open.

Rabbit appeared in the doorway.

"Why don't you take my keys and decide what's for dinner? Make sure you check out all the choices." Zack nodded at me to take the key ring off his neck.

"Sure. You guys want anything special?"

"Whatever, Rabbit." I wasn't sure I'd be able to choke anything down, even after we were done.

"'Kay." His brow was furrowed and his face pale with worry. "How's it going?"

"We're making progress, okay? We're about ready to change the IV bag and that's good—it means he's got fluid in him to fight." I tried to sound encouraging and optimistic.

Rab leaned down and whispered in Twawki's ear, "Fight, boy, please. I need you."

I turned away, blinking frantically so tears didn't fall.

"We're doing our best, Lion Man, go figure out dinner." Zack met my gaze and he shooed Rabbit from the room.

By the time we stripped off our gloves we'd done the best we could. Much less restless, Twawki seemed to sleep deeper. Rabbit's meal consisted of SpaghettiOs with meatballs, green peas, and a jar of cherry pie filling over vanilla pudding. He was becoming creative with the food; it wouldn't surprise me if he ended up a new kind of chef. *Supposing we need careers and jobs in the future?*

With Rab snoring almost as loudly as a jet engine, even if I'd wanted to sleep I couldn't have. Rather than grow frustrated, I gave up and found Zack reading with a lamp outside the room where Twawki snored almost as loud as Rabbit.

"Can't sleep either?" I asked, sliding down the wall to sit beside him.

"Nah, I figure I'll have time to sleep a lot this winter."

"What are you reading?"

Zack turned the book over and showed me the cover. "It's the mechanics of old water pumps—I'm trying to figure out how to restore the water supply here. Or at least find a way to start a new one. How's your brother?"

"Sleeping with Al snuggled on the pillow next to him. Our mom would freak out."

"It's good for him to have a buddy, though." The unspoken thought was if Twawki died at least he'd have the bird.

"How's he doing?" I nodded toward Twawki.

"I just changed the IV—it's the last bag we have, so we're gonna have to get meds into him another way soon."

"Will he make it?"

"He's a tough dog. He made it this far, I think he's got the will to live. That's maybe more important than anything else." There was so much Zack wasn't saying.

"How are you, Nadia?" He closed his book and asked the question with an expression that said he really wanted to know the answer.

I wanted to be flippant, but I couldn't find the strength. "Really tired."

"You can sleep. You're safe here."

"Are we?" My thoughts flashed to the train station, to the grannies, to the nightmare newscasts I'd watched while the world still broadcast media in real time.

"Have you seen others?" Zack asked, as if I was late to the revelation.

I nodded. "We passed a train station about seventy miles from here. Someone lined up survivors and shot them all in the head."

I don't know why I expected Zack to be surprised, but he wasn't.

"You and your brother had a house and food while the world fell apart?"

I swallowed. "I guess. Yes, mostly."

Zack's expression grew distant, like he was shutting off memories before they could surface. "The disease didn't destroy the world—the people were far worse. Panic and fear make people less than animals."

Would I ever forget? "Where were you?" I asked.

"L.A. Los Angeles, the city of fallen angels." Zack snorted.

"And where'd you live?"

"The streets mostly."

My eyes were drawn to the ink that doodled and slashed his arms like inkblot sleeves. No colors, only lots of black lines in shapes that connected and crawled.

"Does that scare you?" he asked, his eyes glued firmly on the book.

There was a time when, yes, I would have been scared out of my mind to sit this close to him. "Not anymore."

"But you wouldn't have talked to me before." Zack shrugged like he'd expected me to be that judgmental.

"Probably not. But you wouldn't have talked to me, either, would you?" I raised my eyebrows.

He chuckled. "Pretty, clean girl like you? Nah, I wouldn't have known what to talk about."

I smiled reply; my cheeks felt stiff and unused. The silence wasn't awkward, though I felt blood rush to my face as he continued to study me.

"Did you get sick?" Zack finally asked.

"Yeah, both of us, but then we got better and stayed that way." While I was sick, Rabbit was too—it all blurred in a fever haze of nightmare-like flashes.

He nodded. "I kept thinking I had a headache, or it was coming on, but nah, just didn't like being left out." He laughed. "How fucked up is that?"

In this world? Kinda normal. I smiled. "Did you ever—" I

125

broke off, unsure how to voice my question. Did he ever wish he hadn't survived? That he could have died just like everyone else and not been left to deal with all this?

"Do I wish I'd died, you mean?" Zack pressed.

I nodded.

"When I was in L.A., the place was ripped apart. Fires burned out of control and there was nothing to find or scavenge in other parts of the city. People started killing people who looked sick and piling up their relatives outside to try to protect those who remained healthy. Stores were emptied. Riots broke out. Looting was normal and everyone in my neighborhood already had guns before this started. Guys started walking around with multiple weapons slung over their arms and shoulders. Every street was guarded for a while by someone. Then fewer and fewer.

"The day my last friend—a guy I'd known forever—died, I took off with a new friend who wasn't sick either . . . not then. Kept walking, moving, stealing cars. Hiding when they did the roundups."

"Roundups?" His new friend must have died too, because Zack was alone here.

"Didn't the soldiers come to your place?"

Those were soldiers? "Once maybe, but we thought they were just criminals."

"Maybe, who knows. Mostly, I traveled at night. Before, my skills took care of me in the city. Not much I knew works out here."

"Nobody is prepared to live like the pioneers."

"Who?"

"Oh, like hundreds of years ago—no power, no appliances."

Zack nodded. "Uh-huh, that's why I decided I needed a

place, a farm and crap. I used to think school was for morons, but now books about history are guidebooks. You know? How to survive without your cell phone or the Internet."

"*How-to for Mega Dummies?*" I offered.

He nodded. "So I found a place with no one left. Named it, started to make it mine."

"There are plenty of farms around here. Why the town?"

"I need to live off supplies for a while, right? Gather information and stuff. I can plant a garden in the town square—it's not like I need acres this summer. Acres, jeez, I didn't even know that word two months ago, let alone what it meant and what to do with it."

I nodded. "I know more about how other people lived now than I ever wanted to." Breaking into people's homes was a necessity, but I still felt like Mom would ground me if I was caught.

"It's kinda fun, too, though, right?"

In a way it was, in a way everything that used to matter didn't, but it was still odd to think about no bills to worry over and no money to exchange. Maybe Zack knew how the gold and medicine currency worked. As I opened my mouth to ask, he interrupted me.

"The thing is, I can't do all that by myself anyway. There are cows down the road and a bunch of chickens I've tried to round up and put in a fence. I need to move them closer before winter—I was thinking the school gym might make a great barn for them all. But I'm no freakin' cowboy."

I laughed at his rueful expression.

"Yeah, I know, a city rat worrying about cows surviving a blizzard. But hey, they survive, I survive."

"I like cows—milk, cheese, ice cream?"

Twawki stretched and we both stood to check on him. The IV bag was empty, so Zack removed the needle and wrapped his leg. Twawki thwacked his tail and tried to kiss Zack's face.

"How'd you learn to use a needle like that?" I asked him.

The smile left his face and he sobered. "If I tell you, it'll change how you look at me. I'd rather not."

"Drugs?" I asked. It made sense, given what he'd told me about his life in L.A.

Zack nodded.

"That's what I thought." I tried to keep my expression clear of anything he might read as pity or revulsion, because it really didn't change how I saw Zack.

He turned away slightly, his shoulders back and his spine straight. "It was a long time ago and a whole other world. I never put that shit in my body, but where I lived, the people I knew—"

"It's okay. I get it."

"I'm not sure you do."

I reached out and touched his arm. Just a whisper-light reassurance, like I'd give Rabbit, only I didn't feel like Zack's sister. "It comes in handy now, right? How am I going to rag on you for that? It's more of a skill than writing an essay on Shakespeare, which was my claim to fame."

"Thanks. Shakespeare?" He grinned.

"Writing essays. I used to make extra bucks writing them for classmates."

"Wow, you must be on the FBI's most-wanted list."

"Essays of mass destruction? Not likely."

"Come on, let's go raid the snacks. Want some pretzels?"

"Sure."

Dawn came much too early each day, but with the rise of the sun, the chores began. *Chores.* Zack called them chores like he was already a farmer.

Over the next few days, the three of us settled into a rhythm of cleaning out all the supplies in the buildings that Zack had already cleared of the dead.

He didn't want me, or Rab, to touch the dead and I didn't feel the need to protest too much. Turned out Zack had different rooms of the town hall designated: bedding, clothing, medical, books (nonfiction only), camping equipment, propane tanks and fuel, weapons, seeds, and gardening tools. We hauled and stashed, making trip after trip with wheelbarrows and hand trolleys. It was exhausting, but it was also a wonderful way to change the pace—working physically helped me sweep more of the cobwebs from my brain. Being in the sun and fresh air, if we were upwind from the body-fire, made me feel a little more alive even as my muscles ached with use. When we finished, we marked the houses done on the maps Zack hung in his command central.

Rabbit became camp cook and took great delight in trying to make new flavor concoctions with supplies in tins, cans, jars, and tubs. The day we found a rooftop garden with fresh lettuce and peas caused joyful happy-dancing among us all. I missed salads and fruit. Yeah, I missed broccoli. Not so much brussels sprouts, but give me time.

In the evenings, Rabbit read from *The Swiss Family Robinson* while Zack and I trolled his how-to library for useful tidbits. We didn't talk about leaving. *Not yet.*

Zack held up what looked like four leather cups. "Hey, do you think you can put these on the dog?"

"He'll let me," Rab said. "What are they?"

"Shoes. Padded soles with rubber on the bottoms."

I picked one up and held it to the light. "You made this?"

"Yeah, thought he might walk around more if his feet were protected a little."

"It's a great idea." My heart thudded at his kindness.

Rabbit leaned down and strapped them on Twawki. After a thorough sniffing and checking, the dog put his head back down. "Guess they're not that different than the socks? Come on, boy, stand up!" Rabbit leapt to his feet and crossed the room. "Twawki, come!"

Rolling to his feet, the dog stood uncertainly, then stepped with more conviction. His tail lifted and wagged and he lumbered over to Rabbit with his tongue hanging low and a long line of drool dripping down onto the floor.

He looked like he was ice-skating, or prancing like a show horse.

We all laughed and he made the rounds among us, giving kisses as he got used to the feel of his shoes.

"We'll still have to change his socks until the wounds are healed, but at least he's got some protection from the elements."

"Thanks, Zack. Those are so cool." Rabbit knocked Zack's knuckles with his fist.

"You're really good at making things," I noted.

"Need is a good motivator."

"What do you mean?"

"Well, I wasn't walking into a mall and buying what I needed, so if I didn't want to steal it, I had to make stuff work for me."

"Oh."

"Don't look at me like that. I'm not a saint, Nadia—I stole plenty."

"I'm sure." *But it means he doesn't necessarily do the easy thing. Easy doesn't mean right.*

By the fifth day, Twawki was a different dog. He started eating anything within reach, walking, and lying in the sun while we worked. He even chewed on a rawhide bone that Rabbit found in a house full of dog toys. Al stayed on Rabbit's shoulder and serenaded us with goofy pop songs as we went about our jobs.

By the end of that week, Zack found four more houses containing no remains, so there was even more to collect and distribute. While I focused on the essentials, Rabbit looked for luxuries he missed. After finding Monopoly, Life, and an ornate chess set, he started teaching Zack how to play chess after dinner.

It was easy to let myself forget about leaving. It was tempting to stay. We could always go next spring. *But what if we get to Pappi's and he's dead and there's nothing at the mine?* At least here we had a place to call home, food to eat, and a good chance of seeing this time next year. *Assuming we don't get sick, or hurt, or a group of criminals arrive to evict us. I need to tell Zack about the plan. Bean's plan.*

Busy sorting medical supplies, I didn't hear Rabbit hovering at my elbow. "Nadia, are we gonna ask Zack to come with us?"

I paused, but didn't look at him. "What do you think?"

"I think we should. He's our friend now."

I nodded. "I've thought about it too. He's definitely been our friend."

"So, when are we leaving?"

"Are you in a hurry?" I swallowed over a sore spot in my throat, trying to ignore it.

"No, but I think as soon as Twawki is better we need to keep going. We've already been on the road for two weeks. We're not even half there yet."

"Let's give him a few more days. His feet are healing, but they're still raw wounds."

"Okay. So?"

"So?" I leaned my back against the cans and turned to study my brother. He'd grown another inch and his hair was going from military buzz cut to a frizzy cloud. Streaks of dirt riddled his arms and cheeks.

He snorted like I was being particularly dumb. "Are we going to tell Zack?"

I wanted to. So badly, I wanted to tell him everything. Every single detail. "Yeah, I think we have to tell him, but we can't tell him why, or where we're going."

"Why not?" Rabbit frowned, shaking his head.

"Because Bean said not to."

"But Bean hasn't met Zack. Why would he leave here if he doesn't know why?"

"You think he might come with us?"

"Maybe. I hope so." Rabbit stuffed his hands in his pockets.

That's a very good point. "I'll think about it, okay?"

"Okay," Al answered me. "Okeydokey, have a smoky."

We giggled. "Al looks better." I noticed he had feathers growing in on his neck. He'd been rotating between both boys' shoulders and Twawki's head. He'd started preening and eating, even bobbing his head to the songs he sang.

"Are we going to take him with us?"

Frustrated that Rabbit kept asking me questions I had no answers to, I snapped, "I don't know."

He blanched and stepped back.

"Sorry. Sorry." I rubbed my forehead.

He nodded but stayed quiet.

"I'm sorry. I have a headache."

Rabbit wandered back to his wheelbarrow and guilt crawled in me. He didn't deserve having his head ripped off because I wasn't sure how to make decisions that impacted everything. If we took Al and Twawki with us we'd have to feed them, protect them, risk having something happen to them. *I'm not sure my heart can survive more loss.*

That night I stared at the ceiling listening to Rabbit, Twawki, and Al all snore. Zack seemed to sigh every now and then. *Will he come with us? Can I ask him to?*

"Nadia," Zack whispered across the darkness.

"Yeah?" I answered, trying not to wake the zoo.

"Can you see out the window?"

I twisted on my mattress. "No, why?"

"There's a ton of shooting stars out there. Come on."

I heard rustling as he got up and tiptoed. I saw Twawki lift his head and then put it back down. He was lying with his back against Rabbit's.

"Where are we going?" My sock feet slid along the floor.

"You'll see. Come on." Zack took my hand and guided me until he could turn on the pocket flashlight so we could see to climb up the flights of stairs. At the very top, he walked us down the hallway until we came to a plain wooden door.

When he opened it the breeze blew across my face, and for

a moment it smelled sweetly of spring and only spring. Then, the waft of smoke drifted over and I lost the warm fuzzy feeling.

Zack guided me out onto the roof.

I didn't hold back a gasp of surprise. "Oh, wow, they're amazing." The stars were breathtaking. So close they seemed like they were hanging within reach and the fingernail of the moon frothed with the bright white of cold milk.

"I know, right?"

We settled against the stonework along the top of the building, dangling our legs like I used to do over the dock's edge at the beach. Below us, in the square, coals of the bonfire glowed, but the smoke was only wisps that floated in the opposite direction from us.

I almost imagined myself on summer vacation, staying up too late. I didn't have curfew anymore. I could stay up here all night, for weeks, and no one would yell at me or ground me. *It's weird to not have rules.*

"You guys are taking off soon, aren't you?" Zack asked finally.

DAY 70

A couple of meteors streaked overhead and stole my words. I inhaled, counting to four, exhaled for four. *Why do I feel like I'm letting Zack down by thinking about leaving?* "Yeah. I think so."

"Well, I think you should stay." Zack's face was turned away from me and up at the sky. As if he couldn't force himself to look at me and say it.

"We made a promise. I made a promise." My voice barely carried from my mouth.

"To who? What?"

"My uncle, my mom. To take my brother to our grandfather."

"Odds are he's dead, you know? Right?"

"Maybe. Probably. But maybe not." I couldn't tell Zack about Bean's research and the shots he gave us.

"You won't stay, no matter what I say, will you?"

I shook my head. "If it was just me. I would. But I can't decide differently for Rabbit and he's too young to decide for himself. I promised."

"You know there are people between here and there who might not be nice."

"That's an understatement." My grimace turned to a laugh.

Zack touched my hand, quickly letting go. "I don't want to scare you."

"You can't. I'm already petrified all the time."

"Really? Never would have guessed."

"I'm not that good an actress." I shook my head.

"I say you are. What are you scared of right now?" he asked.

"Falling off the building trying to see a star." I tried to defuse his question—it would be so much easier to tell him what I wasn't afraid of.

He bumped his shoulder against mine. "What else?"

"The dog dying." I held up one finger.

"I think he'll be okay."

I held up a second finger. "Leaving here for the unknown."

"Then don't leave."

"Come with us?" I wanted to bite the words back as soon as they left my mouth. I dropped my hand to my lap.

"What?" Zack sounded shocked.

"I mean, I know it sounds stupid to leave your very own town to creep across the country with us, but . . ."

The silence was almost unbearable. "Where are we going?"

"Oh . . . I can't tell you."

Zack laughed. "What? You invite me to go and then you won't tell me where?"

"I promised."

"Give me a clue for God's sake." Frustration chewed Zack's tone.

"Across the Mississippi?"

"That narrows it down to a million miles. You gotta give me more than that, Starbucks."

"West Virginia."

"What's in West Virginia?"

"I can't say more. Please. I already shouldn't have told you that."

"But you want me to come?"

"I do. I really, really do." I crossed my arms over my chest and tried to look convincing.

With a nod, Zack put his arm around me. His hand brushed my back pocket. "What is this?" He tapped it. "You carry it around all the time."

I slid the little music player out of my pocket. It was scratched and beat-up and the screen was cracked. I didn't bother with earbuds. I held it out to Zack, who took it carefully.

"Does it work?" he asked.

"I don't know. It was my dad's."

"He liked music?"

I smiled. "Yeah, he'd put in a disc, or plug it in to the car, and he'd crank up these old-school songs and sing along at the top of his voice. Even when he dropped me off at school and picked me up, he'd be blaring Madonna or Lionel Richie."

"Who's Lionel Richie?"

"Yeah, see? Totally lame, but he said it was because his job required so much silence that he needed songs to balance it out."

"Did you run this over or something? Why is it all banged up?"

"He took it with him. His last mission. Afghanistan. He died."

"Oh." Zack frowned. "Sorry."

"It was about two years ago. This came home in his stuff. I don't know if it works. I didn't charge it before the power died too."

Zack laid it back in my palm. "Thank you." He closed my fingers around it.

"For what?" I asked.

"For showing me, for telling me."

I thought for a moment and ripped at the scab a little more, confiding, "He's why I'm here. Why I even left the house when Mom died."

"Why?" Zack paused as if holding his breath.

"He used to coach us in survival scenarios—he loved this game called Worst Case and he'd make up these ridiculous stories and ask us how we'd do whatever."

"Like what?"

"One of his favorite scenarios was an earthquake while we were at school. How would we make it through? He told us to be the cockroach."

Zack chuckled. "I always killed the little suckers."

"Yeah, but there are always more, right? And he'd tell us we didn't have to survive the cause of something, like the earthquake, but the effect. What came after was more about our character than if we were lucky enough to live through something bad."

"Sounds like he had a lot of faith in you."

"Maybe too much."

"So you're letting your dad down if you don't try to get to your family?"

"Yeah, I guess that's it. I hadn't really thought about it, but yeah. This is the effect and he'd be disappointed if I failed my brother." He'd be ashamed of me if I gave up too soon.

Zack pointed out another streak of light across the heavens. "How'd he get named Rabbit?"

"His name is Robert—same as our dad's—but when he was little instead of crawling like a normal kid, he hopped around. Dad started calling him Rabbit and it stuck."

Zack turned his face away from mine. "You're lucky, you know? That he loved you. Your mom too. I'd have let no one down if I died out in L.A. No one would have cared or noticed."

"But you think you would have let yourself down, right?"

He swiveled toward me. "How'd you guess that?"

"Seems like you expect a lot from yourself."

"Now. Not before, I didn't. And I'm not the one trying to get from Seattle to West Virginia with a boy and a dog."

"Before doesn't matter anymore."

"It's all about after, isn't it?"

"Will you think about it? Coming with us?"

"Sure. Maybe." We stayed up on that roof watching the stars until the moon sank and the first glow of morning turned the clouds to slate gray and lavender.

The next few days took on the same rhythm except in the

evenings, when Rabbit and I completely unloaded the Jeep. I wanted to repack with our newly acquired knowledge about trading goods, and we needed a better way for Twawki to ride along. And Al. *Do birds need seat belts?*

We were half done when Zack wandered by. "Photo albums?" Zack nudged the stack. "You gonna eat those?" He continued marching by, toward the tractor.

I sighed. "He's right."

"But—" Rabbit nodded as he shook his head like a bobble-head doll.

"Let's pick a few photographs and leave the rest here. We need room for Twawki—he's gotta be able to stretch out, right?"

Rabbit chose my parents' wedding photo. Dad looked so sharp in his uniform and Mom radiant and young in her poufy white dress. She didn't look haunted or tired. Not yet. I chose a family portrait that Mom set up before Rabbit was born. It was the last day I remembered being the only kid in the family. I picked up the rest of the albums and took them into the nearest living room, setting them carefully on an empty coffee table. I forced myself to turn around and walk out. *Another piece of the past, gone.*

Rabbit was talking to Zack when I came back out.

"Zack, do you mind if we salvage gas for our gas tank? Just enough to get us far enough away from here to look for other supplies?"

"We can fill them all." He picked up the extra gas cans.

I shook my head. "You'll need some for the generators this winter."

"I'll make do. All the cars are in the bank parking lot." He and Rabbit started heading that way.

"Really? Are you sure?"

"Why'd everybody move their cars to the bank?" Rabbit asked.

"No, Wolf, I moved them there early on."

"How? Did people leave keys in them?" I asked, catching up.

"Nah, another L.A. skill," Zack declared, as if it was perfectly normal to know how to start cars without keys.

"Oh." Heat flushed my cheeks. *Grand theft auto?* Who knew that was a handy skill set? I was beginning to think his life on the streets was much more useful than my life in the burbs.

"You're cute when you blush, Starbucks."

As we filled up the gas cans, Zack stared at me. "You've got to give me a good reason to leave here. Why would you leave here?"

"We promised."

I wasn't supposed to tell anyone. But that was before.

Rabbit exploded, "We might have family alive. Like probably they're okay."

"Rabbit!" I rolled my eyes.

Zack's gaze narrowed. "How big a might and probably?"

"I don't know. I really don't. But it wasn't luck that got us through BluStar."

"Our uncle is a doctor," Rabbit added. "He does top-secret stuff for the military."

"Huh." Zack didn't ask more questions and thankfully Rabbit stopped adding his two cents. "You should leave in two days. That'll give us time to pack your Jeep right."

Wow, okay, I think we just got kicked out of Zackville.

DAY 75

Dawn was pink with the promise of a clear sky and empty roads. I swallowed back panic as Zack drove up behind the Jeep in a compact that was one of those cars advertised to get hundreds of miles on a tank.

"What's that for?" Rab quizzed Zack the second he turned off the engine.

"Need extra storage for my stuff."

Rabbit grinned. "You've got a town. How much more do you need?"

"Can't carry a town all the way to wherever we're going," Zack pronounced with a shrug.

Rabbit launched himself at Zack and wrapped his scrawny arms around Zack's neck. "You're coming too?"

I blinked back sudden tears. *He's coming with us.*

Zack met my eyes over Rabbit's head, before wrapping his arms awkwardly around my brother's back, as if he had never been hugged. "Sure, Rooster, I'm coming too."

I mouthed, *Thank you.*

He nodded. "Ya gotta help me load extra stuff in here like food and medicine."

Twawki loped after a ball time and again while we finished packing. After a quick breakfast there was nothing left to do but pour the rain barrels out on the fire. According to Zack there was no reason to risk the town catching ablaze. I wondered if he was keeping it as a backup plan. I couldn't blame him.

"Do you think you can teach Rabbit to drive?" I asked. "At least as we go?"

"Can't you?"

"Yeah, but since I don't really know how to either, seems like a good idea if someone other than his older sister tries to explain it all."

Eyes widening, he choked back laughter at my expression. "Can do."

When Twawki was tired out and Al lounged in a wire cage, we paused as if holding our collective breath. We were really leaving for the unknown. On purpose. *Again.*

"You drive—you need to learn how." Zack tossed the keys to Rabbit. "You take Twawki?" he asked me.

"Sure." I turned away to cover my relief.

"Let's see if we can't make good time since the weather today isn't bad."

I glanced back. "You expecting something?"

"Nah, but there was one dust storm that locked me up for two days when I first got into town. Red dust so thick I couldn't see anything. We don't want to get caught in something like that around here. No idea who's out in it."

Gee, thanks. Feel better already.

I saw the new wire in the dash console. "What's this?" I yelled back.

"For your dad's player. Might as well see if it works, right?" Zack flashed a smile.

"Thanks." I blinked tears. *Sweet.*

🌸 🌸 🌸

I'm doing the right thing. I'm doing the right thing. Watching Zackville disappear in the rearview mirror was more than unsettling. My eyes throbbed and itched. *The stress is getting to me.*

Music filled the car with Simple Minds' "Don't You (Forget About Me)."

"I'll never forget you, Daddy," I whispered as I drove.

We made three hundred miles before stopping for a lunch of canned soup and trail mix. Stretches of fields empty of cattle or horses or crops were interrupted by pockets of cars and the lonely remains of BluStar casualties.

"Where do you want to stop for the night?" Zack asked around a mouthful of raisins and cashews.

"There's a dinosaur park in Ogallala," Rabbit answered him hopefully.

"Dinosaurs?" Zack and I turned to him with our mouths open in shock.

"Why not? Don't think anyone is going to be guarding a bunch of statues, are they? Plus who doesn't like dinosaurs?"

He shrugged, and for a moment I remembered he was still a little boy in so many ways. "I read the maps, remember?"

"How far down the road is it, Eagle Eye?" Zack poked Rabbit's ribs.

Al nibbled on a raisin and Twawki finished a can of Spam. *We should get him dog food. Soon.*

Rabbit reached into his bag and unfolded the map. "About two hundred and twenty miles due east of here."

"It's okay with me." I shrugged and took another long draught of sports drink, trying to drink away the spot in my throat that burned.

"Well, it is my birthday tomorrow," Rabbit confessed while shredding his paper-towel napkin.

"It is?" My stomach dropped. How could I have missed it? Forgotten it?

"Yep, the thirteenth."

"It's already June thirteenth? God, Rabbit, I'm sorry." My stomach twisted with regret. "We camp at the dinosaurs tonight, then you pick something to do tomorrow."

"And what we eat," Zack added.

"I already do that." Rabbit guffawed. "It's okay. I mean, we don't have to do anything special."

I shook my head so hard I felt my brain bounce around. "No, it's not okay. I suck for forgetting."

Zack interrupted me. "I want to see these dinosaurs, let's get moving."

After filling up the tanks with our reserved gas cans, we got back on the road, traveling well above the speed limit.

Twawki let another long, wet fart go and I knew exactly why Zack thought it was a brilliant idea for the dog to ride with me. "Twawki, I'd rather not die of oxygen deprivation at this point."

He ducked his head as if he too was sorry about the stench. "I'll take that as an apology."

Rabbit knew where we were heading, so when Zack passed me and Rabbit held up the map I waved and tried to keep up with the race-car driver behind the wheel. *I sure hope there aren't cops.*

A humongous dino head poked above the tops of the trees, like a giant sentry watching for our arrival. I used to know all the dinosaurs' names and habits. I wanted to be an archaeologist or a fossil hunter, someone who worked outside. *When did that change?*

We drove around the curbs and along sidewalks, heading deeper into the throng of tails and feet. Tree forts for cavemen, or children, were tucked around to be climbed on.

Rabbit flew out of the car and Twawki all but jumped out the window to run with him. "I pick this one!" He scampered up a rope ladder and across the bridge, toward the little arms of a massive *Tyrannosaurus rex.*

I let Twawki out and he stood underneath Rabbit and barked until he found a wheelchair ramp and sprinted up its curves to join Rab. I slipped the MP3 player into my back pocket and shook my head as Al joined in with squawking and bobbing.

Concession stands selling lemonade and ice cream bars were locked tight and looked dirty, like they'd barely survived the winter and no one bothered to clean them for the summer season.

I stretched my back. Too much sitting made me achy.

Zack started unloading supplies for the night without saying a word. Doing it all with the bird balanced on his shoulder like a pirate.

"You sleeping up in the tree fort too?" I asked him as he pulled out a small charcoal grill.

"Nah, I like my feet on the ground."

We worked in silence as dusk began to fall. I half expected the dinosaurs to turn and watch us, but they didn't come to life. *No zombies and no velociraptors.*

"You okay?" Zack watched me chug a bottle of water. "It's not your fault, you know."

"My mom would yell at me for forgetting his birthday."

"Nadia, it's not like dates matter anymore. Besides, what would she do: blow up balloons and bake a cake?"

Not since Dad died. Holidays had grayed and hollowed. Mom had tried, but we all knew the few hours she tried to be happy were as fake as the reheated meals she picked up instead of cooking. Usually, she'd jump at a fill-in shift and escape the house, and us, as quickly as possible.

"No, she'd tell me to." I frowned.

"Look at him. He's okay right now. He's having fun with his new friends." Zack watched as Al swooped and flew up to sit on the railing near Rabbit.

DAY 76

Rabbit was dressed and waiting for us when I cracked my eyes open. I knew that look. He had a plan. "What do you want to do?"

"Let's go to the mall." He'd spread the map out and circled the location

"The mall?"

"Yeah, it's the biggest one in the state and only ten miles that way and you promised."

"I did?"

"Yep, remember? That first day. Besides it's my birthday, right?"

Zack appeared with a Cup Noodles for each of us. "We can try. . . ." Zack trailed off as Rabbit slurped his breakfast.

"What do you mean?" I asked.

"Well, there might be people who live there now."

"Oh, I hadn't thought of that." My stomach clenched and my appetite fled.

"But we can try."

"If people are there we don't have to stay." I knew Rabbit watched my face for signs of fear or trepidation.

Zack glanced around, studying our camp. "Let's take one car and empty it before we go, okay?"

As Rabbit started clearing out the supplies in the compact car I pulled Zack aside. "You think it's that risky?"

Zack's expression was troubled at best. "I stopped at one in California and it was a mess. It was an evacuation center, so there was military. I don't want to scare you."

"Thanks, but you are anyway."

"Sorry. If we take one empty car, we can get back here quickly, or walk back if we have to. It'll give us more flexibility. Hey, Moose, you're gonna need to leave Al here in his cage."

Rabbit nodded and put Al in the tallest tree fort. I listened to him reassure the bird that we were coming back.

America's Freedom Mall got serious play on the highway. Before we'd even passed one sign, we saw another. More cars littered the roads and medians, as if people got only so far and hiked the rest of the way on foot. Or died—there were plenty of pieces, of what used to be people, scattered in the ditches, and in the cars themselves.

The closer we got, the more of a military presence we found. Camouflage trucks and Humvees began lining the exits. Zack paused, taking his foot off the accelerator. Even Twawki tensed and sniffed the air as if trying to anticipate danger. We saw no signs of movement, but we knew that didn't mean much.

"Still want to go?" Zack asked each of us.

"Yeah, we should see, right?" Rabbit answered. I nodded.

"Odds are this show kept people away. Might work in our favor." Zack tried to smile.

We crawled between cars parked alongside the roads and entrances. People had haphazardly driven into trees, other vehicles, even fire hydrants.

A few rows of luxury buses were lined up along the far side of the mall. The heads leaning against the windowpanes told a grizzly story. "They got on the buses and the buses never went anywhere?" I asked under my breath.

"Probably." Zack kept driving until we found a smaller, more obscure set of doors on the backside of the building. Here there were few cars because of the barricade made by sand-colored armored vehicles, piles of debris, and fencing half fallen over, as if it too didn't have the strength to stand tall after a certain point. Rolls of barbed wire were stacked on flatbed trucks as if they had been delivered but no one was alive to unroll them.

"Were they trying to keep people out, or in?"

"I don't know."

Zack pulled as close as he could and shut off the engine. We waited with our ears straining to pick up sounds of human activity. The only thing that whistled was the wind and the honking of geese flying in a *V* above us.

Uniformed piles of used-to-be people told me few had followed orders to the end. At some point, they must have abandoned their posts.

"They were trying to keep people out of the mall." Rabbit's fist was wrapped tightly around Twawki's rope leash.

"No one's been here." The glass doors weren't shattered; chains and locks still strangled the handles.

"This is only one door. I can't imagine looters were too sick. Besides, we can't be the first survivors to come here," Zack cautioned me.

"Why isn't it a town then?" Rabbit asked.

"It might be, we don't know."

"But what about water?" I asked, taking another sip from my water bottle.

"They could truck it in from the lake." Zack pointed in the direction of Lake Ogallala. I nodded, remembering the days when I turned on the faucet and expected a gush of drinkable water.

"Carry the shotgun," Zack instructed, taking a handgun.

"What am I taking?" Rabbit asked.

"You better keep ahold of Twawki's leash—we don't want him getting hurt or thinking we're leaving him."

"Good idea." Rab patted Twawki's head and the dog licked his face.

To me Zack said, "He won't know we're coming back if we just leave him in the car." He pulled a bag with wire cutters from the trunk and cleared a pathway to the door. We followed silently. There was an eerie lack of energy. Malls had been bustling, crazy places where we could never find a parking place—not chained up and locked out like prisons.

Zack sawed the chain off and then picked the lock on the doors. *How did he end up staying out of prison?* With a click of the lock and a hand held up for silence, Zack cracked the doors.

Twawki whined as stale air rolled over us as if the great mall god had been holding his breath and finally exhaled. Under the rotting garbage smell was the scent of new leather and that starchy aroma of unworn clothes. We turned on our headlamps and tentatively stepped inside.

I couldn't believe what I saw. "It's not too picked over. Why not?"

"I heard the National Guard was called out to protect a few capitalist places from rioting, but I didn't think that included malls." Zack's voice echoed off the walls.

"This is supposed to be the largest one in the state." Rabbit's eyes were wide and barely contained his excitement.

"Lots of expensive shops." I scanned the list of retailers, recognizing most of them and knowing we'd never been able to afford shopping at any. I wondered if Mom had known what was coming, if she'd have let us spend a little of Dad's death benefits instead of putting it all in the bank for college. *Nah, probably not.*

We stepped out from the side wing into an atrium. The mall soared up to a glass ceiling three stories above. Most of the stores had gates halfway or almost fully down, like the screens started to fall and then stopped working. Away from the center, the shops and hallways were so dark they seemed like empty mouths waiting to swallow us. Any farther from the center skylight and we'd be blind.

We walked around studying our surroundings and a shiver danced up my spine. The mall was frozen in time. Like it was closed for a holiday. There'd been a little looting by the looks of things, minor messes, but for the most part it looked as though it simply hadn't opened for business yet that day.

I walked on my tiptoes. As if the sound of my footsteps would invite or unleash unknown drama.

"Where should we go first? Any ideas, Goldfish?" Zack tapped Rabbit's shoulder.

I nodded my agreement. "This is your birthday party. You decide."

"Game store?" he asked gleefully.

I laughed. "Why?"

"They might have solar batteries or something."

"Sure, Rab." As if Nintendo was busy retooling their gaming consoles to work in a post-BluStar world. He oohed and aahed over what little stock was left in the store.

"You think employees cleaned this place out?" Zack asked, holding up another empty box.

"Probably. Who knows, maybe they're even playing somewhere and don't know what's happened."

"Best thing that ever happened to them?" Zack smiled.

As Rabbit wandered back toward the entrance I asked, "Where next?"

"Shoes. I need brand-spankin' kicks."

I laughed. "Okay."

We had to fumble around in the stockroom to find sizes, but we ended up with sneakers for Rabbit, hiking boots for me, and black leather biker boots for Zack.

Zack went and checked the kitchen goods store next door and found all the shelves with edibles empty, but he picked up a couple of really sharp, intimidating knives. With a shrug he showed me and said, "You never know."

"Let's go see what Camping Universe has." Rabbit turned down another arm of the mall.

The jewelry stores we passed were empty. *Someone knows gold is the new money.*

At the sporting goods store we picked up sturdy hiking backpacks, clean sleeping bags, and a house-sized tent since

Twawki and Zack took up their fair share of space. We would run into rain one of these days.

Zack headed up an escalator. "I want to make sure they got all the ammo, okay? I'll be right back."

I fingered a pumpkin-colored cotton sweater, then slipped it over my head. The antishoplifting tag clunked against my hip.

"Nadia, look what I found!" Rabbit raced over holding up foil packets, his headlamp perfectly positioned to blind me.

"What is it?" I tried blinking the stinging blindness away.

"It's ice cream."

Twawki barked.

"What?" *There's a working freezer here? We can't possibly be that lucky.*

"Freeze-dried ice cream." His eyes lit up and he held a packet out to me like the true gold it was. "Where's Zack?"

"He's hunting up bullets."

Rabbit shifted, juggling his weight from side to side in excitement. "Do I have to wait? There's three packets."

"Go ahead."

We sat down in display camping chairs. He opened the package carefully, almost as if his life depended on it. He lifted a piece of brown. "Chocolate?"

"Close your eyes and imagine that it's cold," I instructed as he gently placed the square on his tongue.

"Penguins," he said around a mouthful of dissolving chocolate cream.

"Polar bears." I smiled.

In popped a pink, strawberry-flavored chunk. "Ice cubes. Have some." He thrust the bag at me.

"Snowmen." I played along, picking a small crumb; I wanted Rabbit's joy to continue as long as possible. The creamy goodness tasted exactly like ice cream, but the thing I missed most was the cold. "Brain freeze."

A clatter of metal against metal somewhere out in the shadows startled us both. Rabbit dropped the bag on the ground as Twawki turned to face the noise, his head lowered.

I met Rabbit's fearful gaze and clicked off my headlamp, reached over and turned his to dark too. *Talk about having a bright, flashing* Come Kill Me *sign on our foreheads.*

"What do you think that is?" Rabbit whispered, and grabbed my hand.

Where's Zack? He'd call out; he wouldn't deliberately scare us. So who was watching us?

"I don't know," I whispered.

We waited in silence. My ears tried to go into superhearing mode. Twawki thumped his tail and paced, his shoes sounding like sandals on the wooden floor. When he whined, I tightened my hand on his collar.

To our right, a clothing rack tipped, making the clothes sway and the hangers clack against each other. Small skylights above the escalators admitted enough light that we were able to distinguish shapes and textures around us before the edges smudged into blacker shadows. The pitch-black, I still wasn't completely comfortable in, wrapped around us stretching out in every direction.

"There, over there." Rabbit tugged my hand and we moved out of the chairs and between two pop-up tents and a pyramid of rain boots.

"Hello?" I heard a man's voice call.

Twawki woofed a deep, exuberant greeting.

Finally, it clicked that Zack called out. "Guys? It's me. I found a little food downstairs."

Relief flooded me and made my knees weak. "It's Zack."

"We're over here," I called, turning my headlamp back on. Behind us Zack said, "There you are. Not funny."

We'd been searching in the opposite direction from him for the noisemaker. Just as I was about to tell Zack what we were afraid of, something fell to the ground and rattled as it rolled across the wooden floor.

Zack immediately shifted. Dropping the bag in his hands he turned out his flashlight and dove left. I heard running footsteps, and wheezy breathing, as Twawki strained at the leash. He yanked me along in chase.

"Stop! Wait!" Zack called. A door slammed. "It's locked." He reached into his pocket and pulled out a metal stick that he jammed into the lock, then slammed his palm against it until the door opened. The door jerked and crashed into the wall behind us. Cautiously, we poked our heads around, swinging the light to the left, then to the right. Rab took the leash back from me.

A flash of pink swept around the corner of the hallway. Twawki started running and barking, his paws slipping every which way in the shoes. Rabbit hung on for dear life as we gave chase and Zack yelled at the stranger to stop and return. I felt like we were in a bad horror movie. Did we really want whoever it was to come back?

Rabbit bent over and then held up a Barbie dressed in a fluffy ball gown and one shoe. "She dropped these."

"She?"

"I don't think bad guys play with Barbies." Rabbit shrugged, unafraid, if nonplussed.

"Where'd she go, you think?"

I walked around looking at closed doors. The tinkling of keys ahead drew our attention.

Zack placed his finger to his lips and motioned for us to be as quiet as possible as he ventured closer. A tall, tattooed guy with scruffy facial hair, he looked like a criminal—one of those strangers kids aren't supposed to talk to. I grabbed his hand and shook my head. "You'll scare her."

"Don't assume she's alone," Zack said.

"If she wasn't, they'd already have confronted us," I whispered.

While Zack and I argued over the next step, Rabbit and Twawki walked down the hallway.

"She's in here." Rabbit pointed, then lifted his light so we could read the sign.

"How do you know?"

He handed me a matching shoe to the one Barbie was missing. Or it would have been matching if it wasn't squished and twisted. "It was stuck in the door." Rabbit held the door open a crack so it wouldn't shut and lock.

"Cinderella, anyone?" I muttered.

Zack frowned at me.

"Never mind."

Twawki nudged the door and pushed his way inside. I followed, keeping Rabbit behind me in case this was some sort of ambush. We entered what appeared to be a clothing store devoted to everything girl, from infant to tween. Pink and sparkles seemed to be the predominant palette.

"Hello? We found your Barbie? Are you in here?"

Rabbit moved down a side aisle. "My name is Rabbit and this is my sister, Nadia, and Zack. We have food. Are you hungry?"

"Rabbit!" I hissed.

Zack made his way toward the front of the store and then returned to my side. "The gate is all the way down. She didn't leave this area if she came in here."

We peered under the clothing racks thinking maybe she was hiding in the middle of one. Rabbit started playing fetch with Twawki and a Super Ball he took from a toy display by the cash register.

We saved the dressing rooms for last. We'd cornered her with no idea if she had a weapon.

Rabbit tugged my hand and tossed Twawki's ball into the dressing room area. The dog bounded after it. Catching a whiff of scent, he stopped chasing the ball.

All I smelled was bubble gum—that pink, too-sweet, globby chewing gum.

"We think maybe you're inside one of these rooms. We want you to know we're not going to hurt you. We came for supplies today, but we're leaving soon." I hoped I sounded friendly and calm.

"My dog's name is Twawki, you can pat him if you want to." Rabbit was busy turning his head upside down to see under the dressing room doors. At the far end, he gestured me over.

I didn't want to scare her more than she was, but I also didn't feel comfortable leaving her in the mall to fend for herself. We might be the first visitors, but we wouldn't be the last.

I reached into my back pocket and slid out the MP3 player. Folded in its case was a photograph of Dad and me. I smoothed it and put it under the stall door, far enough inside she could see it, but close enough I could grab it back. "That's me when I was eight, with my dad. I'm fifteen now, and this is my brother Rabbit. Zack's the big guy who stomps around in boots like a giant gorilla. He won't hurt you either."

A tiny dirty hand with crystal doodad nail stickers picked up the photograph, then disappeared back into the darkness of the little room. *I'll take that as a good sign.*

Rabbit frowned and made a motion like he'd go in after the photo.

She needed to feel like she was making the choice. I knew it because that was what I might need. Still needed.

"We're going to go to the front of the store and count to one hundred. You can think about it. If you don't want to meet us that's okay, just slip the photo back out here and we'll leave you. Or you can come give it back to me. Your choice. I know your mommy probably told you not to talk to strangers, but now you know us so we're not strangers. Come on, Rabbit."

Twawki's happy tail and bright expression told me she followed close behind us. Probably trying to decide if what I said was honest or not. By the time we got to seventy-seven, Zack jerked his head toward the aisle behind me. I turned around slowly.

There, holding out the photograph to me, was a nymph of a girl, so tiny it was hard to fathom her age. She was skittish and wild-eyed, like she'd been raised in the maze of hallways here. I had no idea what this kind of solitude and fear might do to a child.

I knelt. "Hello. I'm Nadia."

"May I pet your doggy?" she asked.

Rabbit dropped the leash and Twawki bounded over to her and sat while she strangled him in a hug that broke my heart.

Against his fur I heard her mumble, "Patty. I'm Patty."

Once Patty started speaking, there was no shutting her up.

"How'd you end up living here by yourself?" Rabbit asked.

"My mom works here. She's the boss of everyone. She brought me when she got sick."

"Why?" Rabbit frowned.

"The soldiers s'posed to save me."

"How do you get around in here?" Zack asked softly. I knew he was trying to make himself as unintimidating and harmless as possible.

"Lights and keys." She turned on a tiny pink flashlight and showed us a ring of keys she kept tucked in a pink glittered fanny pack.

"Keys?"

"Come on, I'll show you." She leapt to her feet and we followed. Rabbit walked beside her and I let him take the lead. She seemed to bond with him the quickest.

I'd never seen the inner maze of hallways that connected offices and stores behind the scenes. Maybe all malls had them—I guessed I would find out if we went to any others on the trip. Bare yellowed walls and chipped linoleum, empty racks, and cardboard boxes made each hallway look exactly like the last.

"Don't you get lost?" I asked.

"No, I came here all the time—before school and after school. Mommy worked a lot."

"Why were you at the sporting goods store?" Zack asked.

"I eat lunch there."

"You do?"

"Mm-hmm, every day." She turned left into another warren.

Her hair was nested with neglect and oil, but not quite as terrible as I'd expect after weeks of not bathing. And besides the bubble gum cloud, she didn't stink. "How do you take baths?"

"There's a pool at the gym."

"A pool?"

"Yeah, mostly for kids. Mommy told me never to swim by myself, so I stay in the shallow end, but I get clean."

"You don't drink that water, do you?"

"No, there's drinks in the back rooms. Every place has an office." Patty's tone was so matter-of-fact she unnerved me.

"How old are you?"

"Uh"—she held up seven fingers—"first grade."

Incredibly, she'd adapted.

"I have breakfast at Gift Baskets from Heaven." She pointed at a door to our right.

"Why?"

"They have lots of cereal stuff."

"Where's dinner?"

"I change around. I miss hot food. The microwaves don't work."

I can't say I found fault with her mother's plan. Get her kid to a safe place with guards and food, and pray. Her mother must have done a lot of praying.

"Where do you sleep?" I asked.

"The bed d'partment at Macy's. In the monkey bed. Want to pick out your bed?"

"Oh, we . . . um . . ." Rabbit shrugged.

She threw on the brakes so fast we all ran into each other. "You're not staying?" Her chin quivered and enormous tears welled up in her dark pleading eyes. I bent over and opened my arms, and she clung to me crying. "Shhh . . ."

The boys pushed on, checking doorknobs and poking into boxes and rooms. *Like because I'm a girl I know what a mother should say and do.*

"We won't leave you here, I promise, okay? If you want to come with us we'll take you. Can you show me your mommy's office?"

She wiped the snot on her sleeve. "You promise?"

"I promise."

"'Kay, in here." Patty pushed on a door marked Director. The outside office was larger than I expected. A fake tree, bad art posters, and plastic chairs in the corner made a reception area. I kicked something and realized it was a small mountain of plastic bottles. Empty. All of them.

The woman must have spent every last bit of energy stockpiling food and drinks for her child.

"Patty, did you get sick like your mommy?"

"No." She shook her head. "Mommy's in there. She said she was going to sleep forever."

Zack walked toward the door.

"Don't!" Patty shouted. "I promised when she went to sleep I wouldn't go back in."

He held up his hands in surrender. "Okay, kid, I don't have to go in there."

Underneath the stale air I picked up on the unmistakable odor of decomposing flesh. Mommy was sleeping the sleep of the dead.

"Did she want you to stay here? Forever?"

"No, I was s'posed to talk to the soldiers, but they left."

"Have other people come through?"

"Mm-hmm. I hided. I don't like them. They steal rings and sparklies. Mommy would call the police, but I tried and the phones don't work."

Zack picked up a stack of newspapers. "Hey, Nadia, come take a look at this."

The headline read *Will Reactor Near Freedom Mall Destroy Consumer Culture?*

He dropped his voice. "The mall is right by a nuclear power plant. One melted down in Florida when BluStar started."

"Florida? Where? Near Disney World?"

"Yeah, that's not there anymore." Zack shook his head. The newspaper was dated about the time the riots in Seattle gave us all a curfew and shut down the hospitals.

What other massive changes have happened that we don't know about?

"Yeah, people were too scared to come here Mommy said."

"Jesus." Zack swore.

So you leave your kid in a place where she might be safe if you die, but also she could live through BluStar and die because a nuclear reactor didn't survive the no-humans or lack-of-power thing very well. What other catastrophes were going on right now? *What if West Virginia is no longer there?*

"Want to see my favorite place?" Patty asked.

"Sure."

Zack stopped behind the reception area at a locked door with an exit sign. "Patty, is this how we get up on the roof?"

"Mm-hmm." She nodded. "Mommy never let me go up there."

"I'll catch up with you."

Rabbit and Patty started out the door, but I lingered.

"What are you thinking?" I asked Zack.

"I'm going to go up and see what I can see."

"Why?"

"It's the highest place around here. Might give us a sense of what's out there."

"Don't take too long, okay? This place gives me the creeps." I marked turns and directions for Zack on the walls. Bread crumbs weren't as easy to read as "Turn left here."

Patty took us to the biggest toy store I'd ever seen. As she turned on a circle of bright pink Barbie camping lamps I saw the miniature world she'd built. Surrounded by castles and mansions and apartment buildings, I felt like a giant looking down from the heavens. She'd lined the edges with stuffed animals like an audience. Dolls in various states of dress were frozen in time doing countless activities. I could almost let myself believe this was every little kid's fantasy, until she pointed out the pile of dolls in the dump truck on the periphery. "That's the sleeping people."

Zack came jogging in. "Guys, we need to get going." He tried to keep the emotion out of his voice but his tone had my pulse galloping at high speed. He leaned down and whispered in my ear, "There's a cloud of dust headed this way."

"A storm?"

"No, a long line of trucks."

I gasped, turning my face away from the wide eyes of Rabbit and Patty, who were poised to panic at any moment.

"They're miles away, but headed straight here. I don't want to meet them."

"We've got to take her with us."

He nodded agreement. "Grab what you can and let's get out of here." He said in a louder voice, "Horse, we have to go now. Let's go get the backpacks."

"Patty, will you come with us?" I knelt beside her.

"Please?" both Rabbit and Zack reiterated as they lifted the grate enough for us to crawl under.

Her eyes widened. And she seemed to crumple in on herself. "Leave Mommy? Now?" She grabbed my hand and clung as we walked quickly back toward the gear store and the entrance we'd parked near.

I squatted. "You're really brave. And your mommy would be so proud of you. You know how she said to ask the soldiers for help?"

"Mm-hmm?"

"My uncle is a soldier and we are going to his house so he can help us. Will you come with us?"

We heard the roar of engines. It took me a moment to realize what the sound was. There was a time when traffic noises were a thing of normalcy; now they were odd and unwelcome.

"Nadia?" Zack and Rabbit loaded backpacks and bags with our stuff.

"Patty, Twawki wants you to come with us," Rabbit called out.

Zack kept mouthing to me to pick her up. I couldn't manhandle her.

"Okay. But, I gotta get my mommy doll." Patty took off running.

"Wait! We don't have time!" Zack yelled. "Nadia, we can't wait."

Twawki lifted his head.

I listened to her footsteps squeak and pound away from us. "I know! Take Rab and get out of here. I'll find Patty and we'll come to you."

"No!" Rabbit yelled.

"You have to." There was no way we could hide with Twawki and we had no idea if the incoming forces were friendly or not. I couldn't pin hopes on them being unarmed and sane.

"Go," I demanded.

"I'll keep him safe." Zack tugged Rabbit's backpack as my brother cried. Zack tossed me a handgun. "Take this. Shoot first, you hear me? Listen to your gut."

I nodded and tucked it into my pocket.

"It'll be okay, Rabbit. We'll come as soon as we can." I ran over and hugged him quickly.

He sniffed. "Please come."

"I can't leave her here." *Not to face whoever shows up.* "She knows how to hide, we'll be okay. Promise. I'm a cockroach, remember?"

We heard the rattle of chains and a few rounds of bullets echo down the long hallways.

"Go!" I sprinted away from the boys, hoping I'd find Patty with her doll and we could hide well enough to survive. I didn't look back.

I heard doors slam open and bullets fly wildly like a crazy celebration with boisterous revelers. Taking the frozen escalators like stairs, I bounded up to the third floor, pushed along by pulsing adrenaline. My new boots slapped against the tiles. *There, up ahead!* Barely pausing to breathe, I slid feetfirst under the grid of the mega toy store where Patty had built her doll city. My back jeans' pocket snagged on the gate and I couldn't get past it. I struggled until I heard my pants rip, the MP3 player clattered to the floor.

My heart thumped violently.

"Check for critters, bring any here." A voice full of authority, and bitter power, boomed somewhere down below me.

I reached out and snagged the music keeper, tucking it into my other back pocket. I patted the handgun, thankful it hadn't gone off in all my scrambling.

I crawled along the floor hissing, "Patty? Patty?" Where was she last holding a doll? Were we in her mother's office? Here at the toy store? The fitting room?

I heard yelling and ducked behind a partition as flashlight beams crisscrossed and flashed like a deranged laser show. *Breathe in four, exhale four. Keep thinking.*

I made it to the rear door and slowly turned the knob. Holding my breath, I inched into the hallway. No lights. No sounds. I tried to close the door behind me as silently as possible.

I waited for a moment. Two combat breaths. The sounds of shouting and pillaging were muffled behind me.

Where's the office? Zack's directions! I turned on my flashlight long enough at each corner to read the notes and retrace our steps. I flicked the beam down the hallway to check for obstacles, then clicked it off to make the journey in darkness. Until all of this happened, I never realized how bright light shone surrounded by nothing but blackness.

I walked tentatively. I traced the wall with the fingertips of one hand while feeling ahead with my shins and toes. The last thing I needed to do was run into a rack of plastic hangers and knock them across the tiles. It would be like walking up and introducing myself to the gang out there.

Finally, I found the door to the director's office and crawled inside. "Patty? Patty, where are you?"

I heard nothing and skulked behind the reception counter. She didn't answer, or she wasn't there.

Raised voices and thundering yells in the maze of hallways seemed to edge closer.

I need to hide. Now! Where can I go that they won't search too well?

I rattled the doorknob for the roof. Locked. I turned around. There was only one other door. I tripped over empty water bottles and pinched my nose closed. *Sorry, Patty's mom.*

A few flies smacked me in the face as I opened the door. I tasted death and decomposition on the back of my throat, even with my nose closed. My eyes burned and as I turned on the flashlight I tried not to think about the lumps and mess to my right. I ducked around the door and spotted a nook between the filing cabinets. They'd have to come in and study the room to spot me. I prayed they had weak stomachs and greedy eyes. I cradled the gun in my hand and took the safety off. I'd shoot. I'd shoot anyone to save myself.

I made the mistake of breathing through my nose. Bile rose as my gag reflex worked overtime to unload my stomach. I clenched my jaw and pressed the inside of my elbow to my mouth. *Please don't puke. Please don't puke.*

I was so focused on not throwing up that I missed hearing the outer office door open.

"I swear I heard something in here."

"Yeah, dead people. Whatcha, one of those psychics now?"

Today's lunch filled my mouth. I had to breathe through my nose, which only made me throw up even more. I pursed my lips as the footsteps drew closer. I tried swallowing, but I couldn't make my throat take it back.

The door cracked and I felt as though my body was made of thin glass—one move and I'd shatter.

"Shit, man, bodies in here."

"Anything of value?"

"You know how I feel about touching 'em."

"You want me to?"

"Nah, just looks like a dog who crawled into bushes, you know. Not hoarding goods."

The door clicked shut and I heard their voices and steps recede. I held my position until I leaned over and spit out the vomit. The relief brought the rest of my lunch up, and I continued puking until all that was left was air.

My stomach cramping, I crawled over to a stack of bottles behind the desk and saw an unopened water bottle. I swigged my mouth out, trying to chase away the acidic taste of vomit. I spit onto the floor. Cold sweat beaded my forehead and brought shivers in waves across my spine. I felt goose bumps rise along my arms.

I had to check the fitting room. That was the only place left to look. I tried every door along the hallways until I found one unlocked. Shuffling through the stockroom, I realized this store used to sell teen costume jewelry. The cartoon characters and tubes of glitter cosmetics mocked me.

All over the mall I heard glass breaking and shouts. How many were there? *Sounds like a herd of looting elephants.*

I snuck toward the gate, trying to spot a landmark or store

to help me place my location. Peering through the chains, I realized I needed to be down a level and then head left toward the clothing store.

I slithered under the fence and crouched behind garbage cans, then potted trees, and benches, as I worked my way over toward the escalators.

When I heard a man yell, "Come back! We won't hurt you!" I thought maybe I'd been spotted, but the running was in the opposite direction. *Patty?*

I changed course and headed toward the center atrium, where most of the chaos originated.

As I scrutinized the commotion below me through glass partitions, my stomach twisted.

"Look what I caught!" one man yelled to his pals.

"Patty!" I whispered.

Patty struggled in his arms, and the more she wiggled, the more he laughed. "It's not like we're going to eat you," he said. "Yet."

I ducked down. There were several smaller groups of men, unshaved, dirty, and greasy. Maybe a dozen men. They were heavily armed and looked slightly ridiculous yet completely dangerous. In suit parts and baseball caps with flashlights duct-taped to the bills, they weren't wearing I'M A CRIMINAL signs. And months ago I would have said they didn't look like the types to carry automatic weapons and harass children. *But looks are very deceptive.*

I glanced overhead. Evening was falling; the light paled, taking on a sickly, greenish-gray pallor. I needed to wait until full dark, or they'd see me coming. Even armed I was no match for a dozen men with automatic weapons and greed blinding them.

In a never-ending cycle, the leader dispatched groups to hunt up different supplies, even as they all returned to the center with their treasures.

With a nod to one scraggly lounger, the leader commanded, "Keep on an eye on her—Jonah will trade good for her."

Patty quit struggling rather than let him touch her. She huddled with her knees drawn up to her chest, bundled tightly into herself, as if she might be able to disappear completely by shrinking.

"Hang on, Patty. I'm here," I whispered.

The leader instructed his latest set of goons, "You have forty-five minutes to gather what you can. Meet back here. We'll take the girl to the rendezvous spot and trade her to Jonah for more ammo. Make sure there aren't any others around here hiding. We don't need any surprises." As they scurried off like mice, I knew I needed to get down the escalator before I ran into any of them.

The guy guarding Patty grew bored with teasing her, but even in the low light I saw his eyes were bloodshot and yellow. He seemed like he was drunk or high. He fidgeted and twitched, checking his watch and glancing over his shoulder as soon as he was left alone. He outweighed me by a hundred-plus pounds.

He eyed Patty like she was on the menu.

Finally on the ground floor I watched, and waited, while the sun sank and the light coming through the skylights blued, then faded away completely. Our only chance to escape once outside was the darkness. If they couldn't see us, they couldn't follow us.

When her captor turned around to light a cigarette, I tried blinking my flashlight at Patty to get her attention. She didn't move or even acknowledge my light. I tried to memorize the layout and floor plan. We had to escape without the benefit of sight.

The next time he started pacing, he picked up Patty and sat her on an art-installation cube. "Stay."

He wandered over to a store that sold jerseys for sports teams. With the butt of his rifle he smashed at the window. When his back was turned, I tried to creep closer and get Patty's attention. I kept one hand tight around the handgun.

She saw me and couldn't hold back the squeal.

Shit!

He spun around. "What's out there? Billy, you there?"

There wasn't a way to get any closer and stay under cover.

"What's going on?"

I knew the others would soon return. I unfolded and marched forward. "Let her go."

My fingers cramped as I held the gun tightly in my fist. *Be the cockroach. Breathe.*

"Oh goody, you're real purty." He tossed his cigarette on the ground and stamped it out. He wore a tool belt stocked with bottles of water, cigarettes, and rolls of duct tape.

"Come here, Patty," I said, but didn't take my eyes off the man. She didn't move.

"I can't let you leave." He started sauntering toward me.

"Patty! Hurry!" I tried to use the you're-in-trouble-now voice my mother had perfected. I didn't know if the man simply didn't see my gun or ignored it. If he assumed I'd never use it, he assumed wrong.

I would use it. I had to.

But I was afraid to shoot and hit Patty. I needed to be as

close as possible. *Hold down the trigger. Don't jerk, there'll be a kick.*

I took a few steps in her direction and, as if a switch was thrown, she skittered across to stand behind me. Her little hand twisted around my ripped back pocket.

The man shook his head. "You're not going to get out of here. Jonah wants all the girls."

Who the hell is Jonah? "Jonah doesn't get everything he wants." I hid the fear I knew might crack my voice. I pretended like I had the power and the means to pull this off. I knew without thinking too much that I was going to have to shoot him. We'd have to run because the others would hear all the shots and come to investigate.

I wouldn't have a second chance.

"Don't move," I said, lifting the gun so it was clearly visible in the beam of light he aimed in my direction. As night stole all the ambient light, his body became an outline behind the LED blaze pointed directly at me. *Aim for the light and lower. His trunk. Hit his trunk.*

He stopped moving, but started talking loudly, almost to the point of yelling. *He's calling them back to help him.*

Patty huddled behind me, crying. Her sniffles were muffled as if she was trying to stay as quiet as possible. "Get ready to run," I said as quietly as I could, without taking my eyes off the man. "I'll be right behind you."

"Okay," she whispered.

"Can you run? Go toward the doll city you showed us?"

"Uh-huh."

I'd take that as a yes. *A very scared yes.* My heart thumped so crazily against my ribs, it felt as though it was trying to push its way out of my chest. The gun wavered, shaking with my nerves.

The man inched toward me again.

"Please just let us go. Don't make me shoot you."

"You ain't going to shoot me."

"I will." *Breathe in, exhale with the trigger.*

"No, you won't." He lunged.

"Run!" I screamed, and then pulled the trigger. I felt the air move and Patty's hand disappear.

I held down the trigger and used both hands to steady the weapon. I flinched with each quick boom. The scent of hot metal and the tang of gunpowder made me want to sneeze. But thanks to the games Bean had sent us I knew how to aim. The light fell sideways; the sound of the man's girth crashing into potted palm trees and his moans of pain, of surprise, cut through the air even as the gun quieted.

I'm out of bullets. For a moment, I stood there, paralyzed, my fingers frozen on the trigger. *Cockroach, Nadia.*

Then I ran. Keeping my flashlight off, I couldn't go as fast as I wanted to. I heard shouts and roaring around me, but I kept moving. With quick leaps I took the escalator steps two at a time. Up ahead I saw the pink flashes of lights come from Patty's sneaker soles.

Chaos erupted as the gang found the man dead. They shouted demands and curses. Fired weapons in rapid fits. But I didn't stop.

One hand on the wall, I pushed on until I touched a giant teddy bear and knew I'd made it to the toy store. I slithered under the grate, my breathing labored, adrenaline singing through my blood.

Crawling deeper into the shadows, I whispered, "Patty?'

"Here." She shook a glow ball and it lit up with the faintest soft pink. My eyes were so adjusted to the darkness that it felt as though she held the sun in her hands. I grabbed a T-shirt from the rack and tossed it over the ball.

"We have to get outside. Can you get us to an exit away from those men?" We hid behind a counter. They wouldn't leave until they found us. That I knew. We needed the vast outdoors to disappear into, or we'd find out who Jonah was and why he wanted girls.

She nodded. "There's an exit at the end of the hall, back there." She pointed.

That's not too far. We might make it. "Let's go. We have to be quiet, okay?"

We crawled and made it from the back stockroom to the warren of hallways behind the stores. I saw the fire door as we turned the corner. Ordinarily lights and sirens would sound if it was opened. Not anymore.

We exited on the opposite side of the mall from where Zack said the trucks came. Maybe luck was on our side. *Maybe.*

"Where are we going?" Patty asked.

"Do you know where the dinosaur park is? That's where Zack and Rabbit are meeting us."

"Mm-hmm, it's that way."

That lined up with the direction I thought they were too.

Please let them have gotten away. I knew Rabbit. I trusted Zack. Twawki wouldn't let anyone hurt them. But I feared Rabbit, or even Zack, might come back inside the mall to rescue us if they didn't see us soon.

Zack won't let anyone hurt Rabbit. I know that.

Staying behind abandoned vehicles and motorhomes, I kept my flashlight pointed at the ground. Patty's shoes lit the pavement with each step. We crossed the parking lots at a jog. Once we made it to the road we climbed into an army truck to catch our breath. Patty was hanging in, but she drooped with each moment that passed.

Finally in the hush I heard her ask, "Why did they want to hurt me?"

"I don't know, Patty. Did your mom ever tell you about bad people in the world?"

I felt her enthusiastic nod. "She told me to talk only to people in uniforms. Policemen."

"That was a good plan." The insides of my nose and throat were still coated with the stink of Mommy's decomposition.

"Where are the police?"

"I don't know. We just have to be super careful from here on out. And rely on ourselves."

"Where are we going?"

I repeated, "Do you know the dinosaur park around here?"

"Mommy takes me there to hunt for fossils."

"That's where we're meeting Rabbit and Zack."

"Okay, but where after that?"

"To my uncle's house—the one who's a soldier?"

"Oh, right. Okay." She nodded as if this was normal.

I felt the urgency drain out of my body like a receding tsunami. All I wanted to do was close my eyes and sleep. Fear of discovery and fear for the boys had me climbing back down to the road sooner than I wanted.

One step became two, then one hundred, then one thousand. We slogged on. I saw no lights behind us and heard no sounds of activity other than owls and dogs howling.

We trudged along the road, but I stayed in the ditch and

along fence lines—as close to cover as possible while keeping on the right path.

Patty slowed until she almost dragged each foot. Until she was almost going backward. "I'm hungry."

"Me too." I sighed.

"I'm thirsty," she whined.

"Me too."

Eventually, I lifted her onto my back, piggyback-style. I needed her to keep going, no matter what.

The moonlight came and went behind a light layer of clouds. Not so much natural light I worried about being seen, but enough I saw the outline of my feet. The last thing I needed was a sprained ankle.

I felt Patty relax against my back. *She fell asleep? Kids sleep anywhere.* I remember thinking that about Rabbit when he was little—one moment he'd be playing and the next drooling on the carpet, his Star Wars toy clutched in his fist.

I hoped Rabbit and Zack made it out. Wouldn't we have seen them if they'd been caught at the mall too? Or what if they gave up and decided to move on without us? What if they'd already left? Already decided that we were lost?

A throbbing behind my eyes reminded me that I hadn't drunk anything for a while and what I'd put in my body came out long ago. My growling stomach heaved at its hollowness and my tongue, fuzzy like slippers, stuck to the roof of my mouth.

We rested under a sign declaring that the dinosaur park was another two miles away.

Patty snuggled into my arms and I hugged her close. If I closed my eyes, I heard the gunshots ring in my ears. The spray as bullets exited his body. I remembered his expression as the light slipped from his forehead and spotlighted his face.

"I had no choice," I whispered. *I had no choice. I had no choice.* I scratched at my itchy scalp. I wanted a hot shower, clean clothes. *I want to hug my brother. I want to take back killing a man.*

I staggered to my feet and lifted Patty until she clung to my front, her frail arms locked around my neck and her legs wrapped around my waist.

I kept slogging, shuffling, and as I turned a twisty corner road we were so completely sheltered from view that I took the pavement to ease the energy I used. My tongue felt swollen and stiff against my teeth. Dizziness made the trees sway without a breeze.

Finally, a brontosaurus head rose out of the darkness, and for a moment, I thought it looked at me before breaking off a tree branch to gnaw.

"Here, I've got her."

I tightened my hold.

"Nadia, it's Zack. You made it. You're safe. Let me take Patty."

"What's wrong with her? Nadia, what's wrong?" Rabbit's voice sounded far away and underwater. I wanted to tell him nothing was wrong, but the words wouldn't come out. . . .

Mom was too sick and tired to notice when I crept into her bedroom to check on her. I held the syringe that Bean brought, to give her the same shot he injected into us. Can I do it? What happens when I give her the shot and she's already sick? Will it kill her? Will it make her better? Dad? If you're out there, I need your help. Tell me what to do. Please.

"Nadia?"

"Mom?" I leaned down. "What do you need? Are you thirsty?"

"Tell me again, what did Bean say?"

"He wants us to go to Pappi's."

"You should." She passed out. Her fever had reached 104 degrees. I didn't know if the shot was still good. I didn't know anything. Not really.

I rubbed her arm with an alcohol wipe and she shivered. Before I could change my mind I stabbed the needle into her arm and depressed the plunger, slowly, carefully. She didn't even move.

"You gave her the shot?" Rab said from behind me.

"Yeah."

"Will it work?"

"I don't know, Rabbit."

DAY 78

"Drink this." Zack leaned over me.

I lay on my side in one of the little dinosaur caves, someone's coat draped over my torso. I swallowed the cool liquid as quickly as I could, but a stream of it dripped down my chin and soaked the collar of my shirt.

I blinked, trying to focus under the glaring beam of the camp lantern. Patty gripped Twawki's neck while Rabbit unpacked the backpacks from the gear store.

"We need to leave. They might find us here." My throat sounded raspy and ached.

Zack and Rabbit shared a look I couldn't interpret.

"What?" I asked, too sick to brace myself for their answer.

"The Jeep is gone."

"Gone? All of it? Everything?" I struggled to sit up, closing my eyes against the dizziness that rushed toward me.

"Yeah. Even Al is gone." Rabbit frowned.

"We have nothing?" I swallowed quickly against my reflexes.

Zack leaned down and gripped my face until I opened my eyes. "No, we have the backpacks of supplies from the mall. Frog and I made it back with those."

Rabbit nodded. "We have enough for a few days. You're sick."

"No, I'm not."

"You feel like you're running a fever."

"They took everything? Why would they take Al?" My brain couldn't make sense of any of this news.

Rabbit scooted around to my other side. "They left the cage. Maybe they didn't want him to starve and opened the door."

Zack's quick shake of his head told me he'd tried to spin it for Rabbit. For all we knew, someone ate African gray for dinner.

"We're so far away from Pappi's." I sighed.

"We're over halfway there, Dia."

I shook my head, despair cracking my ribs and stabbing my neck. "We'll never make it."

Zack pressed his face against mine and, into my ear, scolded, "You cannot talk like that."

I leaned away, wanting to slide down into a puddle. "You're right, I'm sorry."

"What do we do now?" Rabbit asked.

"We start walking and we investigate every house, and

every car, we find until we gather new," Zack answered with conviction.

"What about the bad men?" Patty asked.

"Or the Jeep stealers? Will they come after us?" Rabbit added.

"Nah, they were headed in the other direction. We'll be okay. Right, Nadia?" Zack asked, but all I could think was that our supplies, all the work to hoard and find them—all of those were gone.

"Right," I agreed as my eyelids slid closed and the world faded to black. . . .

By the third day Mom's fever broke, soaking the sheets. She was weak, shaky. The circles under her eyes bags of bruises. Her lips were chapped and bleeding. Her skin felt like cooked chicken, but scaly and dry, shedding like snakeskin.

"How long was I out?"

"It's been a week."

"I'm getting better?" she asked.

I nodded.

"Thank you for taking care of me," she said, before closing her eyes and sliding back into sleep.

"You gonna tell her?" Rabbit whispered.

"Yeah, maybe." I was afraid to let go of the breath I held in my lungs like a security blanket. Would she get better?

For a week she ate and grew stronger. And just about the time I thought I should show her the box, Bean's letter, and the gun, I found her collapsed outside the bathroom.

"Rabbit!" I shouted.

He helped me drag her back to her bed.

Tears ran down his face. "It didn't work. It didn't work," he muttered to himself.

Her temperature skyrocketed, and fireworks of blood and fluids began erupting under her skin until she looked like she was covered in blue cheetah-print pajamas. I waited too long.

"Nadia, listen to me." She grabbed my hand to still my motions.

"What?"

"Sit down. I'm lucid, but the dreams are bad, so what's my fever, 104?"

"Sometimes."

"Sore throat, headache, canker blisters, cough, blue star-shaped bruising. The only thing I don't have yet is the bleeding from my nose and ears. But that won't happen until the end."

"Don't say that. You're getting better." Tears streamed down my face.

"I have at least two broken bones from the coughing. We have to talk about what to do when I get too sick."

"Mom—"

"Nadia, I know what I have; we both know what I have. I'm going to die, so we need to talk about what you're going to do next. Like we should have talked when your daddy died. I'm so sorry, honey. I couldn't face a day without him. I couldn't talk about life without him."

"Mom—"

"I'm sorry, Nadia. I should have sent you to Bean when he came to see me at the hospital."

"What?"

"He tried to tell me."

"I didn't know."

"I wouldn't listen. But get paper, you should write some of this down. Let's talk about how long you can stay here."

As I shivered and slept, sweated and dreamed, I vaguely recognized hands soothing me, pressing cool cloths to my face, spooning pine-flavored soup into my mouth.

"You're going to poison her with that stuff."

"No, I'm not. It's spruce tea. Very high in vitamin C. Dad made it for me once."

"How do you know which tree to use?"

I wanted to ask that too, but I didn't hear the answer.

I sank back into oblivion.

The whoop of helicopters dropping giant confetti papers in all colors. First they were pale green, then yellow, then orange, and red. *Do not go to hospitals. Stay in your homes, doctors will come to you soon. Evacuate to the nearest landmark—the Space Needle—for relocation and medical care.* Then the helicopters stopped coming. . . .

Boil all water before use to stop the spread of the pathogen. . . . The European Union has closed its borders; all air travel has been grounded. The President of the United States will be making a State of the Union address tonight. "My fellow Americans, we face the greatest health crisis of the twenty-first century, perhaps of all time."

The lights blinked out and the water stopped running from the faucets.

. . . "Oh God, make it stop." Mom cried in pain as blood dripped out of her ears.

"Mom, Bean gave me pills for all of us. Do you want them?"

"Medicine?" she croaked.

I couldn't bring myself to say it out loud. *To kill you. Us.* "To stop the pain."

"Show me."

I went to my room and brought out the box. She was sleeping when I got back to her room, but she wakened. "Read me the labels."

I did the best I could to pronounce the drug names and read her Bean's written instructions. I thought she wasn't listening until I noticed the tears leaking down her cheeks.

"I'm so sorry, Nadia. So sorry."

"Mom?"

"I should have trusted Bean and taken the shot. Put those away. They're too tempting." She groaned again as another wave of pain twisted her limbs into unnatural angles.

"Mom? Are you sure?"

"I can't, Nadia. Your father would hate me if I gave up and left you. If I die, then I'll die, but I'm not leaving you to have to pick up the pieces and carry the guilt of giving me those meds."

"Should I give them to Rabbit?"

"How can I ask that of you?"

"I'm asking you."

"Keep them. But try. You have to try. Then, if you think you have no way to survive, then yes, you need to know that your dad and I wouldn't want either of you to suffer needlessly. We'll wait for you and if that means we see you when you're old and have grandchildren, we'll be there. And if that means we all spend Christmas together this year, then we'll be right there with you."

"You're talking like you're already—"

"I've watched patients with this for days now. I know what's coming. Sleep. Now I'll sleep."

I dragged myself back to my bedroom and put the box back into my underwear drawer. I slid to the floor. I pulled my knees up under my chin and tucked my head against them. "Daddy, I can't do this. Why do I have to do this?" I cried deep racking sobs.

My tears burned my sensitive skin like acid as I blinked my eyes open. I closed them quickly, wishing for oblivion again.

Someone put liquid to my mouth and told me, "Drink."

"Let me go." I pleaded in my stupor with my father, my mother, my brother, even Al, who danced and sang, "When you call my name, it's like a little prayer. . . ."

DAY 81

"I'm not hungry." I shoved the instant oatmeal away without opening my eyes.

"You have to eat."

"Come on, Nadia, eat!" Rabbit pleaded.

My eyelids were caked and cracking with gunk, as if they'd been glued together ages ago. I rubbed my hands on my face. My skin was scaly and chapped. I caught a whiff of my body odor and illness stench.

"Eat, drink, get married!" a squeaky voice proclaimed.

"Al?" I asked, trying to turn my head toward the sound.

"Yeah, he came back." Rabbit smiled. "I guess he flew out, but didn't go far."

Where would he go? Where can any of us go?

My bladder screamed in protest with my movements. "Um, I need to—"

Zack leaned down and tried to help me stand. My legs felt like barely set Jell-O. He all but carried me outside and over to a clump of bushes. My head felt as if I wore a cement helmet.

"How long have I been sick?" I mumbled.

"Three days. I found an old minivan about five miles from here plus some Tylenol that seemed to help your fever."

"I can do it from here." My face burned with the knowledge that I had to pee in front of Zack.

He turned around and gave me his back. If it hadn't been such a dire necessity I'm sure the pee would have climbed back up inside me rather than tinkle and splash within his earshot.

I used a couple of leaves to wipe. I barely got my pants buttoned back up before my energy flagged. I stumbled into Zack and he caught me.

"We have to get going tonight," he said, as he helped me back toward our little cave. "We've stayed too long and most of the farms around here have been picked clean. I think it's a high traffic area."

I nodded, not trusting myself to speak.

"We're almost out of water and food. I'm sorry, Nadia, I wish we could stay here longer. Give you time to rest more."

"It's okay."

"Hopefully, we'll find beds and supplies to clean up with."

"I know I smell." My nose wrinkled.

"We all do." Zack laughed. "Cancels it all out."

"Good to know." I tried to smile. "How is Patty?"

"She's a trouper. I found coloring supplies in the van and she's been 'colorfying' princesses for you. You're her hero."

I stumbled. "I had to shoot a guy."

"I know. I'm glad you had the gun."

"I wish . . ." I trailed off. I couldn't do it differently, could I?

"Don't." Zack stopped and pulled me tight against him, partly to prop me up and partly to emphasize his words. "I've killed too. It's necessary for survival. Maybe more now than ever. You can't carry guilt, or wishes, or anything. You have to let it go. You didn't have a choice. Focus on that."

"I'd do it again, but that doesn't change the fact that I wish survivors were good people and we could work together to rebuild."

"Welcome to Realityville," Zack said. "Maybe somewhere we'll find good peeps."

I leaned against a bench, getting a sense of how little there was left at camp. "Let's load up and go. Now."

"Are you sure?" Zack frowned.

"Yeah, I am."

I slept in the backseat of the minivan while everyone else packed the meager remains of our supplies, including Al's cage and a bleached bone Twawki had dug up from a garbage pile behind the concessions.

"We'll go as far as we can on a tank of gas. Keep your eyes peeled for other travelers or supply haunts, okay?" Zack instructed Rabbit and Patty.

Miles rolled past. I didn't have the energy to do more than sit in the backseat with Patty and watch the countryside cruise by. Rabbit rode shotgun and navigated with a map that he found crumpled up in the glove box.

Zack shook his head. "Hawk? Why the love of maps? It's kinda strange. Helpful, but weird."

Rabbit shrugged and I listened carefully for his answer. "My dad. Didn't like the GPS things, said they made people stupid. He wanted me to be able to get around. Took me up into the mountains to camp."

"You're not supposed to call people stupid," Patty chimed in. "*Stupid* is a bad word."

"Okay, kid. No one's stupid," Zack assured her with a barely suppressed laugh. I wondered if he'd ever spent time around little girls who thought the world was filled with unicorns and castles.

"Cars up ahead." Rabbit pointed.

At the first cluster of cars we stopped, checked the trunks for gas cans and supplies. There was one can and half a tank full of gas among all of the cars. We split a gallon of water and had half an energy bar each. Zack took a bite and gave Patty the rest of his share.

We slept that night with the seats folded down, huddled against each other, our stomachs vying for whose-growled-the-loudest. The jangling of the ride drained what little energy I had and I fell into a troubled sleep faster than the rest.

I was not sure Zack slept at all that night. When he saw me watching him in the early morning light, he tried to smile before we set off again.

I must have slept more in the heat and the rhythm of the drive, because the next thing I heard, Zack declared, "There's a town up ahead. I think we have to check it out."

I heard Zack's stomach rumble and mine answered. I thought only yawns were contagious.

"We have to go into the next town?" Rabbit's voice was part surrender and part trepidation. I understood his desire to avoid any surprises.

"Odds aren't good we'll find anything or anyone." I didn't

want to say much in front of Patty, but we were learning that the farther into populated areas we moved, the more stripped the world became. More people meant more survivors, which meant less to go around.

"I know, but we have to try." Zack switched off driving with Rabbit. I knew I didn't trust my weakened state behind the wheel, so I was glad I wasn't asked.

Starting in the outskirts, we drove in blocks searching for any people, any signs that there might be danger. Nothing. Not even packs of dogs or cats.

"There are big stores way down there in that shopping center."

"We can try 'em. Maybe something was overlooked."

Twawki's stomach rumbled louder than the rest of ours and Al picked through crumbs between the seats before unearthing an ancient French fry to gnaw on.

We turned into the main parking lot of an old strip mall that was several city blocks in length. Besides stores that used to sell books, clothes, and groceries, there was a chain pet store anchoring the far end. Most were boarded up and had spray-painted notes on the walls declaring EMPTY, or REPENT, or FORGIVE US. *Lovely.*

"Look! What are all those?" Patty leaned forward in her seat, pointing.

As we drew nearer, we saw stainless steel and porcelain bowls of all sizes lined up along the walls and under the covered walkway. The doors of the store were boarded up like the others. Sprayed in red paint across it was the word EMPTY.

The entire complex seemed deserted behind the plywood and I wasn't sure how we were supposed to get past the grocery-carts, metal cans, and lumber scraps barricading the doorway.

Rabbit sighed. "Should we try to go in and see if there's dog food, just in case?"

Zack nodded. "Yeah, I think we should."

"We don't have the right tools," I said.

"We have a bar and our hands. Come on, let's try." Zack hopped out and listened for others, any sign that someone considered this their territory and might protect it. Who knew what or who made the laws these days, let alone enforced 'em.

Rabbit and I climbed out, putting Patty on watch while the rest of us tried moving the piles of cardboard, carts, and wood scraps out of the way.

I dragged a puny stack of cardboard away. A dripping sweat reminded me that I was nowhere near fighting form.

"Take a seat," Zack commanded, and I didn't have the heart to argue. I squatted next to Patty, trying to stay focused and awake.

We heard bells, a million twinkling, rattling bells. Howling and barking erupted in the distance.

"Um, guys?" I asked, wondering if I was hallucinating or if they heard the bells too.

"Let's get back in the car." Zack grabbed Patty and sprinted toward the van while Rabbit clung to my hand and pulled me along.

DAY 82

We scrambled back into the front seats as what seemed like a herd of antelope crested the earth berm in front of the pet store. Dogs. Toy poodles and purse Pomeranians, Labradors and giant schnauzers vaulted over debris and careened across the parking lot. The cats came next. Long haired and short, smashed faces and those pointy aristocratic ones that looked like they originated in a fantasy novel. Some ran with the dogs, others leapt onto towering heaps or slunk along the walkways and hid under boxes.

A few of the animals limped, injured, covered in mud and snarled fur. Others looked like they'd just come from the spa, with expressions that disdained the mass of peasants around them. I wished we knew what they were thinking. *What do they tell each other about BluStar?*

"Nadia, what is this?" Rabbit breathed, watching the wave of domestic animals flow toward us and the storefront.

"I don't know." I'd say I was on the set of an animated movie if I didn't know any better. At the least, it was a group hallucination and not my fever skyrocketing. Small comfort.

The bells rang louder and Patty grabbed my arm, her tiny nails digging deep. I was not sure if we expected an army of fairies to fly in with magic dust, or a talking dalmatian wearing a crown and scepter to come out from the Pet World doors to greet his court. But I didn't expect to see an old man, wearing a crimson coat, pushing a grocery cart covered in bells. Jingle bells and sleigh bells, cowbells, triangles of rusted metal, and the kind they ring on ships. With his head down, the man trudged along as if he made this trip in his sleep.

We sat unmoving, waiting to see what would happen next.

"He has to know we're here, right?" Rabbit whispered. "Shhh, quiet, Twawki." With a muffled whine our dog laid his head on the back of the seat and watched without barking.

How can he not?

In addition to the raincoat, the man wore a baseball cap with Navy insignia and an aircraft-carrier patch. No hair stuck out from the sides or back. He wore gold-framed glasses repaired at the temple with duct tape. He slipped off his coat, revealing corduroy slacks and a dingy button-down shirt that completed his outfit. He looked cleanish and healthy as he yanked on yellow rubber gloves, the kind Mom used when cleaning the bathroom with bleach.

"Can you tell what's in the cart?" Zack asked.

It looked like carcasses. *Dead animals. Roadkill?*

"I think there are dead animals in there," Rabbit answered.

"Really?"

Patty whimpered.

I nodded, patting her with what I hoped was comfort and reassurance.

Pausing at the length of bowls along the outside of the store, the man began to unload the cart. It looked like he removed rabbits, rats, even a raccoon from it. He carefully laid the animals in the bowls like he was doling out kibble at a pet buffet.

A few dogs dove in along behind him. Others stood back and watched.

He went down the line, putting smaller rodents in the smaller bowls. A couple of dogs began playing tug-of-war with legs or tails, but soon all were covered in the blood of their "prey" and, even in the car, we heard the crunch of bones.

With a nod of satisfaction, the man walked back to his cart and dragged out a cardboard box from its underside. With no wasted motion or jerky movements, he deliberately made his way away from the dogs and closer to where the cats congregated along the barricade. He knelt down and gently turned the box on its side. A dozen or more mice and smallish rats poured out right at the cats like a mini wave. The felines began pouncing, picking up, and running away with their catch. Then, from the bottom of the box, the man shook out a pile of dead rodents that other cats poked and sniffed as he walked back toward the dogs.

"He's feeding them." Rabbit's voice was awed.

Zack agreed, "I think he is."

For several minutes the man stood and watched while the dogs munched and the cats hunted. He stooped to pick up a kitten who tried climbing his pant leg. A few of the creatures were much more interested in getting attention and affection than in the meat smorgasbord he provided.

"Should we say something?" I asked.

"Wait, what's he doing now?" Rabbit tensed.

The man went over to the plywood over the door and lifted it off, disappearing inside. I guessed there was some sort of optical illusion, because at our first glance the whole thing seemed impenetrable. He returned dragging a huge unopened bag of dog kibble.

"I guess it's not empty, huh?"

"Guess not."

"Do you think he knows we're here?"

"Of course, he has to. It's not like the minivan has an invisibility shield or anything."

The man scooped kibble into the bowls like it was a second course. A lot of the dogs who ate meat began to play and paid no attention to the food, but those who hadn't touched the fresh meat moved closer and ate the dry kibble as quickly as they could. Cats meandered in and snaked to bowls too. He kept refilling the dishes until his bag was empty and then he disappeared back inside, coming out with brushes and bones and toys. He passed these out and romping began. He turned a bucket over and sat down to give love and attention to those who crowded around him.

A golden retriever lifted its nose and ran toward us barking. Tail wagging, jowls flapping, happy hellos.

"Can we go say hello now?" Rabbit asked.

Twawki smacked his tail against the back of my seat with a deep woof.

I snorted. "I think that's a yes."

Rab and I opened the car doors. "Leave Twawki here. We can't have him get into any trouble."

"Okay. Sorry, boy, stay."

"Patty, do you want to stay in here?"

She nodded vigorously. I shut the doors and the three of us started across the parking lot. Soon we were enveloped by excited pets wanting to play.

"Howdy." The man raised his hand, but didn't stand up and didn't stop brushing out knots from a shih tzu's mangled coat.

"Hello," Zack answered.

"Where you folks from?"

"Seattle."

"Long way from home. I'm Frank."

"I'm Nadia, this is my brother, Rabbit, and Zack."

"What brings you through here?"

Zack relaxed a little. "We have an injured dog we picked up two states over and now a bird. We were hoping to find food for them, and antibiotics."

Frank nodded. "Figured you needed something. The Pet World parking lot isn't the most happening place to park these days. From the looks of things, seems like you need human supplies, too."

"Are all these yours?" Rabbit held a Siamese cat who was so busy rubbing at his face, Rabbit looked like he was growing a mocha-colored beard.

"Nah, never was much into pets," Frank answered.

Rabbit frowned. "But you're feeding them."

"I'm alone in this town. Lost my wife, kids, and grandkids.

What neighbors survived headed south toward the evacuation points. But everyone left their animals behind, one way or another. Somebody has to teach 'em what they're supposed to do. They have to start hunting; they can't be house pets and survive, there aren't any houses left for them to live in."

I heard the pain in his voice when he told us about his family.

Several cats rubbed against my legs and a couple of dogs sniffed us like they were trying to inhale our whole story with one breath.

"But you gave them kibble," Rabbit pressed.

"I've got it figured out to slowly wean them off it—increase the amount of meat I bring them, start bringing more and more live prey. I got traps set up all over the place for rats—all that garbage and death was good for their population. I need the cats and dogs to step up and restore a bit of order."

"Will it work?" Zack asked.

"For some, I think." The unspoken was that come winter there would be more death. More animals. More people. Survival of the fittest would go up a notch. Again.

"Let's see what we can hook you up with." Frank stood. His arthritic knees popped and complained. He clicked on a flashlight and showed us where he'd hidden the latch and hook on the plywood. The back of the barricade swung open like a door.

"This is pretty fancy." Zack bent down and studied the construction.

"Once upon a time I was a carpenter. There's a couple of choices left—take whatever you need. There's treats down that aisle. Rummage up whatever you can find in the staff break room. I don't need any of it."

"Don't you need them? The treats and stuff?" Rabbit asked.

"Nah, these animals have to stop thinking like pets and more like their wild ancestors. Treats remind them too much of where they came from. Besides, I'm an old man. Birdseed and the like is in the back over there—" He pointed, then stopped. "We may have big-box stores, but don't you be fooled, we were a small town. Mayor told everyone to let their pets out when the whole family was sick. Those who were healthy or recovered took care of 'em. Just like all the families with young children gathered at the local high school. Didn't want healthy babies to die because they couldn't get care. Loaded the survivors up onto a school bus and took off last month for the capital."

"There were survivors in your town?"

"Course there were. Not many and can't tell you why— families, singles, all ages. Lot of older folks lived after being real sick."

"If you don't like pets, why are you doing this?" Rabbit picked up a leash and collar.

"My Lyssa was a receptionist at a veterinarian's office. Always came home with the animals that needed extra TLC and nursing. She'd want me to do what I can."

Rab's expression broke my heart. "Thank you. If they were my pets I'd want you to know—thank you. Do you need anything in return from us? We don't really have much, but . . ."

Frank stopped and considered Rabbit's question, as if he understood that Rabbit was trying to adjust to this new world just like the puppies and kittens out there. "Well, if you'd help me haul a few of these playpen things outside, I think they'd be good at collecting rainwater for the animals who hang around here."

It took all of us struggling with the plastic and cement

structures, originally intended to make life for reptiles and tortoises all Taj Mahal-y, to haul them outside. We finally managed to get them into the parking lot.

Zack loaded a medium-size bag of kibble into the van and checked on Patty.

Frank glanced up at the position of the sun. "I'd best get home before dark. You need a place to stay tonight?"

"Thanks, but we'll keep moving."

"If you take a left down Maple, the fancy houses in town are in that neighborhood. Would be a good place to scavenge supplies on your way out, guessing tornado shelters didn't get picked over. The old gas station has a hand crank, if you need to fill up your car."

Zack shook his head. "We don't want to take any from you." There was a limit to what we felt comfortable taking from other survivors.

"Don't worry about me, kid." Frank's eyes were sad and full of loneliness. "I don't eat much these days."

"Thank you," I said.

"You take care of yourselves."

"You too. You'd make your wife happy." Rabbit smiled.

"Ah, kid, I get more out of it than the animals do." We pretended not to see him tear up.

As we headed toward the van, Frank called out, "Hey, wait!" He walked back over toward us. "My sister—she's got a farm on the other side of the Mississippi. If anyone can survive this thing, it's her." He wrote a note that included her address. "If you go near, would you deliver this to her? I know it's a lot to ask, but she'll feed you. She's a tough bird, she'll have that place running like a military boot camp."

I took the paper and ignored the tremor in his hands. "Yeah, we'll do our best."

"Thanks, never thought I'd have a chance to say"—Frank glanced at the kids and changed his words midstream—"'see you soon' to her."

We waited for a moment as he pushed his bell-covered cart back around the building. The herds and flocks hung around for a while; some even followed his path and then dispersed as if they'd never been there.

We were silent as we drove. Turning down Maple we picked a modest-looking mansion to explore first. Or Zack picked it; his intuition was much better than mine as to where to hunt. Unsure if others had already come this way, it seemed as though the neighborhood was mostly untouched.

Starting in the garage, we found a tricked-out hybrid SUV. It was a car that once cost twice what my parents' house did.

"Let's stay here tonight?" I asked, my energy drained completely by the time we struggled into the main hallway of the house.

Zack pointed at a chair. "Sure. Hey, Kangaroo, Patty, there should be a secret room around here, wanna help me find it?"

I peeled off my nasty boots and socks and realized the stinging came from open and seeping blisters. "Secret room?"

"Tornado shelter. Frank's suggestion. Most of the upscale houses in the Midwest have them. Could have supplies, too."

Zack's expertise at finding hidden caches of water and food continued to shock me. It was like he had a built-in finder system. *Maybe his "before"?*

Rabbit and Patty ran around the downstairs tapping on walls and checking behind paintings.

I padded into the kitchen checking the obvious places for food. They were bare and dry. My stomach heaved with hunger. Unfortunately, the faucets didn't drip water magically when I turned them on.

I checked the pantry and saw nothing but a door handle at the back of the small room. "Hey, Zack?" I called out.

He peered over my shoulder. "Booyah!"

We crowded into a room the size of a large walk-in closet. Cases of bottled water, wool blankets, light sticks, medical supplies, and nonperishables were loaded around a sleeper sofa and side chairs.

We sat down, passing around water bottles and energy bars. "Don't eat too fast, we'll get sick," Rabbit warned.

My teeth ached from the fever, and my gums were a mass of sores and divots. I couldn't eat quickly even if I wanted to.

The next thing I knew Rabbit was bending over me, shaking my shoulder. "Nadia, wake up. It's time to wash up." The water from the toilet tank could be drunk, if necessary, but also heated for bathing.

Once I made it to the bathroom, there were rows of lit candles along the tile shelves and Zack brought in a pot of warm water. "There's not much here, but enough to get the dirt off. There's more cold if you need it. Just yell."

He hesitated.

"I'm okay." *I must look frighteningly bad to warrant that much of a stare.*

"Here's clean clothes." Rabbit deposited a stack on the toilet. Noting the predominately pink color, Rab frowned. "Not a lot of choices, plus Patty helped pick 'em out. Come on, Zack, dinner's almost ready."

I started on my hair without undressing. I rummaged

around until I found little bottles of hotel shampoo, a disposable razor, and a fresh cake of soap. This was clearly the guest bathroom because most of the drawers and shelves were empty except for ridiculous knickknacks and shell-themed crap.

The tangles in my hair were shellacked with oil, grime, and sweat. "I give up." With little trimming scissors I cut out the tangles, until I ran my hands over my hair and felt only tight curl frizz, not masses of nasty. I shampooed twice, not bothering with conditioner. By the time I dried off, my skin was red and shivers racked my body. Dressing in pale pink stretchy yoga pants, a fuchsia T-shirt, and a pink hoodie with silver sparkle stars along the sleeves and back, I felt like one of those marshmallows in breakfast cereal. Patty's taste was a little too pink, but the clothes were clean, though a size too big. I no longer smelled and I didn't have the insane urge to scratch every inch of my skin.

I found a down throw across the bed and wrapped up in it.

With a flashlight, I followed the noises back to the main level of the house.

Everyone's hair was wet or drying, including Twawki, who no longer smelled like old skunk. He had much more white on him than I had realized. We all wore borrowed clothes, though none of them fit well. Zack's red polo hung long; the designer jeans, held up with a leather belt, must have come from a big-and-tall store. With his closely shaved face, the combination made him look years older.

The fire crackled and Zack added what looked like chair legs to the glow.

"Do you want beef stew or beef stew?" Rabbit glanced up at me. He was wearing pink sweatpants and a ladies' black long-sleeved henley, and his expression dared me to comment.

Patty was the only one who looked like the clothes were bought with her in mind.

"Not big on choices?" was all I asked.

They laughed. "Two cases of beef stew. Two cases of canned tomato juice. Two cases of dried apple slices."

"Really?" *Odd.*

"I don't think they really thought they'd have to eat it." Zack shook his head.

"Stew, please." I cradled the steaming bowl, inhaling the fragrance of real food.

Patty scooted closer to me. I saw constellations of freckles across her freshly bathed nose. Her hair was pulled back with mismatched barrettes. Relief that she managed to bathe and dress on her own surged through me. I couldn't imagine having to be a mom to her.

"Your hair!" Patty combed her fingers through my botched hair as if she was a stylist and I'd ruined her best work.

I shrugged. "It'll grow back."

Later that night, Rabbit and Patty pored over maps they'd found in the library office. Patty colored in the margins while Rabbit kept tweaking the route we'd take next. Zack and I kept our distance with the dog and the bird.

"Your brother seems obsessed with knowing where we're going next." Zack scratched under Al's chin as he talked quietly to me.

"Every time Dad came home from a tour he'd load up Rabbit and their packs, and they'd take off into the woods, or the mountains, for a few days. One time, Rabbit told me they didn't speak for three whole days."

"Was your mom worried, or anything?"

"No, she knew what Dad did. At least, what she *could*

know. I think she knew he was worried about not coming back from a mission. He didn't want to die before teaching Rabbit how to be a man."

"He didn't ever take you?"

"He tried. I talked too much." I shrugged. I was too into girly stuff for him, but too headstrong and tomboyish for my mom.

"Not the outdoorsy camping type?" Zack asked.

"Nah, I like the burbs. Used to. Now?" I shook my head. The corners and hallways of any building, even this house, felt like they hid the next horror. I liked open spaces, sky overhead, earth under my feet. In retrospect, I understood what Dad had tried to teach me.

Zack prodded, "Now, what?"

"Now, I'm almost afraid to stay inside, like anything with the roof might be a trap."

He nodded, staring into the fire. "How long did you hide in your house?"

"A couple of months. But we could go outside after the exodus."

"That's still a long time."

I know.

❀　❀　❀

In a choreographed dance that felt like déjà vu, we packed the SUV with anything remotely usable. Zack commandeered extra gas from high-end sports cars in the garages around us. With two days of driving we camped in the car at night. Eating the last of the beef stew, and dried apples, rebuilt my strength to the point I rotated back into taking turns driving.

"Hey, guys? What's that smell?"

"Ew!" Patty chimed in, clamping her fingers over her nose. My nose wrinkled.

As we got closer to the river, the smell intensified. We passed a couple head of cattle chewing grass, in green spaces, along the banks of the river.

Staring out at the vast expanse of the Mississippi River we might as well have stared across the Pacific Ocean. Bloated bodies of all kinds swirled through its muddy currents.

"Are you sure this is a river?" Zack asked out loud to Rabbit.

"Yep, map's got it right here. It's the Mississippi."

"It's what kept pioneers from flooding the West," I murmured. *How do we cross it?*

"Thanks for that history lesson." Zack grinned. "I missed that chapter."

A blush crawled up my neck. I wanted to blame the fever for my asinine comments, but knew I couldn't.

"Did they dump the dead into the river rather than bury them?" Rabbit asked.

"Your guess is as good as mine." Zack shook his head and turned Patty away from the flotsam and jetsam that used to have names.

"Aren't there bridges?" Patty asked.

"We can continue down the river and see," Zack said.

Rabbit shook his head. "They started blowing them up as people ran."

I wondered which breaking news segment put that image in my brother's head. "All of them?" I questioned.

He nodded. "The big ones for sure."

"As if it mattered," Zack muttered.

"Yeah, it didn't really do any good, did it?" Rabbit frowned.

"I guess we need to find a boat?" Zack started scanning the shores.

Quietly I joined him and tugged him aside. "Have you ever driven a boat?"

He shrugged. "How hard can it be?"

Can he even swim? Can Patty? When was the last time Rab or I did?

"Looks like a marina on the map five miles south," Rabbit said. "Boats there probably."

"Hopefully a yacht." Zack grinned.

"Sure." Rabbit's lips twisted up in a broad grin.

🌸 🌸 🌸

It took Zack four tries to find a small boat that had the keys in it. From the smell clinging to everything, I think he evicted the previous owner over the side. We made several trips from the SUV to the boat, with our blankets and meager supplies.

"Should we wait until morning?" I asked as the sun set in a fiery bow.

"I think dark is probably better." Zack pointedly glanced at a body snagged on a propeller near us. It would only be worse if we could see them all.

"I go with now."

"I'm cold," Patty complained, and I wrapped the blanket tighter around her.

"We should all put on life jackets." I handed them out.

"Yes, Mom," Rabbit teased.

"Hey, you want to fall in and have to swim across?" I groused.

Zack and Rabbit shared a grin at my expense, but I didn't

care. Al was tucked into Zack's cargo pants pocket—the last thing we needed was a gust of wind to pick up the bird and send him flying out over the river. I sent a quick wish out that we made it across safely.

"Are you heading anywhere in particular?" I yelled at Zack as we got underway.

"Over there, where the water stops and dry land begins." He pointed. "Doesn't matter if she runs aground, right?"

"I guess not."

Zack turned the headlight on low and kept it pointed directly in front of the boat. The fear of running into something bigger than us stole my breath. We hit floaters as we crossed. I was glad that the darkness hid their identities.

After an eternity Zack shouted back, "Hold on, this might be bumpy!"

I clutched Patty around the waist and put a hand on Rabbit's shoulder. He sat low in the boat braced against Twawki's wind-shielding girth.

Kathunk. Whoops.

I hit my head, and the whine of the motor stranded above the waterline made my ears ring.

Zack turned off the engine but left the light on so we could see to climb out. "There. Piece of cake."

Twawki's nose scented the air and his hackles rose. I was just about to ask what was wrong when the darkness lit up with spotlights and headlights.

One second we were alone in the world and the next it was like we stepped onto a stage.

DAY 84

Behind the lights a voice called out, "You got food?"

Zack held his hands up. "Check our bags. No."

"What's your business here?"

"We're just passing through. Crossing the river."

I listened to hushed voices arguing. I had a feeling whoever was interrogating us hadn't ever done this before. The spotlights made it seem like us against a crowd, but the longer they talked, the more I thought it was us against a couple.

"You're not planning on staying?" a male voice shouted.

Zack pretended he was meek and not a threat. I'd never heard him so polite. "No, sir, just needed to cross the river. We're heading to Miami."

"You keep going, we'll let you pass."

"We'd appreciate that," I spoke up. "That's all we want."

"You touch nothing, you take nothing from town, or we'll have a problem."

I nodded. "That's fine."

"You need wheels?"

"Please?" Rabbit spoke up, and I wanted to shush him.

The man nodded and sounded like he was giving orders. It was so hard to tell what was happening on the other side of the lights. Blinded, I didn't think I'd see clearly for weeks to come. Several minutes passed and a couple of kids about Rabbit's age wheeled two bicycles into the circle of light. One of them had a family cart attached to the back that I strapped Patty into along with Al's cage. I checked my pocket for Dad's MP3 player and Frank's note. *Safe.*

"You can have these. Stay on this road until you're outside the city limits. If I see you back here, I'll shoot first. Leave the stuff in the boat alone. Let me see your hands."

"Understood." Zack nodded, taking Twawki's leash in one fist and a bike in the other. We walked the bikes into the black with only a single flashlight to give us direction. Zack made Rabbit ride the bike so he could walk Twawki in the darkness. I wasn't sure, but I thought maybe Zack didn't know how to ride.

"Was that a family?" Rabbit asked, when we'd exited the city blocks and the night once again embraced us.

"I don't know." I was sure I felt eyes on us for miles as we rode the bikes in patchy moonlight that came and went with drifting clouds.

"There's a tractor in that field." Zack pointed out the shape.

"So?" I barely acknowledged his words.

"So you're falling over. Rabbit's tired. Wait here."

We collapsed against the side of the road while Zack leapt the fence and headed for the tractor. When it started up, he drove it straight over, through the fence, to get to us. We piled up into the cab and settled in. Patty and Rabbit fell asleep instantly.

As dawn cracked open, we started looking for farmhouses. We had figured out that there was usually an old-time water pump and a barn that we could pull into and park in out of sight. If we were fortunate there were supplies like jam, pickles, and jars of peaches or tomatoes abandoned and overlooked in cellars.

I knew we'd been lucky in finding a boat and only losing stuff, not each other, on the other side. But I didn't think it was luck, as much as Dad and Mom guiding us. Watching out for us and helping us to know where, and when, to go on.

We slept in an empty dairy barn, and Zack got the family's station wagon to run after tinkering under the hood. We filled containers with water and found a jar of peanut butter in the warm fridge that wasn't growing mold. The added sugar and preservatives kept it quite delicious.

"There's a country school up ahead." Rabbit pointed out the sign. "Maybe there's stuff in lockers or something. At least a lost and found with clothes that might be cleanish."

"You're getting the hang of this." Zack grinned.

"And crayons?" Patty asked.

"Definitely crayons." I didn't think anyone would hoard those.

The one-story rambling brick building peeled off in arms and legs like an octopus from a central office.

The scent of chalk dust sucked me back to elementary school.

"Uh, guys?" Rabbit asked.

"What?"

"I think that's today's date on the chalkboard. Isn't it?"

"Someone's here." Tension whipped through me.

DAY 86

We froze and started listening to the building around us. I imagined whoever was in here with us held the same breath.

I whispered to Zack, "What if they're kids, too?"

"Or teachers?" Rabbit asked.

I moved toward the door.

"What are you doing?"

I shook off Zack's question. "Hello? Is anyone here? We're just moving through. Looking for crayons, maybe a change of clothes," I shouted. "We don't want to steal from you, though, so we can go on. Just tell us to leave."

Okay, I feel like an idiot.

Creak. I heard a door opening along the hallway and a man poked his head out.

"Hello." Relief and new trepidation stole my breath. I

forged ahead, acting brave for Patty's and Rabbit's benefit. "I'm Nadia. There are four of us."

He paused. "Let me see you all?"

I motioned and Zack, Rabbit, and Patty came out. I saw Twawki and Al and recounted. "Sorry, there are two more if you count the dog and bird."

"Hang on a minute." His head disappeared and there were sounds of furniture moving as if they'd barricaded themselves inside the room.

Twawki wagged his tail, and Al sang a jazzy rendition of "Joy to the World."

Finally, the man walked out with a woman and a young girl. "I'm Bruce Angelo. This is my wife, Gail, and our daughter, Emma."

As we made introductions, Emma held out a box of crayons to Patty. The girls were about the same age, and started chattering about their favorite colors in the big box. They giggled and danced and acted like they'd known each other forever. I wished for that kind of resilience.

Rabbit wandered off to check out locker contents after Bruce acknowledged they hadn't explored them yet.

Zack, Bruce, Gail, and I moved toward the front doors and the fresh air.

"How'd you survive? Your whole family?" Zack asked.

"We didn't all. Our son died," Bruce answered, the pain in his voice raw and fresh.

"I'm sorry."

"Bruce is a homeopathic physician. His knowledge is what gave us a chance," Gail asserted. "His patients also had a higher survival rate than most."

Bruce shook his head. "Gail's background as a psychiatrist kept us grounded and looking forward."

"You had to keep us alive first," she argued with a small smile.

"How did you know what to do?" I asked, as we sat on the steps of the building in the sunlight.

"I used accounts of the 1918 influenza pandemic to base a treatment protocol. I'm not the only one, we were all trying. Before communications went down completely, there was a doctor in Germany who thought he had a miracle treatment. I don't know what it was." Bruce's shoulders sagged.

The Angelos were heading east hoping to make it to Washington, D.C. They thought there might be rebuilding and a working government.

"Are you ill?" Bruce asked, staring intently at my eyes. At my nod, Bruce retrieved his bag of medical supplies. Zack disappeared on an amble around the playground with Gail.

When he saw my expression Bruce shrugged. "Shrinks come in handy in disasters. He's not the first person we've met who's needed to talk."

But when they came back to join us it wasn't as if Zack seemed happier. He seemed more depressed, darker. He began studying me with a troubling expression I couldn't decode.

By mutual agreement, we traveled on together in a caravan of sorts. Emma and Patty rode with the Angelos, and the two girls became inseparable. We headed toward Frank's sister's farm. It wouldn't take us much out of our way, and kindness was all we had to give in this new world. Besides, the idea of hot, fresh food was a selfish motivator.

Without warning, a horse and armed rider cut us off on the

country road. Visions of the grannies stealing everything had Rabbit and me cringing.

"Everybody out of the vehicles where we can see you!" the gunman called. "What are you doing here?"

"We have a note from Frank Lanson for his sister, Ms. Lindy, if she's still alive. We thought this was her farm." I spoke up before Bruce, or Zack, played man-in-charge.

"You've seen Frank?" She lowered her gun with a squinting disbelief. "He made it? Why isn't he with you?"

"He's feeding a bunch of animals," Patty inserted from behind me. "Kittens."

She nodded. "Ah. His wife?"

I shook my head. "I'm sorry, but he said no one else in his family made it."

Her shoulders dropped with her sigh as she dismounted.

Rabbit stepped forward. "Here, ma'am." He'd been using the note's scribbled address to navigate us to the farm. "Ms. Lindy, here's the note."

She took it from him with shaking fingers. "I'm sorry for the gun-in-your-face greeting, but we can't be too careful anymore."

"Don't worry about it. We won't stay," Bruce said.

She ruffled up, offended. "Of course you'll stay. We always have food to share with friends and family."

"You don't know us," Zack said.

"You were kind enough to deliver a note from Frank. He wouldn't have sent you unless you're good people. That's friend enough in my book." She swung up on her horse. "Just follow me along the driveway up to the main house. We'll roast up a chicken and have fresh cherry pie."

We shared a look that had our mouths filling in anticipation.

The farm ran like a small city. People hurried and scurried, barely stopping to stare at us, as if everyone's job was more important than new arrivals. Can't say I blamed them. "There are about twenty of us. None from the same family. Mostly old women and a few kids. There's fish in the river. Vegetables in the fields. We have chickens, pigs, cows. It's a full farm—we cobbled it together with what we all had. You'll rest as long as you need."

By the third day on the farm, we had chores like everyone else, but at dinner that night the atmosphere was quite serious.

"We voted. We'd like you to stay with us," Ms. Lindy said, as she passed the sourdough loaves around the picnic table. *Bread. See, Rabbit?*

The Angelos wept with obvious relief at the invitation. There was no question they'd stay.

When all eyes turned toward us, I shook my head. "We can't."

Rabbit didn't hesitate. "Our uncle is waiting for us."

Ms. Lindy didn't argue. "If you change your mind, you come back here. There's plenty of work, but we'll make it through the winter all fine." She stared out across the land and toward the horizon.

"Yes, ma'am," Rabbit answered.

Patty and Emma read each other storybooks and braided each other's hair before falling asleep in a tangle of pink. *I can't take her away.*

Late that night Zack and I snuck off to talk. "We have to leave her with them, with Emma. She's happy as part of their family," I said without preamble.

Zack squeezed my hand, wrapping me closer. "I thought you'd argue with me. I agree. Bruce made it clear to me that they'd like to adopt Patty and make her part of their family. Emma and Patty are like sisters. I think it's what her mother might have hoped for, maybe more than she could imagine—two parents, food, shelter. There are worse places to grow up than on a farm like this." Zack talked on, giving me time to try to stanch the ache that grew and grew.

Tears rolled down my cheeks and I dashed them away, frustrated with myself. "I don't know why I'm crying."

Zack tucked me into his arms, letting me cry it out without trying to make me feel better. "Because it's another goodbye, Starbucks."

DAY 89

Patty took the news much better than Rabbit did. With a quick hug for us humans and kisses for Al and Twawki, she linked arms with Emma and skipped away. As much as I would miss her, there was a certain inescapable relief that came with not having to worry about one more little human.

For his part, Rabbit huffed and cried silently into his elbow as we drove along. He didn't want comforting, not that any of the arguments Zack and I had for relinquishing Patty made sense to him. Maybe he'd liked not being the baby of the group. Maybe he'd liked having another girl who thought he hung the stars instead of just his sister.

As we continued east, we began switching vehicles rather than siphoning gas. It wasn't as if we had many supplies to transfer. On our second truck Zack snuck another glance at me.

"Zack? Why are you staring at me all the time?" I whispered, hoping Rabbit wasn't paying attention.

"'Cause you're pretty," he answered, turning away and dropping his eyes.

I snorted. "By now you should be a better liar than that."

He paused, then reached over and lifted my chin. "You are pretty. You're beautiful." The intensity of his gaze made me fidget.

"That's not why you're watching me all the time," I argued.

He shrugged. "Why not?"

Rabbit called out a direction from the backseat and the moment was lost.

We'd barely crossed into Kentucky when it sounded as though a thunderstorm was barreling down on us. The cloudless sky told me there had to be a different explanation.

The earth rumbled. Vibrated.

"Is that an earthquake?" Rabbit asked.

"I don't think so," Zack said. "Sounds different."

I saw the horizon wiggle and undulate like it was alive. "Are those cows?"

Zack leaned out the window. "Horses?"

"Both?" I squinted, trying to make sense of it.

Rabbit tensed. "Um, guys, we're in their way."

Suddenly realizing he was right, I yelled, "Back up!"

Coming straight at us were a million cows and horses. A herd that stretched from the left horizon to the right.

"We can't outdrive them. Besides, we have to go that way." Zack pointed toward the oncoming animals.

"Turn off the car, at least?" I suggested, my fingernails digging into the upholstery of the dashboard.

We had to shout over the noise. The pounding jiggled the car, shaking us all.

"They'll go around us, right?" Rabbit clung to Twawki, who growled low as if he wasn't sure exactly what the threat was, or where it was coming from.

Zack looked at me. I could see the city-kid fear in his face. He usually acted as though he'd seen and done everything, but facing a herd of hooves—that rocked his facade.

"We'll be fine in the car," I reassured all of us. *Really? Are you sure?*

The first wave was close enough that I saw the whites of their eyes. A bull with a massive set of horns whacked his head against the headlights as he ran by and the racket of broken glass was drowned by our screams as the truck was hit from one side and then the other. We rocked like a dinghy in a hurricane. I heard metal crumple.

Dust filled the air and flies buzzed into the windows with splats. The pop of gunfire made us duck and search for the source of the noise. Last time I checked, horses and cows didn't fire weapons.

The last noses passed and the thunder began to recede behind us. I heard the unmistakable sounds of repeat gunfire, engines, and men shouting approaching from our right.

"They don't look friendly," Rabbit said, as men on motorcycles surrounded us.

I wished this mob was all tattooed, black leathered, and scarred with weird piercings—that they looked like bad guys. Jeans and khakis, T-shirts and striped button-downs, board shorts, and flip-flops looked more like a men's clothing catalog than a motorcycle gang. And guns. Minus the weaponry, they could have been surfers, or accountants, or college kids.

"Hey, guys, we got one!" Surfer dude strode over to a young cow lying on the ground. He shot it one more time in the head, up close.

Rabbit cried out.

"Get out of the truck!" One of the guys knocked on the windshield with the butt of his rifle.

"I don't want to," Rabbit said quietly. Twawki growled.

"Nadia, take the dog's leash and hang on tight." Zack held up his hands and let them see he was unarmed. "We can't take them all."

I knew Zack was right.

"Rabbit, hold tight to Al, okay? Don't let him swear at them."

Please keep the bird quiet for once.

I opened my door, then whispered to Twawki, "Easy, boy, easy, quiet."

"Load the meat up in the back there."

In our truck? Why do all these groups seem to have a dictator? Is democracy another fatality of BluStar?

"Where are you headed?" The question was directed at me.

"South," I answered as Rabbit shuffled behind me, both hands clasped around Al's wings and a towel draped over the bird's head.

Zack stepped in front of us. "Toward the gulf."

"Why?"

Zack shrugged like having conversations at gunpoint was

totally normal. "Heard it was where the government's setting people up. Jobs and food. Vaccines."

The surfer yelled from the truck bed, "Hey, is that why we're going—"

"Shut up, Gary."

"Man, but—"

"I said shut up. Whatcha have in that truck?"

Please, God, don't take the truck. My blisters are getting blisters.

"Clothes, toys for my brother, dog food," Zack answered.

"Yeah, but how come you don't look like you're starving? Clear out the crap." He whistled and two more men rushed over. "I suggest you get out of our way, or we'll help you move."

In seconds they dumped our clothes and the dog food, found a couple bottles of sports drink we were saving for an afternoon snack. They tossed them around and drank it all.

The leader pointed the gun at Twawki. "He's big, he'd be a good sidekick." He reached like he was going to take the leash and Twawki lunged and snapped. I'd braced my feet against the earth, but the leash tore into my hand. Zack reached over to help me as the gun went off.

"Damned dog, next shot I won't miss." The leader shook off his missed shot and stepped back as if he'd planned to incite the dog to kill. "Too much to feed him anyway. We should roast him up instead of the cow."

The group guffawed like scaring kids was a fun new hobby. They took everything. Surfer guy and a few more threw the carcass into the truck bed, loaded their bikes next to the cow, and started the engine. Without saying anything else they followed the stampeding animals.

As the rest revved their motorcycles, I watched a passenger on one of them drop a piece of paper behind him into the dust.

They left us standing at the side of the road. Twawki pulled at the leash to go after them.

As the gang disappeared the way we'd come, Rabbit sat down on the ground and cried. "I'm not moving. I'm not taking another step."

I leaned down next to him. "I can't say I blame you, but can we go sit under that tree and out of the sun?" I pointed.

We needed a moment to catch our breath.

Zack picked up the paper and read it out loud. "'Two miles back, farmhouse with water pump.' Seems like not all those guys are in agreement."

"Why help us?" I asked.

"Who knows? But maybe hooking up with a gang is the only way to make it here. People do crazy things to survive."

Drops of red splatter on Zack's shirt and pants drew my attention. "Uh, Zack?"

"What?"

"Did you get shot?"

I stripped off the flannel overshirt I wore as a jacket. "Sit down."

"I'm fine." Zack flinched, but stopped arguing as I began peeling off his shirt.

I gasped. His bicep had been tunneled by a bullet that left jagged edges of muscle and skin and lots of oozing blood in its wake. "Ruined your tattoo," Rabbit declared with a sad shake of his head even though his face was a greenish white.

Zack chuckled, and I couldn't stop my own laugh. The tattoo was the least important part.

"Did they roll the bullet in dirt first?" I wrapped my shirt-sleeve tight around his bicep to stanch the blood flow.

"Is it still in there?" Zack twisted, trying to see the extent of the damage.

"No, I don't think so. It just burrowed a half-pipe in your flesh." Rabbit nodded as if he was a doctor.

"Can you walk at all?"

"It's my arm, Nadia. Of course I can walk," he snapped.

"Sorry." I wanted to ask for my head back.

Pushing to his feet in a show of superhuman strength Zack demanded, "Let's go find this farmhouse." He took off, with Rabbit slugging along behind him.

"But—" None of the boys paid attention to me and I struggled to catch up.

We made it to the house, but it had been cleaned out, ransacked, probably by the same group.

Come on, Nadia, think. Be the cockroach, what have we learned?

Rabbit turned in circles. "There has to be a cellar. Where do they go for tornadoes?"

"Maybe they don't have one."

"They have to have one. It's a farm. They put garden stuff in jars."

"Rab, we're not in the 1800s, you get that, right? Not every farm had to be useful. Maybe they bought pickles at the grocery like the rest of us."

"No. You don't run a farm and not feed your family off the land."

"Where are you coming up with these things?" I asked.

"Zack's books. Kinda boring."

I laughed. "Okay, go find the cellar."

I dug around in the lady's sewing room and found a large needle and sturdy thread to sew up Zack's arm. There was a water pump against the side of the house. The water stank of rotten eggs, and tasted worse after we dropped bleach into it to kill any bacteria.

Rabbit ran back to us. "It's in the barn, under hay. There's full jars."

"How did you find it?"

"I'm brilliant and determined." Rab grinned.

"That you are, brother mine." I shook my head with a smile.

We made a meal of dill pickles and blackberry jam, crunchy green beans and corn chutney. I wanted to forget the feel of sewing Zack's skin with the needle.

The next morning, I checked Zack's arm and the wound was an angry red, with streaks away from the sutures. My stomach dropped. It didn't take a genius to see we needed to open it up again, clean it out, and restitch it.

"I vote no," Zack said.

"You're outvoted. Until we find antibiotics we don't have a choice."

"How are you going to disinfect it, Starbucks? Pour bleach on my arm?"

"That would eat your skin, not clean it," Rabbit answered, as if Zack had asked the question sincerely.

"We have to pee on it." I grimaced.

"Huh?"

"We don't have any antiseptic, do we? It's a nasty wound, there'll be bacteria in there."

"And pee is better?"

"It's a nurses' trick." I frowned.

"I can see why it's not better known," Zack grumped.

Rabbit backed away. "No, I am not peeing on him."

"Rabbit, please," I pleaded.

"You think it's a brilliant idea—you do it."

"Fine." I grabbed a bowl and walked into the bushes. "For God's sake somebody talk loudly, this is hard enough without silence!" I yelled. *Once again, wishing I was a boy.*

The steaming, fragrant bowl held anything but broth. I swallowed a gag.

"Don't think about it, just do it." Zack held his arm away from his body.

I dumped a steady stream of still-warm urine along the wound. *Dear God, please don't let him die because of my pee. How the hell would I live with* that *guilt?*

Al started singing, "Tinkle, tinkle little star."

Zack guffawed. "Funny bird."

"We have to keep moving."

Over the next two stops, we found school backpacks and scavenged a few bottles of water, a last jar of olives, a pan, lighters, and a couple of knives. "I wish we had at least one gun."

I nodded. There was something more comforting about a gun than a knife.

Rabbit found an atlas from 1995 in a dead car. "At least the big roads are probably still on here."

This was farm country. Miles upon miles of acres with occasional farmhouses, or carcasses of ones that had burned down. Two sun ups, two sun downs, and lots of shuffling feet because all the vehicles were on empty. Semi-trucks that once hauled freight were empty when we found them.

After the seventh charred residence, Rabbit voiced what we all were thinking, "Would someone deliberately burn down houses?"

"If they were trying to force people out, I guess."

"We have to keep moving."

Twawki stopped by a mud puddle and dipped his tongue into it. Al said, "Yuck!"

I almost considered doing the same thing. I was so thirsty my tongue felt swollen and crusted.

"There's a pigeon." Rabbit sounded beyond excited.

"Great," I mumbled.

"Yes, it is great. There's a whole flock. Which way are they flying? Pay attention," Rabbit demanded.

"That way." Zack pointed, and I agreed.

"We need to go that way."

"Rabbit, that's off the road, off the path. It's the wrong way."

"Are you thirsty? Come on."

"Why are we following a flock of pigeons into the forest, Shark?"

"Keep your eyes peeled for finches, too."

Zack turned to me. "What the hell does a finch look like?"

I shrugged. "Um, it has feathers and wings."

"Thanks."

Rabbit recited, "Grain eaters like finches and pigeons stay near water. If they fly low and straight they are going toward the water source. Dad said."

Well, if Dad said it . . . It wasn't Rabbit's fault I felt bitchy, so I didn't let the thought escape, but Dad also said nothing was going to happen to him and he'd come home. Alive. Dad said a lot of things that were never going to happen.

"Wait. Stop. Quiet." Zack grabbed my arm, while Twawki sat and cocked his head.

There, at the outmost range of my hearing, was a trickling sound like water running.

"He's right?" Zack shook his head. "Lead on, Mouse."

When we found the pond and the stream bubbling into it I wanted to submerge my face and lap it up like a creature of the forest.

"I want to jump in and drink." Rabbit lay down along the banks.

"We can't. We have to disinfect the water."

"I'd give anything for a cherry ice."

"Don't say ice. That's cruel." Sweat kept our clothes sticking against our skin.

"Sorry."

We all stripped off our shoes and socks and dipped our toes into the water. Then we filled empty bottles with water, measured the last of the bleach in, shook them up and let the water sit.

Finally, we sipped, measuring our intake against the horrendous need to chug it all down. The discipline it took bordered on insanity.

"Slowly." The last thing any of us needed to do was puke up any of the precious liquid.

By the third round of bottles my headache had eased. Rabbit moved and I could hear his stomach slosh around.

It struck me as funny and a giggle escaped, along with a slightly chlorinated belch.

I dug my toes into the cool mud, letting it seep the throb from my blisters, and slapped Zack on the head. "Sorry, mosquito."

"Oh, really?" He quirked an eyebrow up.

"Scout's honor." I smiled.

He flicked water at me with a grin. "You look a little hot."

We'd walked miles without seeing a car, a house, or even much wildlife.

Poised to turn this into a full-out water war we froze when Rabbit said, "Hey, guys? Is that a tree fort?" He pointed up behind us at a stand of old trees, the kind with peeling white bark.

The breeze shifted, and lifted the branches again. We saw a ladder of boards nailed into the backside of a tree trunk. It was either falling apart or had never been finished, but it was definitely human construction.

DAY 92

"It looks like kids made it." Zack raced after Rabbit to get a closer look.

"Well, where there are kids, there might be people and a house, right?" Rabbit offered.

"Rabbit, you're brilliant." I hugged him. "Nice eyes."

We quickly dried off our wet and muddy feet. I hated wrestling my stiff socks back on, but the idea of a house with untold treasures egged me on.

"How far away might the fort builder live?" I asked as we trudged along what might have been a deer trail, or simply a path we were desperate to see that didn't exist.

No one answered me; I hadn't expected them to. The trees thinned, became sparser and more scraggly, as we went. The light clarified and brightened.

There, in the distance, I spied a roof. I think we all saw it at the same time. We started walking more carefully, quieter. When we got close enough we sat against trees and peered out at one of those preplanned neighborhoods filled with cookie-cutter McMansions and culs-de-sac. "There are houses out there. Seven," I whispered, as if staring at a mirage.

And a lot more planned. There were asphalt roads and carved driveways. Dirt piled lots were littered with little pink flags and wooden stakes marking off unbuilt houses.

"I don't even care if there are zombies. We can sleep in a bed tonight, and maybe they have food." Rabbit started forward until Zack held out a hand.

Surrounded by fields, and forests, the actual neighborhood was a long way into the open without cover.

"We need to wait until dark, see if anyone comes back here for the night. Or lights a candle," Zack cautioned.

"I agree. We need to be careful. I'm hungry too, but at least we're not thirsty anymore." I tried to focus on the positive.

Rabbit sat in the shade and rubbed Twawki's head. Al chased a shiny black beetle in circles at our feet.

With my stomach full of cool water and the heat of the haze a lullaby, I fought drowsiness even as I watched Rabbit drift off.

"We've got movement," Zack whispered in my ear.

My eyes snapped open and I instantly went on alert. "Sorry," I mumbled as I watched a woman come out of one house dressed in a very stained tennis outfit and sneakers. A sun visor covered her face, and she'd pulled her hair into a slick and tangled ponytail that stuck out of the top. When she picked up the hose and started to water a row of brown and dead bushes, Zack and I shared a glance. There wasn't water coming out of the hose, nor did she seem to notice the bushes—roses, maybe?—were dead.

She carefully hummed and tended as if seeing a lush and verdant garden.

"She's snapped." I rubbed my face.

"But is she alone?" Zack asked.

"I'll go."

"No, I will," he insisted.

"No, I'm a girl. If she's alone you might scare her. I'll wave if it's safe, okay?"

"I don't like it."

"I don't care, you know I'm right." I brushed off my butt and walked out of the woods with what I hoped was a friendly-looking wave and jaunty step.

The woman didn't pause in her watering, but smiled and waved me closer. She yelled, "You must be part of the new family in 5325. I'm right, aren't I? I can't believe I've been too busy to bring you cookies and welcome you to the neighborhood."

"Hello!" I shook her hand, trying not to let my unease show.

"Is your husband with you? You must come in for refreshments."

"Oh, we don't want to interrupt your plans," I said.

"Nonsense, it's only a silly tennis game. They'll understand. Not every day I get to meet the neighbors."

I waved toward the woods and Zack joined me. I knew he kept Rabbit and Twawki away on purpose.

She prattled on, "I can't tell you how nice it is to meet you. Jack will be so happy to see you when he gets home at six.

I do hope you like to play couple's tennis? When we moved out here our usual duo couldn't make the drive—such traffic these days. Would you like some lemonade?" We followed her inside.

She continued as if pattering on and making invisible lemonade was part and parcel of normal. She served us very dirty, very empty glasses and then laid out a plate of invisible cookies served from an empty box in the cupboard. "Please help yourself. I know they're not home baked, but I simply haven't been able to get to the market this week." We ate and drank, like one of Patty's tea parties, and made small talk about the weather, local schools, her husband's job as a traveling sales rep for medical devices.

The overwhelming smell of human waste inside her house made my eyes water. I guessed the toilets stopped flushing weeks, or months, ago.

After the most bizarre pantomime ever, we walked over to "our" house and waved to her as she disappeared back into her living room. Zack checked the ground and found a faux rock that held a spare key. "Lesson number one: if you don't have any other plastic rocks in your landscaping, your key hide is probably pretty obvious."

I laughed. "Thanks, I'll keep that in mind."

Rabbit came out from the woods behind the house. "That was creepy! What took you guys so long?" His voice full of worry. "There can't possibly be anything left in here, can there? She has to have scavenged everything."

"Not if she really thinks her world is normal. She's not going to break into her neighbors' houses," Zack disagreed.

A finished pool in the backyard was green and slimy, but

with a little ingenuity, the sacrifice of five-hundred-thread-count sheets, and an inflated kiddie pool, we cleaned out the chunks and got clearish water boiling over the built-in fire pit in the backyard.

The pantry was still fairly full, but we started with bland crackers and added fruit punch powder to the water to cover the nasty taste.

"Why doesn't she raid these houses?" Rabbit asked.

I didn't answer. I knew there were people who simply couldn't handle change, who shut down. She was stuck in a weird *Groundhog Day* replay. How she managed to live this long I didn't know and I really didn't want to ask.

Taking turns cleaning the water from the pool for each other took hours. However, the squeaky-clean and scrubbed feeling afterward was worth all the work. With crazy-high humidity, the feeling only lasted a few minutes before sweat replaced shower dampness. We washed up, dressing in designer-label cotton pajamas. No air conditioning, but we ran a battery-powered fan and opened windows to keep from smothering in the heat.

I slathered ointment on my blisters and stuck Band-Aids on all of them.

I knew I'd have to wrestle Zack to get him to let me poke at his arm again, so I went on the offensive first and found rubbing alcohol, bourbon, and supplies to stitch the wound. I gathered them together in a basket and took them downstairs.

"I found the gun safe," Zack greeted me.

"That's good, right?" I asked.

"It's locked."

"Oh . . ."

"They have to have written their combo somewhere, right?" We hunted through desks and drawers.

"Hey, guys, this mail—it all says the same thing." Rabbit held the mail up and flicked on a flashlight as if he wasn't sure of what he was seeing.

"What are our names again?"

"No, not that. We've made it into West Virginia." The awe in his voice was part puzzlement, part excitement.

"Really?" I shuffled through the stack, checking both the mailing and return address sections. *West Virginia.* "You're right." I went to the desk in the kitchen and pulled out the massive Yellow Pages phone book.

"We did it! We're in the state!" Rabbit squealed and tossed unpaid bills in the air, doing a happy dance. I joined him bouncing around. Twawki barked and chased his tail with enthusiasm as Al did a head-bopping, leg-lifting dance to his own tune.

Zack waited until we calmed down slightly to ask, "So, uh, where's Pappi from here?"

I wasn't sure, but I knew it depended completely on how far into the state we'd come.

Rabbit's face fell. He held up a single finger. "We're here."

Zack nodded. "Okay?"

He lifted another finger and held it at arm's length from the first one. "Pappi's mine is here."

"Shit." Zack closed his eyes. "We've made it this far—can't you clue me in on why we're going to Pappi's?"

"You want to tell him or should I?" Rabbit asked me. "You're better at it."

"Let's heat up the lobster and artichoke bisque for dinner and I'll do my best."

"Why couldn't they have canned chicken soup like normal people?" Rabbit grumbled. "This is so chichi."

"It's food. You're hungry. You'll like it, Rodent." Zack ruffled his hair.

I glanced at Rabbit, unsure of what to say and how much to leave out of our family's story. I must have hesitated too long because he shrugged at me and said, "I heard all the fights too. I probably know more than you think I do. Besides, I'd like to know too."

I nodded and decided to start at the beginning.

"Uncle Bean joined the navy first because he wanted to be a doctor and the marines don't have them on staff. Dad followed him into the military two years later. He was already a marine when my mom met him; she hated that he refused to give it up when I was born. He wouldn't consider changing careers. When the terrorists struck New York, he not only decided to stay in but went for extra training. I don't really know how it worked, but he became special ops. He was called away more than he was home. When Mom got pregnant with Rab, I remember her telling me that Daddy would have to stay home now." Sadness broke in waves over my heart. What would our family look like today if he'd left the Corps?

"He said a desk job would kill him. Didn't he?" Rabbit whispered.

I nodded. "Yes, on your fourth birthday they had a huge fight because he had to leave before you'd had your cake."

"So your parents weren't perfect. They loved you both, right?" Zack asked.

"As much as we fought, I know Mom loved me. Dad too," I answered.

"You have to remember that more than the fights." Zack spoke toward Rabbit, who nodded.

"I think Mom had this idea from television that we'd spend holidays around a table and get dressed up and everyone would laugh and—"

"Like a movie," Rabbit agreed.

"Yeah, like a movie. Only she didn't have much family at all. An older sister who maybe lived in Florida and she never talked about her parents." Did we ever have photos of them? *No.*

"Ah, so your dad's family had to be the picture-perfect one?"

"Yeah, I guess she thought Dad would get out of the military if his brother and father would let him."

"What about his mother?" Rabbit asked. "Did I ever meet her?"

"No, she came to visit when I was little, then she died. She lived with Pappi, though for only a few years when they first married. I didn't know about most of this until Mom explained it to me. After we were stuck at home."

"When?" Rabbit asked.

"Those last few days. She made me write stuff down so I wouldn't forget. Pappi was a medical doctor, and a virologist, who worked in bioweapons warfare during the Cold War in the '50s and '60s. He went to Vietnam. Mom says she thinks he was CIA or something, and a spy in Russia. Something bad happened, because he came back to the States and started selling cars."

"He sold cars? That's weird. Why come back and work as a car salesman? Why not be a regular doctor?"

"I don't know. He started talking about secret experiments

and caches of weapons. He wrote letters and tried to get politicians to meet with him. Then when Dad was in high school he snapped. He left his family and disappeared. He showed up at Dad's college graduation ceremony. Pappi had purchased an abandoned mine and was preparing for the big event. Dad visited him every six months or so to bring him new stuff, even when we were little. Bean did too."

"They just accepted his crazy?"

"I guess Mom went with him once and it scared her so badly she wouldn't let Dad take us to visit. Pappi never left his mountain."

"You've never met him?"

"Nope. If things were different, I know Mom never would have told us to go to him."

"So why?"

"I guess he's brilliant, and planned for every catastrophe known and unknown. Mom said if anyone could make it through this thing alive *and* thrive, it was Pappi."

"Is he dangerous?" Rabbit asked in a little voice.

"No, Mom said he hates the government, and most people, but he will protect us. He's never hurt anyone and he loved us. Dad took him photos and videos on his visits."

"Am I in danger?" Zack asked.

"Uncle Bean gave us permission to bring friends. I don't think so."

"Maybe you should have mentioned paranoid relatives before I left my place." Zack frowned.

"I'm sorry. It didn't occur to me that he might not welcome you."

"We'll make him." Rabbit's conviction eased the tension in Zack's face.

"Mom said if Bean knew enough to get us shots, then he knew enough to make sure Pappi's mine was fully equipped for the next phases of civilization." *Whatever those might be.*

"Why didn't he take you back with him then? I don't get it. Why make you risk so much getting there now?"

"He couldn't," Rabbit answered.

I frowned at my brother. "How do you know?"

"I talked to him, remember? When he called, a second time, to wish you a happy birthday months early?" Rabbit shrank with each word as he remembered.

Oh, that's right. I forgot.

"What did you talk about?" Zack asked in a soft voice, as if Rabbit's recollections could be startled like a butterfly.

"He said he couldn't take us to Disney World because Pappi was right and there were eyes everywhere."

"They must have been listening to his phone, too."

"He promised he'd meet us at Disney World next year no matter what."

After a moment Zack asked, "Who else had the shot?"

I shrugged. "I don't know."

"No one we've met has mentioned it."

"No, Bean thought there might be people with a genetic immunity."

"But if there's a magical vaccine don't you think they'd have given it to the president, or rich people, or celebrities?"

"Probably. Maybe that's why people are heading south. Maybe there's a city of survivors."

My stomach fell. Maybe Zack didn't want to continue on with us. Maybe he wanted to try to find another place. "I mean, if you don't want to go to Pappi's with us, you don't have to—"

240

His quick grin preceded "Nah, I'll take my chances with crazy grandpa over the freaks running around with guns and too much power. You're stuck with me."

I exhaled the breath I didn't know I had been holding. *I count on Zack being here.*

Rabbit slurped the last of his soup. "I say we stay here for a few days—let the blisters and arm heal a little before we venture on."

"Sure. We need to figure out the combo to the safe so we have guns, too."

I agreed. We were so close, and yet getting here took more out of all of us than I could quantify. If we headed off into the unknown without taking advantage of a respite with shelter, water, food, and medical equipment we might not make it the rest of the way.

"Vote on it?" Rabbit brightened.

"We don't need to vote, Coyote. It's the smart thing to do." Zack shook with laughter.

"Good, now strip off your shirt, drink this bottle, and lie down on the kitchen table," I said, handing Zack the bottle of booze.

He lifted his eyebrows like I'd asked him to do nastiness. I knew he was simply trying to embarrass me about being demanding, but it wasn't going to work. *I need him.*

"I thought about peeing on you again, but since they've got rubbing alcohol and ointment, sterile bandages and good thread, I vetoed that. It's gonna hurt, though. I mean, if you don't want to be drunk first, that's fine, but . . ."

Zack lifted the bottle and chugged a few swallows without even hissing. There were things about Zack I didn't know, a history that moments like this made me wonder about. But it came back to one thing and one thing only—he'd had my back, saved my life, was an extra set of hands to make my burdens bearable. That was all I needed to know. . . .

The phone rang. I grabbed it.

"How's the birthday girl, Nadia?"

Why is he speaking in code? Confused, I replied, "Hi, Uncle Bean."

"How are you feeling?"

Had I told him I'd been sick? "Better, I think."

"Good. Rabbit?"

"He's on the mend too."

"Did your mom take the medicine?"

I snorted.

"Are you sure you can't convince her?"

"It would help if I knew what it was."

"Just migraine medicine, kiddo. Like we talked about."

Are people listening? He sounds odd. "I know, but you know she flipped out."

"You tell your mom about the birthday present I left you?"

"No." I sobered.

"I know it's hard to keep a secret from her. Thank you. Count down seven, okay?"

. . . Mom stumbled into my bedroom. "Nadia, I need to talk to you. It's bad." She hung her head as tears fell down her cheeks. "They sent us home tonight. Cancelled all shifts for the rest of the month. They closed the hospital. Even sent patients home." She hugged me tight against her and mumbled into my hair. "It's not bird flu or swine flu. It's hemorrhagic with blue star-shaped bruising."

"Mom, what's that mean?"

"It means there isn't medicine to fight it . . . It's everywhere in the world all at once. I've never seen anything like it. . . ."

. . . "Should we go to the evacuation sites? Should we, Mom?"

"Nadia, you can't go. You have to control your own destiny. Those will be refugee camps where you'll be dependent on handouts and the whims of other people. I want more for you and for your brother. You do what Bean told you to. You're smart. You're resourceful. You make decisions for yourself and you'll survive."

DAY 95

I gathered up a box of food, including a bunch of full water bottles, and took it all over to the tennis wife before we left.

I practiced my lines on the walk over.

"Hi, Marcy!"

"Nadia, so nice to see you again. Would you like to come in for more lemonade and cookies?"

"I can't. We've decided to take little Robert on a road trip. He's always wanted to see Shenandoah and we keep promising him. But I stocked up the pantry this week—would you mind terribly using this food? I'm afraid it won't keep until we get back and I'd hate for it to go to waste."

"Are you sure? You can't possibly be gone that long."

For a moment, I was sure I saw a flicker of reality behind her eyes; then it was gone, replaced by a glazed denial.

"I'm sure." I held out the key to the house. "Would you mind terribly checking on the houseplants while we're gone?"

"I'm happy to."

"And please, help yourself to anything you need. Our casa es su casa." I gave her my best faked Hallmark smile and backed away.

"Sure. Sure. See you when you get back."

"You don't want to come with us, do you?" I couldn't not ask. I shouldn't have, but I had to.

She pooh-poohed me. "Jack will be back in time for dinner. He wouldn't know what to do without me for the weekend."

"Okay, thanks!" I waved, while she stood there holding the box of food. I climbed into a commandeered sedan Zack had repurposed from a half-finished house construction site.

"Will she be okay?" Rabbit asked from the backseat. "Never mind." He shook off his question. We all knew the answer, but we'd done what we could.

We'd decided to travel light, staying on country roads that Rabbit plotted and planned.

The houses grew farther apart, and the poverty would have been heartbreaking in another time. Dead mining towns and shut-down factories rusted through with neglect were common sights. This wasn't land that was easily self-sufficient. This was land that those people, who could, passed through on their way to something better. Miles of silence rolled by.

"We're running low on gas, guys. Better keep eyes peeled." The rusted-out Cadillac we rode in had a hole in the floorboards and duct-taped plastic sheeting for two windows. This wasn't a country of flashy SUVs or European imports, this was a use-it-up-until-it-falls-apart world.

Maybe we're all of that mind-set now? How many years of my life will be using up until it all falls apart?

With the gas needle dipping toward E and hiking seeming like a looming possibility, Rabbit pointed. "There's a driveway."

"Turkey, where are we from Pappi's?" Zack asked, slowing.

"Twenty-two miles, but those are all in the Allegheny Mountains, so they'll be slow going."

"We have to chance it and see if there's gasoline here. Yes?" Zack asked.

"Yes," Rab and I answered. Even Al agreed on cue.

Pausing to prepare for confrontation, I switched positions with Zack, who held a handgun in his good hand. Rabbit clutched a shotgun and aimed it out the plastic window, more for show than because we expected him to use it.

The driveway was more pothole than road and children's plastic toys like tractors and bikes littered each side. As we drove around a curve, a patched and decrepit mobile home came into view. I turned off the engine at Zack's nod. We sat in the car for long minutes waiting to see if anyone came out, or shot at us. *Nothing.*

Finally, we unbuckled and stepped out.

"I can't go in there," I said as flies bit my neck and curtains blew where glass once was.

"I'll check inside." Zack nodded, as Rabbit and I walked toward several sheds. When he came back all he did was shake his head. They hadn't had anything before BluStar.

"There are a couple of four-wheelers plus gas cans," I reported.

"We've still got a few miles in the gas tank. It doesn't make sense to switch now. Plus, if we fill up the tank with whatever gas is in those cans . . ."

"We can tow them if we run out. At least they're better than walking." Zack and Rabbit tied the quads to the back bumper and somehow managed to rig them so they'd roll behind the car without having to be turned on.

"Let's go." Zack made it down the driveway to the main road before what was a great idea in theory fell apart when we started up a hill. The sound of grating metal and popping bolts preceded a crash.

We all turned to look behind us.

"Oops." Rabbit snickered.

The back bumper lay on the ground for a moment, until gravity grasped the four-wheelers and they began rolling down the hill, the bumper towed along behind them.

Rabbit's giggle was contagious. Maybe we'd been traveling too long, or maybe it was because we were two days from showers and real beds, but I joined in.

Zack shook his head and seemed to take the failure personally. "It should have worked."

I tried to bite back my chuckles because I didn't want Zack to think we were laughing at him. "Just think, someone may come along and thank God that there's a rear bumper tied to a couple of four-wheelers."

"Maybe I could—"

"You know this car is held together by a prayer and two rolls of duct tape. I say we keep heading forward and don't worry about it." I squeezed his forearm.

Behind us there was a large crack and crash as the vehicles

fell into a ditch and the bumper clanked on top of them. Even Zack gave in to the giggles at that point.

As night fell, the Caddy coughed on the last fumes of gas and expired near the turnoff to the entrance of the Monongahela National Forest.

"We want to head that way to camp tonight?" Zack asked.

"No, I think we should skirt it," I answered.

Rabbit nodded. "Dad would say stay to the edges, it's a perfect place for crazies to build an empire."

I could almost see Zack thinking, *Like your Pappi?* But he didn't say it.

We loaded up the backpacks, Rabbit and I carried most of the weight. Zack wasn't complaining about his arm, but it looked swollen and painful. I worried we hadn't gotten rid of the infection.

"There's a historic site in two more miles." Rabbit perked up.

"What is it?" I asked.

"Pearl S. Buck's birthplace." Rabbit looked up from the flashlight beam shining on the atlas page. "Figure it has to be a house, right?" We'd found that historic sites didn't tend to have squatters or dead.

"Good call, Toad. There's enough moonlight to keep going until then."

Under a full moon we trudged along, keeping to the middle of the road. With more ups than downs, curves, and inclines I understood why these were called mountains.

My blisters recracked and the warm ooze of blood and fluid made my socks stick to my skin uncomfortably.

Al rode on Twawki's back, who continued wearing his

shoes. Though the dog's wounds were healing, the pink skin was fragile and not callused. He didn't seem to notice them anymore, though. The last thing we needed was him getting hurt again so close to the end of the journey.

"There's a sign." Rabbit pointed.

Zack grunted. I watched as he staggered a little and sweat poured off his face. I was afraid to touch him. He blazed with fever and he'd started to smell funny. Not just the usual smell of dirt and sweat, but the sickly sweet of infection I knew by heart.

At the sign, we trudged up another hill. Football fields away, a large two-story white house reflected the moonlight, but a smaller, less fancy building was closer to us.

"I vote for the closer one," Zack said, pausing for us to deliberate.

"Me too." We marched on.

I flipped on the flashlight and swept the place to make sure no one else was living there. The structure was part white shingles, part log cabin with mud chinking. The inside was minimally furnished, but there were two rope beds with stuffed mattresses and quilts.

"We're probably destroying George Washington's favorite quilt," Rabbit grumbled as Twawki leapt up on the bed.

"Yeah, well, I don't think there will be field trips here anytime soon. I'm sure Pearl, or George, will understand that we're being cockroaches and using what we need to survive."

Zack swayed.

"Lie down." I led him to the bed and helped him get situated. He was a deadweight of weakness and illness.

"Rabbit, can you figure out what we're eating? Find the

bottle of Tylenol, too, okay?" I asked, as I started to peel off Zack's boots, socks, and long-sleeved shirt. *Yep, definitely feverish.* The waves of heat radiated off Zack's skin like a paved road in the middle of summer's heat.

"I wish we had water." Rab sighed. Worry in his eyes with each of our movements told me he was grouchy because of Zack's condition. Grouchy and exhausted.

"They have to have a well and pump." I sat back on my heels as Zack's eyes fluttered closed.

"Want me to go look?" Rabbit's wide eyes pleaded with me as he handed me the pills and a juice box from a backpack.

Shaking Zack awake, I shoved two pills at him and made him drink all the juice. "No, figure out the food and I'll go see what I can find."

"I wish we had the walkie-talkies." Rab sounded impossibly young.

"I know. But I'll be fine." I grabbed a big cast-iron pot from the kitchen area and removed the fake carrots and potatoes. Dusty and unused for who knows how long, I had to evict a spider, but the pan would hold water. *Please let there be a well, a working pump, a pond, anything, pleasepleaseplease.*

I left Rabbit huddled over our supplies and headed outside toward the picnic tables, keeping my ears open for any noises out of the ordinary. I heard a pair of owls and the pinging of bats above me, but nothing human. Nothing sinister. In the valley below there weren't any lights. No campers, no fires, no threats.

Taking deep breaths to battle my brain fog, I kept my eyes on permanent scan, making sure I didn't miss a detail. *No tunnel vision, Nadia. Fight it.* "Bingo and a gold star." I found the old pump in the center of a picnic area with a small cement pool at the base, presumably for dogs to drink from. "Please work, please work." I set the pot on the ground, gripped the handle, and primed it up and down. Seemed like it was here for visitors to use, so hopefully it had only been unused for months, not years.

My arms burned and my hands ached from clutching the handle. I paused to catch my breath and wipe sweat from my face.

No water.

I kept moving the handle up and down. *Pleasepleaseplease-pleaseplease.*

Finally, a few drops leaked out. I pushed harder, using my whole body. Zings sang up into my shoulders. In a great gush, then a steady flow, icy cold water filled the pot. The first rush was muddy, so I rinsed the pot and refilled it until the water was clear. I wanted to strip down and bathe right then.

I cradled the pot in my arms and lugged it back to the cabin. "Rab, it's me. I've got water."

"Really?" Rabbit was bent over a tiny camper's flame heating up pork and beans. Twawki whined excitedly as I gave him a bowl of cool water.

Zack was sound asleep snoring. Al sat on the headboard and watched Zack as if willing him to be okay.

I rummaged around in the bedrooms and found fragile cotton nightshirts, the kind I'd only ever seen in old movies. I also found sheets and towels in simple homespun textiles. Whoever stocked this house for the public tours tried to stay authentic. I grabbed a big copper washtub to put our clothes in.

We ate and then Rab helped me strip Zack's outer layers

251

so I could get cold cloths on every inch of his body. He didn't notice or wake.

"Is he going to be okay?"

I didn't answer. I wouldn't lie, but optimism felt false. In the moonlight I sat with my back to Rab while he washed and put on a nightshirt. Then he sat with Zack while I did the same. Making multiple trips to the pump, I filled the tub with water and swished our clothes around again and again until they no longer stood on their own. We hung them over the railings of the cabin's back porch to dry.

Together, we lugged more water in to bathe Zack again. Rabbit, Twawki, and Al took the other bed and soon the snores outnumbered the crickets and nightlife that buzzed around the cabin. I was afraid to take my eyes off Zack. *Please don't let him die this close. Please don't die.*

DAY 98

It took three days of Tylenol, lots of water, and all of our food supplies, but when Zack opened his eyes he was ready to head on.

"Um, uh, thanks." He caught my hand.

I nodded. My throat closed.

Rabbit wheeled out two very vintage bicycles, one of them a tandem. "I found these in the shed back there." Enough seats for all of us.

After pausing and taking a deep breath, Zack said, "I don't know how to ride a bike." His expression full of doubts.

"You get the backseat of the two-person, then. I'll take this one with Al and Twawki." Rabbit grinned.

I tried to instruct as best I could and we started hobbling

along, Rabbit and the animals taking point on the expedition. At least the bike was tandem and Zack simply had to balance and mimic my movements.

I could almost hear Bean egging us on. *We're so close.*

Around us green hills rolled and climbed until they appeared blue, then black.

"There's a cabin up ahead." Rabbit circled back to stay close to us.

The tiny log structure was surrounded by old, smooth white grave markers and didn't have a single window. A stagnant pond down the hill was covered with Canada geese and ducks making enough noise to qualify as a hard-rock concert.

Someone had turned the ancient cabin into a fishing retreat during better days.

An old cooler was stocked with three different kinds of beer, none of them cold. We were thirsty enough to consider drinking it regardless of the temperature or the alcohol content.

Zack walked around to the back of the cabin. "Uh, guys?"

"Yeah?"

We came out holding cans of warm beer.

"Do they have gas in them?" Rabbit asked, as Zack removed the tarp on two four-wheelers.

Zack nodded. "And keys."

"But where's the bumper to drag along?" Rabbit grinned. "I'm bummed."

Zack's face turned red. Not all ideas could be good ones.

"I know you really wanted to ride bikes for another day," I said to Zack, who rubbed his ass.

"Uh, no. How is that fun? My butt will never be the same."

He shook his head while Rabbit giggled. Twawki chased a few geese and jumped into the pond to swim in the muck and algae.

We ate stale granola bars, shared a bag of chips, and drank a couple cans of beer each, even though none of us liked the taste. We'd all consumed worse in the last months. It was liquid and calories—both of which we needed.

Rabbit burped, then asked with a smile, "Does this make me drunk?"

"Just don't drive," Zack replied with a straight face.

That night I couldn't sleep, even though the alcohol made me drowsy. *We're so close. So close. We might make it. We might actually make it.*

Fog greeted me as I tried to stretch the kinks out in the early morning light. The chill of morning belied the heat I knew would rise up by noon.

Zack joined me. "What's today, Nadia?"

"I don't know." I wasn't even sure if it was a new day, or just a superlong moment pieced together.

"Come on, hop on." He pointed to the back of the four-wheeler and handed me a helmet.

"We can't leave Rabbit—"

"Hey, Spider, you good for a few? I need to show your sister something."

"No problem, Zacky-poo. Thanks for not kissing her in front of me." Rabbit made exaggerated choking sounds and wiggled his tongue like it was a worm.

"Nice." I rolled my eyes, and climbed on behind Zack. "You feel hot—are you okay?"

"Why, that's the nicest thing you've ever said to me."

Blood flooded my cheeks. "I meant a fever. What's your arm look like?" I touched the edge of the bandage.

He tried to cover his flinch, but I saw it. "Zack?"

He revved the engine and refused to answer. Talking over the engine noise was impossible. When we crested a hill overlooking canyons and brush he turned off the engine. "Get off."

"Here?" I didn't move. I'd never find my way back to camp.

"Here. Get off." Zack held out a hand.

I peeled off the helmet. "What are we doing here?"

He leaned back against a boulder and stared at me.

Do I have a booger hanging out? A weird stain on my face? Smell bad? Why is he staring at me? "What?" I almost shouted.

"We're almost there," Zack answered me quietly.

I surveyed the view, trying to see an imaginary flashing light marking Pappi's cave. "We are, aren't we?"

"So says your brother, and he's rarely wrong."

Dread filled my stomach with rocks and snakes. *What if Bean's not there? What if they're dead? What if there's nothing at this mine but more questions? What do we do then?* I felt limbs begin to shake as goose bumps broke out along my arms.

Zack continued, "Tomorrow's July Fourth."

"It is?" *How can it be?*

He nodded. "How are you?"

"I'm still standing. I'm the cockroach. We're the roaches." I tried to smile. "That would be a good band name—you play anything?" I tried to change the subject. I didn't want to talk about what happens next. *There is no next—it's Pappi and Bean and everything will be okay.*

"Spoons. Okay, you're still standing, but you're falling apart on the inside. I can see it. And if I can see it, your brother . . ." Zack let his words hang.

I closed my eyes as the shaking grew worse.

"Scream," Zack said into my face.

"Huh?" My eyes snapped open to meet his. He'd moved silently until we almost touched and I was sure that with the fever Zack had lost his mind.

"Come on, scream," Zack demanded.

"What? Why?"

"Scream. Primal. From your gut. Dammit, Nadia, don't look at me like that. Just do it," he snarled, shaking my shoulders.

I tried a roar and it sounded more like a vacuum cleaner dying a painful death than a primal scream.

He shook his head and sneered, "You can do better than that. It's not like anyone's going to film it and put it on YouTube."

All the things that were so important once upon a time were gone. No Internet. No school. No popular kids. No college. No parents pushing me to be the best I could at everything. I tugged the MP3 player out of my pocket and held it.

"Come on, climb up." Zack helped me climb up onto the top of the rocks. I saw an empty world in every direction.

Zack prodded my side and pointed at the player. "You're stuck here. They're not. That sucks."

"I'm still here," I whispered. Anger at being the head of the family, the person tasked with making sure we lived, seared my heart. I growled.

"Now, scream it!" Zack yelled next to me, and his voice echoed around us.

"I'm still standing!" I belted the words out as if shouting to be heard over a jumbo jet engine. I grabbed a rock and hefted it into the chasm below. "I'm still here!"

"More! More!" Zack danced around me, egging me on. "Your parents—what'd they do?"

"They died," I answered.

"What? I can't hear you?"

"They DIED!" I yelled.

"How does that make you feel?"

Shouting, "Alone!" *Repressed. Responsible. Careful. Deliberate. Ready to explode.*

"Scared?"

I nodded.

"Terrified?"

"And if Rabbit dies?"

"I'll die, too." My shoulders dropped and breathing became impossible.

"No, you won't!" Zack shouted.

"It would be easier."

"I know. What about BluStar? How do you feel about it?" He kept coming at me, not letting me think before words tumbled out. All I could do was feel and weep.

"I HATE it. It took everything. Killed my mother. My life."

"What are you scared of right now?"

"What if Uncle Bean isn't there? What if Pappi is dead, too?" The words tore from my throat as if by releasing them into the world the ideas took tangible form.

Zach reached out and grabbed my hand. His grip on my fingers was twin to my stranglehold on his. *I won't know what to do.*

I didn't realize I'd spoken out loud until he answered. "You'll figure it out."

I sank to my knees, crying out my fear. He smoothed my

hair and didn't let go of my hand. When I sighed, Zack sat down next to me and wrapped his good arm around me in comfort.

"Feel better?" Zack studied my expression.

I opened my mouth to tell him no, but stopped, shocked. "I do. I actually do."

"Good." He nodded. His expression spoke of extreme self-satisfaction.

"How'd you guess that's what I needed?" I asked.

He hung his head. "I didn't. Gail suggested it. She thought maybe you were bottling it all up. And that was before you started obsessing about my arm."

I laughed. Of course Zack hadn't talked to the shrink about himself—he'd talked about me.

"What?" He snapped his question, and his eyebrows together, in defense.

I did my best to draw back toward serious, but giggles kept popping out like Coke bubbles. "I think it's funny you talked to Gail about me." I knew it came out wrong as soon as the words left my mouth.

He frowned and dropped his arm.

"It's nice. Sweet." Everything I said made it worse. "That you care. It's, um . . ." I touched his leg. "Thank you. That's what I meant. Thank you for caring."

He nudged my shoulder with his. "Just watch the sunrise."

Along the horizon, a glorious burst of pinks and oranges and reds and purples painted the clouds as cotton-candy ribbons. "It shouldn't be colorful. Not anymore. Nothing should be beautiful," I whispered.

"The world should be gray?"

"Or black. Anything good seems rude and disrespectful."

He nodded. "I don't think that's the way it works. But I hear you."

I felt my parents, my dad, prodding me to open up to Zack, to trust him with more of my story. "Did I tell you who I'm named after?"

I felt him shake his head.

"Dad promised me someday he could tell me the whole story." I paused. Now I'd never really know.

"What *did* he tell you?" Zack asked.

"He was on a night mission and his parachute failed to open all the way. He fell completely off course. He broke both legs and his right hand falling into trees, broke them so bad all he could do was drag himself along. He wasn't exactly in friendly territory.

"There was a cave nearby, so he tried to crawl to it. When he saw a shadow coming toward him, he stopped to hold his gun in his left hand. He never said it, but I think he was going to shoot himself rather than be captured. But he heard a whisper—'Peace'—that made him hesitate.

"It was a young girl; Dad said she was probably older than she looked. She pointed at the cave and repeated, 'Peace,' several times. She balled up his parachute and carried it while he dragged himself up the rocks into the tiny cave. The sun was rising, but she stoked the little fire and cut pieces of the parachute until it was all burned up. He knew if he could stay alive his guys, his team, would find him. But he didn't know if they had time before Tangos found him first. The girl tried talking to him, but she wasn't speaking a language he understood. He thought it was maybe one of the nomadic dialects—he tried all the languages he knew, but all he got was that her name was Nadia. He gave her the food in his pockets and drank the milky tea she gave him in exchange.

"When he heard a helicopter in the distance, she checked and came back to him saying, 'Peace good.' She helped him get to the cave entrance and signal with his mirror, but then she disappeared among the rocks. They weren't the only ones who heard and saw the chopper. The armed gangs in the countryside raced toward them firing and there was a firefight as he was loaded into the chopper. He looked for her, but he knew that the gangs were as deadly to a girl on her own as to an American marine.

"She disappeared as if she was never there. He found out later her dad was an interpreter at a nearby base for several years and had been killed in action. After he recovered, Dad tried to find her every mission that brought them close to the same place, but she had vanished into the land.

"His team didn't understand how he'd survived that day. The local guerillas had announced the capture and killing of an American special forces soldier—he was the only unaccounted for at the time. He was less than a mile from their hiding spot. They should have gotten him. He says she saved his life and he hoped I would be as brave and caring as she was. I wonder if she lived through BluStar?" I gave up fighting the next wave of tears.

"That's a lot to expect a little girl to live up to. My mom named me after a hot guy on her favorite cop show." Zack brushed my tears away and smiled.

"Really?"

"Yeah, I don't even think she was sober when she had me.

I don't know who my father is. I've never had a family or foster parents or lived in group homes—kids on the streets were my family and most would have shot me over a cookie if it suited them."

Tears dripped off my chin as I pictured Zack as a little boy on the streets. I licked snot straggling down my lip as I rooted around in my pocket for a tissue. Nothing.

Zack handed me a plastic-wrapped period pad.

I held it in my hand, frozen. *Does he think I'm PMSing?*

"At least it's clean and sterile. Super absorbent." He smiled.

"I don't have— It's not my—" I didn't know why my period stopped. Maybe it was BluStar, but at least I didn't have to deal with that out here. *Yippee.*

"They make good bandages. Maybe they make good tissues, too, when you don't have anything else. Right?" Zack laughed at my stammering and embarrassment.

I blew my nose and folded the wings over without making eye contact.

Zack continued, "It's a new world, Nadia. There are no rules. You can use tissues or leaves or nothing at all and tell generations to come that's the way it should be."

Rays of gold caressed the world, slapping at shadows, and pushing the last pinkish gray away.

"We're close. We should get there by the end of the day." He kissed my head, right above my ear.

My heart stuttered. By this time tomorrow, we'd know if this was worth it. If Bean lived. If Pappi was the crazy man Mom always claimed, or if he knew more than the rest of us combined. If there was home to build onto the next to come.

I stood. "Let's go."

Day 100

July Fourth.

Once we passed Minnehaha Springs with its curved hotel stairway to nowhere, I didn't need Rabbit to tell me we were closing in on the last few miles.

We turned off the main road and onto a gravel track that was overgrown and looked completely unused.

"We can't take the bikes farther," Rabbit declared.

"We sure this is the right place?" Zack asked.

"Bean gave us explicit directions in his letter."

"That we don't have to check and make sure you're remembering correctly."

"True," I answered.

"I can see the end of the road up there. Then, it's just woods."

"That's the point, isn't it? It's hard to get to."

"This hard?"

"You haven't heard enough stories about Pappi. We're lucky we don't have to ride magical mountain goats to find the mine."

I shot Rabbit a glance and he shrugged. "What? You think you're the only one who eavesdropped when Mom railed about him and Bean?"

"Okay." I held my hands up.

"Besides, there's a camera over there in that tree." Rabbit pointed.

Zack peered up and shook his head. "I thought your grandfather lived off the grid?"

"Yeah, well, I guess surveillance doesn't count." I shrugged.

"Let's just hope that someone friendly is on the other end of that camera." Zack bumped his arm and swore.

"I don't see a red light. Maybe it's not even working." Rabbit slung on a fanny pack and tried to pick up Zack's backpack. He almost fell over. "What's in here?"

"Food. Water. Rocks." Zack took the bag and slung it over his good arm. I could tell he was trying to put on a brave face, but he flinched with every step and wouldn't let me look at his arm again.

Rabbit took the lead with Al on his hat. I grabbed the pack from Zack, who didn't argue with me at all, then wrapped Twawki's leash around my wrist. Zack took up the rear and didn't seem to mind. We set a slow and deliberate pace, even though my heart sped along, tripping over itself in nerves.

"North side of the tree, white *J* at the base. We're on the right trail, guys. Come on." Rabbit nodded and started counting his steps.

The deciduous trees spread their arms around and over us, acting like umbrellas in the sunlight. Insects filled the air with buzzing and biting. I gave up trying to swat them all and simply itched where the mosquitoes left welts.

The humidity made it feel twenty degrees warmer than it was and not a single ounce of breeze blew through the forest to cool us down.

At one hundred steps, Rabbit checked the trees for an *O*. By the sixth one he'd found the letter.

By the time we got to *S*, we were so deep into the mountainside that I had no idea where we'd left the bikes.

"Guys?" Zack asked, turning in circles, surrounded by brambles and branches.

"Rabbit?" I asked, also unsure about the next step. I thought we'd find the last tree and it would lead us to the mine.

"Now we sit and wait." He plunked down onto a tree stump.

"We what?" Zack asked, incredulous.

"We wait for sunset." Rabbit held up a roly-poly bug for Al to peck at.

"You think that's what he meant?"

"Yep. Bean will come at sunset every day to see if we've made it."

Zack glanced at me and seemed appalled that after all this we would sit and wait. With a sigh he sank into the shade and swatted at the biting no-see-ums.

I couldn't bear to look at either of them, let alone make small talk while we waited. Twawki lay in the dirt and took a nap with his belly in the air and his tail draped over Rab's legs.

I felt like crawling out of my skin, when a quiet voice said, from almost on top of us, "Red lights on cameras make them visible to Tangos. They work. Had to make sure you were mine and not just wandering in. Welcome home, kids."

I think I squealed as Zack leapt to his feet.

"Pappi?" Rabbit's chin quivered as the man leaned down to help him stand up.

"Robert Jr., aka Rabbit, I assume? And Nadia?" Pappi was tall and lanky, like Dad and Bean. His face was darkened by the sun, wrinkles around his eyes and bracketing his mouth. His green eyes blazed under bushy white eyebrows and close-shaved white hair. His camouflage cargo pants seemed to have something in every pocket and his olive-green cotton T-shirt matched any in Dad's closet. His boots were shiny black leather and he carried a bladder of water slung across his back, a machete on his thigh, and a shoulder holster for a handgun.

"You need water?" He handed me the straw. "We still have a hike up to the top. I'm their Pappi; I assume you're a friend of theirs?" He eyed Zack.

"Zack saved Twawki and helped us." Rabbit started babbling, spilling the story in mixed-up torrents. It was odd after all this time to have a new person to talk to.

Al flew to Pappi's shoulder and after a moment Pappi simply shrugged and let the little bird cling.

I waited until Rabbit paused for breath to ask, "Uncle Bean?"

"He's here. Sleeping. Had the night shift, so I let him sleep. Figure you're a present to wake up to. Thought you'd be here weeks ago."

"Mom," I said with a glance at Rabbit. I shook my head, I'd explain later.

"Sorry, kids." He immediately turned to Rabbit and asked, "So how the hell did this dog get stuck with a call sign like Twawki. He piss you off? Sounds like you're spitting out a hair ball every time you say it." Pappi demonstrated until Rabbit was laughing too hard to miss Mom. "He stinks like geese shit—he bathe in it?"

"Pappi!" Rabbit giggled at Pappi's gruff language and demeanor.

Pappi took all our bags on his shoulders even though he and Zack seemed to tug over possession a little.

"Your wing broken?" he asked Zack.

"Yeah, something like that."

"You pee on it?" Pappi asked me.

"Yes, it didn't really help."

"His arm fall off yet?" Pappi quirked an eyebrow at me.

"No?" I answered, checking quick to make sure it was still attached.

"I say it worked." Pappi turned away.

Rabbit chattered up the mountain to what looked like a pile of rocks from a rockslide.

"Home sweet home."

Zack paused and I knew what he was thinking. When Pappi stepped to the side and seemed to disappear in front of us, I realized the rocks were positioned to completely obscure the entrance.

Rabbit was next. "Bean!" he yelped.

I walked to the rocks, and it wasn't until I was right on top of the doorway that I saw it.

"Impressive," Zack said from right behind me. He tugged on my hand.

A low hallway opened up into a cavern with smaller hallways branching off to other rooms and other tunnels.

"We got cockroaches in this family," Pappi called to Bean. "A family of survivors." He nodded at Zack and me in obvious pride and delight. "All of them," he added as Al started to sing "La Cucaracha."

My feet froze to the ground for a moment. I'd forgotten that Uncle Bean looked like Dad. Sounded like Dad.

Bean hugged me. "You made it. I knew you could do it."

I fell into his arms and clung. Hugged like Dad. "We made it. We're here."

"Your father's so proud of you. Your mom, too."

"She tried to come," I gasped into his shoulder. "I didn't inject her with it soon enough."

I felt my legs give out as Bean held me. How many steps had we walked? How many moments of thinking this was it, the end of it all? How many times had I reminded myself to be a cockroach, to live up to my name, to do what Dad and even Mom tried to teach us?

"It's okay, Nadia, I've got you," Bean repeated, until I felt the rest of my fear and worry slip away.

"Come on, son," Pappi said to Zack. "Follow me down to the infirmary and let's see what we need to do for your wing. You too, Rabbit. I'll show you where you've gotta bathe that dog. Won't have our house smelling like a geese latrine."

"You have a bathtub?" Rabbit sounded awed.

"Warm water from the sun, shower and laundry. Even have a wood oven to bake up bread once a week. Maybe even a pizza."

"Ice cream?" Rabbit chattered excitedly as he followed, until it was just Bean and me in the entrance.

"When you're ready you can brief me on your adventure, okay? Right now I think you look like you could stand to clean up and then sleep for a week. Sound good?" Bean asked.

I nodded, my tongue too big for my mouth, my story too big to know where to start.

He must have sensed my frustration. "Take your time. Now that you're here there'll be some adjustment necessary. It's called letdown. You have to reacclimate to life standing still."

"It's over? It's really over?"

He nodded. "You made it. We'll have to work hard each day, but we'll be fine and we'll thrive in this new life. Tell me about Zack—do I need to clean my guns in front of him and question his intentions toward my niece?" Bean's smile was Dad's for a moment.

I grinned and blushed.

We were safe. We were home. We'd be ready for whatever came next.

AUTHOR'S NOTE

I have always been fascinated by viruses and how they operate. I read *The Hot Zone* by Richard Preston when I was in middle school, getting my first taste of the power of viruses and the intricacies of studying them. I followed that by reading one of my all-time favorite novels, *The Stand* by Stephen King. In another life, I would have loved a career studying viruses and vaccines or working for the Centers for Disease Control out in the field as an epidemiologist. It's normal to wonder what might happen "if," whether that "if" is being locked into a mall, surviving a *Titanic*-like disaster, or witnessing an alien invasion! Lots of people dream about those what-ifs! I do it all the time when I'm writing. With Nadia and Rabbit's story I got to live out one fantasy of a worst-case-scenario pandemic.

The BluStar virus in this story is a conglomerate of viruses like Marburg and Ebola that cause hemorrhagic (meaning bleeding) fever and an influenza strain like the one that killed millions of people early in the twentieth century. BluStar doesn't exist outside the pages of this book, but something like it could exist at some point in the future. Viruses mutate all the time on their own—it's part of what makes them so fascinating! For the purposes of this story, I gave BluStar a very high kill rate, one that has never been seen in a global pandemic, so this should not be read as anything other than a fictional story of survival.

Viruses are geniuses when it comes to survival—much better than humans! Everyone gets sick. When bacteria are the culprit, doctors can prescribe antibiotics. Viruses, however, are not always treatable, which is what leads to fears about pandemics. An infectious virus can cause either an epidemic or a pandemic, depending on how many people in the world are affected.

A pandemic is "a worldwide epidemic of a disease," according to the World Health Organization. There were influenza pandemics in 1918, 1967, and 2009. Other historic pandemics include the plague, which ravaged Europe from the fourteenth to the sixteenth century. Current large-scale pandemics include HIV/AIDS, polio, tuberculosis, and malaria, to name a few. In this book, BluStar killed many more people than would be likely should we have an influenza pandemic during your lifetime. If you're interested in learning more about viruses, careers working with disease, or the history of pandemics, I highly recommend these books: *Flu: The Story of the Great Influenza Pandemic of 1918 and the Search for the Virus That Caused It* by Gina Kolata, *Virus Hunter: Thirty Years of Battling Hot Viruses Around the World* by C. J. Peters and Mark Olshaker, and *Panic in Level 4* by Richard Preston.

None of this information is supposed to scare you. There are plenty of times in your life when you or someone you love will get sick, and they will get better because they will receive medical attention and their bodies will fight off the disease. What can you do? First of all, don't panic if someone in your family gets sick. Odds are good they will get better with rest, drinking lots of fluids to help their body fight off the attack, and most importantly getting medical care from a doctor of medicine, or a homeopathic physician. Nothing in this book is intended to be applied to real-life scenarios—always seek medical help when someone is sick.

I know you've heard this a lot, but you can do a lot for

yourself, your friends, and family if you wash your hands regularly, rubbing them for twenty seconds each time under running water. If it's not possible to wash your hands, try to keep antibacterial gel in your backpack or purse and use it before and after you eat, shake hands, touch money, or blow your noise. The big thing is to prevent the spread of germs if you're sick, and to avoid infecting yourself with someone else's germs. It sounds silly, and too easy, but if everyone washed their hands, far fewer people would get sick each year. However, you don't need to go overboard—everything should be done in moderation and with common sense. If you have questions, find an adult you trust and seek out information. Information is always the best tool!

Again, you probably won't face a pandemic like Nadia and Rabbit but you may live in a place where there are earthquakes, hurricanes, or other weather-related disasters. You'll go a long way to helping your family, and yourself, if you know ahead of time how best to handle a situation. If you're interested in learning more about how to survive, these are a few of the books I'd highly recommend: Cody Lundin's *When All Hell Breaks Loose: Stuff You Need to Survive When Disaster Strikes* and *98.6 Degrees: The Art of Keeping Your Ass Alive!*, James Wesley Rawles's *How to Survive the End of the World as We Know It: Tactics, Techniques and Technologies for Uncertain Times,* and John "Lofty" Wiseman's *SAS Urban Survival Handbook.* If you're interested in reading about people who have survived extreme experiences, check out Ben Sherwood's *The Survivor's Club: The Secrets and Science That Could Save Your Life,* where you can also take a quiz and learn what kind of survivor you are and how to maximize your strengths in any situation.

All of these books contain potentially scary information—

it's hard to think about bad things happening to our world and the people we love. It's normal to feel fear, especially of the unknown, which is why I've included information about these other books. You don't need to be afraid, and in most cases it's my hope that adults and authority figures around you will help you not only survive, but thrive in any circumstance. Information is the best tool for fighting fear—we fear the unknown, and often our imaginations run wild, making things seem much worse than they are.

If you find yourself passionate about any of these topics, there are great careers out there for you to explore. But if you feel you're not ready to read on in any of these subjects, then don't! I don't want anyone getting nightmares after reading—that's horrible!

I hope you enjoyed reading Nadia and Rabbit's journey as much as I enjoyed writing it. And remember, BE THE COCKROACH!

ACKNOWLEDGMENTS

Special thanks to:

Barney Wick for lending his call sign to Uncle Bean and for sharing his love of all things USMC with me. A special thanks to my early readers from all over the world: Danielle Mitchell, Karlee Roberts, Anne Jablonski, Tristan Wisont, Livia Lomne-Licastro, Gail Laforest, Lisa Bjork, and Sue Wiant. An important part of my writing process is finding a candle scent that my brain recognizes as a match for a story—when I first smelled Brian Paffen's "Dirt" candle, I stashed it for later. It was perfect for this story—like digging in sun-drenched spring earth, it helped grow this book in my brain and on the paper. Thank you, Brian! (Check out HerbalArtOnline.com.)

All of my Facebookers and the students at Langley Middle, in Mrs. Kizer and Mrs. Bakeman's seventh grade, for the title assistance and opinions. You guys rock!

Thank you to my local independent booksellers Josh Hauser and Nancy Welles for their continued enthusiasm for this island girl's work.

Trudi Trueit's "Water Coolers" are much needed and endlessly appreciated "office" talk—I'm so grateful to have your optimistic and sunny spins in my corner! Thank you!

I have to acknowledge the hard work of everyone behind each title at Delacorte Press/Random House Children's Books to produce the best books we can. Thank you all! And to my agents who spread the world internationally and do the behind-the-scenes so well—thank you too! Readers—you make my job so rewarding, and as for your fan mail, email, posts, blog entries, tweets, and hand-selling of my work—thank you isn't big enough or grand enough a phrase, but it will have to do! Thank you! While I wrote this book, men and women proudly wore the uniforms of our volunteer military in stations all around the globe. I am grateful to you all for your service; your dedication makes my job possible. Thank you.

Finally, I end with the acknowledgment of acknowledgments—a hearty and head-turning laugh of appreciation for my mom, who puts up with hearing about everything this business brings, including me saying to her, "I had the best idea last night and no, don't ask me to tell you what it was. Cuz it's not ready yet." I love you.

AMBER KIZER has been fascinated by viruses and epidemics since she first read *The Hot Zone* by Richard Preston while in middle school. In an alternate universe, she would love to be an epidemiologist or working in a Level 4 laboratory studying tiny and complicated organisms. As a vector, she often hosts tea parties and all-night raves (depending on the virus) for infectious diseases in her neighborhood . . . she's not sure why she's so lucky to be on their call lists and would like to remove herself. Amber is the author of a New York Public Libary Best Book for Teen Age, an Arkansas State Best Teen Book Finalist, and a Cybils Award nominee. The best part of her job is hearing from readers, so please reach out (after you've washed your hands). More information about her writing life and work can be found online at AmberKizer.com.